THE FAIR PURITAN.

AN

HISTORICAL ROMANCE

OF

THE DAYS OF WITCHCRAFT.

BY

HENRY WILLIAM HERBERT

("FRANK FORESTER")

AUTHOR OF "THE WARWICK WOODLANDS," "THE CAVALIERS OF ENGLAND," "MY SHOOTING BOX," "CROMWELL," "THE BROTHERS," ETC.

PHILADELPHIA:

J. B. LIPPINCOTT & CO.

1875.

Entered according to Act of Congress, in the year 1875, by
CHARLES C. SAVAGE,
In the Office of the Librarian of Congress, at Washington.

AUTHOR'S PREFACE.*

THIS, the only *American* Romance of the author, is truly a historical romance; many of the persons being genuine historical characters, and the facts generally and the spirit of the age carefully preserved. The period is one of the most interesting of the early times of North American history, being that of the subsidence of the terrible excitement of the Salem witchcaft, the tyrannous government of Sir Edmund Andros, and the first organized and successful resistance to the authority of the crown.

The author respectfully submits it to the public with the hope that it will be found a worthy companion to his other works of historic fiction, whose scenes and characters have been gathered in foreign lands.

*Mr. Herbert prepared this romance for the press in 1856. It had been stereotyped, when commercial disaster interfered with its publication. The plates were afterward mislaid, and only recently discovered. Meanwhile, the accomplished scholar and novelist has rested from his literary labors and passed beyond the tomb.

C. C. S.

December, 1874.

THE FAIR PURITAN.

A Romance of the Bay Province.

CHAPTER I.

THE FOREST DWELLING.

ὦ κόρα, ἤλυθον, Ἠλέκτρα, ποτὶ σὰν ἀγροτέραν αὐλάν.

In the latter part of the seventeenth century, the capital of Massachusetts, or, as it was then usually termed, the Bay Province, was the largest, as it is still the most beautiful, of American cities.

Already, at that early period, it had done more than laying the foundations of that reputation which she still possesses, as the metropolis of transatlantic letters, if not of wealth or of commerce.

It was a peculiar trait, and one the most redeeming, among much bigotry, much stupid and fanatical intolerance, much hairsplitting and strife of ultra-creeds—it was, I say, a peculiar and most honorable trait in the character of the hard old Puritans, that wheresoever they set foot, they left their track permanently stamped, not as their Dutch contemporaries of the Nieu Netherlands in warehouses and factories, but in the nobler work of schools and colleges, adapted to the future wants, not to the present means of their sparse population.

No part of what are now the United States was peopled from a stock so sound as Massachusetts.

Virginia, indeed, had to boast a nobler lineage, a race imbued with the noblest sentiments that grace humanity, the highest chivalry, the clearest sense of honor, qualities for which, to this day, her sons are deservedly renowned.

It may not be denied, however, that soldiers rather than scholars, adventurers rather than statesmen, were her settlers; while, in addition to the vast advantage she derived from the character of her first governor, the moderate and admirable Winthrop, Massachusetts had among her founders, "many of high endowments, large fortune, and the best education; scholars well versed in all the learning of the times; clergymen who ranked among the most eloquent and pious in the realm"* — men equally removed from intolerant bigotry and sectarian license — men equally averse to arbitrary power and democratic anarchy — men, in short, than whom none could be found better suited to their great office, as the forefathers of a mighty nation.

Cambridge was founded almost simultaneously with the city to which it is still the brightest ornament; and it is worthy of remark that the oldest born is yet the most eminent of American colleges, and that — right consequence of noble causes — Boston alone yields as of right to mental power and literary eminence, that social rank which the less elevated spirit of her rivals grants to superior wealth, or to success and enterprise in traffic.

Nor were the fruits of this higher civilization displayed only in great features, in the grandeur of public institutions. They

* Bancroft's History, vol. i., p. 355.

were as manifest in the humanities of the domestic circle, as in the morals of the forum.

And it is not incurious to observe, that, as if to disprove, on the very face of his country, the general though most unjust assertion which would attribute to the New-Englander a genius peculiarly money-making and gain-loving—to observe, I say, as every one must observe who has travelled in the pleasant places of his land, that the New-Englander *alone* has spared time from his gainful toils for the adornment of his household gods—for planting trees in his village ways, and cultivating flowers in his cottage-gardens, and making his home—sure test of a refined and gentle spirit—not rich alone in those creature comforts, the taste for which we share with the brutes that perish, but in those nicer charms, which fill the eye with pleasure, the heart with patriotism and with love—which last is virtue.

Nor is the culture, which we now behold, laughing out, under the brilliant suns and cloudless skies of America, in the sweet villages and glowing fields adjacent to the metropolis of New England, as it laughs nowhere else on this side the Atlantic, the tardy growth of progressive centuries.

The English elms, which lift their heads still green and comely and untouched by age above the roofs of the old city, were planted there before one generation had elapsed, after the pilgrim's foot first trod the rock of Plymouth.

And the log-cabins of the first settlers displayed, unlike the shanties of the west, the cultivated taste which had been nursed in remote and polished regions, by the red-berried mountain-ash planted before the door, by the sweet-scented creeper trained round the humble casement, and by the rose or pink brought from beyond the sea to bloom in the bleak precincts of the New England clime.

In the year 1688, for it was at that period that the great

events occurred, with which were interwoven the humbler threads of personal adventure, to which my narrative relates—in the year 1688 the province of Massachusetts, which then included Maine as far as the Piscataqua, could boast a population of about forty-four thousand souls; of which at least a fourth part were inhabitants of Boston, and the beautiful villages about. These latter, at the first landing of Winthrop, having been well described as abounding in "sweet and pleasant springs, and good land, affording rich cornfields and fertile gardens,"* had justified the choice of their first settlers, and had already, in the little space of half a century, acquired much of the elegance and yet more of the comforts of an old country.

And if the population, which filled those pleasant seats, was not sprung from the "high folk of Normandie," neither is it altogether true that they were of the "low men," although they were indeed of Saxon origin.

Had they been such, they would not have brought with them the love of letters and the intellectual tastes for which, from their first arrival on the shores of the New World, they were conspicuous, howmuchsoever they might have brought the love of regulated freedom, whether in politics or in religion.

Many, and those the best and the most useful, of the new settlers were of the better class of yeomanry, or of the smaller gentry, with not a few able burghers from the country towns, persons of ample means and sufficient mental cultivation. And a clear proof of this is to be found in the fact that they brought with them a considerable number of bond-servants, to whom, not long after their landing, perfect freedom was granted, not so much from any love of liberty in the abstract, as because their labor was less valuable than the cost of maintaining them.

It is a great mistake, yet not on that account less general, to

* Bancroft's History.

imagine that the first inhabitants of the Bay Province were either absolute dissenters from the church of England, or strong opponents of a kingly form of government, however they may have resisted the corruption of the one, or the undue extension of the other.

Winthrop, the first governor, was a royalist, and an enemy to democracy, a churchman, and a moderate aristocrat. For very many years the church of England was the church of Massachusetts, though in a milder, and, as the colonists averred, a purer form than in the mother-country. The government, in the first instance, was one of "the least part," though as they fondly believed of "the wisest and the best."

Between the foundation of the colony, however, and the period concerning which I write, it can not be denied that changes have been in constant progress, tending to absolute independence in the church, and to republicanism in the polity of the embryo nation.

It was to check this growing spirit, that the charters of the New England states were abolished; that, on the succession of the second James, it was proposed to send the notorious Colonel Kirke, whose infamous renown had not yet been acquired fully, as a fit person to coerce and crush down the growth of puritanical and democratic principles; and, to conclude, that in the winter of 1688, Sir Edmond Andros landed at Boston, glittering in gold and scarlet, surrounded by a body-guard of flaunting cavaliers, as governor of all New England, and destined to rule with a rod of iron those whom his creature Randolph had designated as "a perverse people."

Those were the evil days of New England. Then there began a series of vexatious and tyrannical oppressions, as violent as ever were endured by an English population.

Nor was it merely under the oppressive system of public measures that the people groaned indignantly. For private insolence, extortion, and licentiousness, were let loose in aid of public tyranny and persecution.

The vilest men that could be found in all New England, as being the only men who would lend themselves to the measures of the new governor, were those selected to fill the highest office. And, while the tenure of their posts was dependent on their zeal and determination in the extinguishment of every spark of civil or religious freedom, the due performance of this odious duty was a sufficient plea whereby to defend every act of personal revenge, or sensual gratification.

Liberty was indeed trodden under foot throughout the Bay Province.

The schools of learning were, as the best foundations of that liberty, with a tact as odious as it was farsighted, discouraged, and allowed to decay.

The churches were reduced to extremity, by interference with their means of support.

Vote by ballot was forbidden under penalties.

Town-meetings for deliberation were proclaimed as an overt act of sedition.

Domestic rights were scarce less oppressively invaded than public privileges. No man's house in New England was his castle. The right of *habeas corpus* was denied, and men were calmly told that the laws of England would not be found to follow them to the world's end.

But widely did they err, who fancied that with liberty itself, the love of liberty could be extinguished in the bosom of the pilgrims.

The very violence of the means adopted to abolish it was, under Providence, the cause of its establishment; and in the despotism of Sir Edmund Andros will be found the match which fired the train, that smouldered long, to blaze out in unextinguished brightness, after a century had passed, on the same spot which saw it kindled.

It was at this period of the history of the Bay Province, when the oppression of the English governor was at its height, and the depression of the popular mind at the lowest, that there might be seen at the eastern end of Boston bay, among the rocks, which wall it toward Nahant, a small cottage of singular construction, yet most romantical withal, and indeed beautiful.

Midway the cliffs, which project so far above it, as to admit of no access from the land-side, there was a small, green ledge or platform, containing about an acre of land, nearly level, though sloping gently to the southward, where it was bounded by a sheer descent of fifty or sixty feet, scarped by the hand of Nature in the living rock.

On every other side, it was surrounded by dark crags rising abruptly as a rampart from its grassy margins; for it was then clothed with a carpet of short mossy greensward shadowed by half a dozen giant pines, the sole survivors of a colony, which had occupied all the platform previous to the invasion of the white man.

In front of this platform, otherwise inaccessible, there rose from the sandy beach a huge, round heavy rock, entirely isolated at high water, and separated from the cliffs, whence probably in some remote age it had fallen, by a space of fifty feet.

On the side facing the shaggy shore, this rock was precipitous and sheer, its head overhanging its base, and its slippery sides unscalable by the most adventurous foot. To the seaward, however, it was ledgy, and broken into several stages, like a huge flight of steps; and this had most likely suggested the occupation of the platform above, which was some ten feet higher than the insulated rock, as a place of residence.

It was on this platform, then, nestled close into the recess, and actually overhung by the cliffs above it, that the romantic cottage stood, wherein not a few of the incidents occurred, which I purpose to secure from oblivion, as types of an age, the memory of which is but too rapidly evanishing.

Built of rough logs, and but one story high, it resembled somewhat a Swiss chalet; but yet more an English cottage of the Elizabethan era, allowance being made for the difference of material, and the absence of skilful architects.

Like the former, it was entirely of wood, with eaves far projecting beyond the walls of the building, and with a roof, bark covered, highly peaked, and overgrown with gray lichens.

Like the latter, it was irregular in shape, having been built without any definite plan in the first instance, and increased, with the increasing exigencies of the family that occupied it, at random. It had, therefore, at least half a dozen stacks of chimneys, and as many gable ends, three doors with a rustic porch over each, and eight or nine windows, opening in the lattice fashion with small diamond panes set in frames of lead, which, by their appearance, must have come evidently from what the colonists were still proud to call HOME.

The little space, in front of this old English cottage, was laid out as a garden, partly in level turf smooth shaven as a lawn in the old country, partly in flower-beds neatly trimmed, and bright with flowers which never had their birth on this side of the Atlantic. A little walk, firmly compacted of sea-shells beaten into powder, led down from the principal entrance of the cottage to the brink of the cliff, directly opposite to the insulated rock I have described.

Here a bridge of a single arch spanned the rough chasm, framed like the house itself of unbarked timber, and guarded at the sides by parapets, if they may so be called, of gnarled roots and branches from the forest.

The lower rock itself had undergone certain improvements also, which had rendered it not only more accessible, but more picturesque, and pleasing to the eye.

Rude flights of wooden steps, with balustrades of pine branches, led from one platform to the other; and a bold breakwater of trunks piled fantastically one upon the other ran out from its eastern end, making a small but secure harbor, between the island and the shore, wherein two or three fishing-boats of various sizes, a long, light skiff, and an Indian canoe, lay moored, safe from the wind or tide, when it was up, and snugly beached on the white sand at low water.

Such was the scene on which the setting sun was casting its last level rays on a lovely summer evening of that disastrous year. The diamond panes glittered like gold in the ruddy beams; the column of blue smoke, which curled its way slowly upward, relieved by the dark background of the granite rocks, assumed a palpable and solid form, as its edges were gilt and rounded by the rich light; the gaudy flowers laughed gorgeously beneath the influence of the time and season; and even the old weather-beaten pines, which sheltered the low roof, assumed a juvenile and jocund air in that sweet summer's eve.

The sea, for miles aloof, lay crisped in millions of small laughing ripples, flashing and twinkling to the cloudless skies. The rocky and wood-crested isles, checkered the wide expanse of gold and azure with their long purple shadows; the distant shores and the bold headland of Cohasset loomed like a hazy cloud against the western sky, shrouded in the soft mists of the summer sunset.

Thousands of snow-white gulls were on the wing, soaring and diving through the transparent atmosphere, or plunging down upon their scaly victims among the flashing spray of the small wavelets.

But save these, no living form enlivened the bright scene; until, when the sun was already half sunken in the glowing ocean, there stepped out from the cottage-porch, shading her eyes with one hand against the horizontal rays, a girl so beautiful, and, to me at least, so interesting in her child-like innocence, and her strange fortunes, that she merits a better introduction than the end of a long if not tedious chapter.

CHAPTER II.

THE FOREST MAIDEN.

Λαμπρὸι γὰρ εἰς γένος γε. Χρημάτων δὲ δὴ πένητες.

The girl, who stepped forth from the rustic porch, and gazed out so eagerly, as if expecting some one, over the sunlit sea, was one of those exquisite creations that we sometimes behold, though rarely, on earth, recalling all our thoughts toward heaven.

She was very young, yet not perhaps so young, as would have been imagined from the expression of her features, and her whole air, which were singularly juvenile and almost child-like.

Her hair, which was luxuriant, almost beyond the reach of fancy, though the simple mode, on which it was arranged, dissembled much of its rich redundance, was of that beautiful and unusual hue, so difficult to be described, which the old poets were wont to call golden. Without one shade of red or auburn, it was in fact of that soft, light sunny brown, which, catching as it did now, the last slant sunbeams, glitters indeed like threads of virgin gold.

Divided on the brow, and laid smoothly down over each cheek, in a broad, glistening fold, the wavy lines of which showed clearly that, if suffered, it would have wound itself into a maze of natural ringlets, it was collected into a knot at the back of her beautifully-formed head, so dense and massive that it required no practised eye to discover that, unbound, it would have fallen nearly to her feet.

The girl's complexion was such as might have been anticipated from the color of her hair; that is to say, it was fairer and whiter than anything to which it can be well compared, yet with an under-tint of sun that showed how healthfully and warmly the pure blood circulated under that snowy skin.

Save this faint tinge, her cheeks were nearly colorless, unless it were when some quick thought or transient feeling flooded them with brief crimson.

As if to make up for this deficiency, however, her lips, exquisitely arched and wooing, were of the warmest and most vivid carnation.

What was most singular and striking in her aspect was, that her eyebrows and long, silky lashes were of so deep and well-defined a brown, that, when contrasted with her light hair and lucent skin, they looked almost black.

Her eyes, which were very large and bright, though softer even than they were brilliant, were also very dark, not black, indeed, but of that full deep hazel so common to the peasant-maids of England.

There was, however, something in the whole aspect of this girl which denied the inference that might have been drawn thence that she was of lowly birth—that indiscribable and nameless something, which certainly is not manner alone, nor the mere effect of mind, by which the eye at once distinguishes the gently, if not nobly, born.

That the qualities of both the mind and body are in some

sort hereditary, I can not imagine be disputed. Still less can I conceive when it is perfectly in accordance with the rules of nature that it should be so, why it *should be* disputed. In animals, we see clearly that blood will tell; the horse, the hound, nay the inferior brutes, transmit their qualities with absolute precision; and if, in man, the descent of virtue or vice, strength or debility, deformity or beauty, is less evident at first sight, it is that, in man, education has power to modify that, which it can neither create nor annihilate, the natural bent and bias of both mind and body.

Be this, however, as it may, no one can have mixed much with the English in their own land, without coming to the conclusion that there is a marked and perceptible physical difference between the upper and lower classes of society. The upper classes, as a whole, being the handsomest race in civilized Europe, tall, well-formed, delicate, and slender, though at the same time muscular and strong, with small hands, feet, and ears; while the lower classes, though robust, healthy, and not uncomely, are square, thick set, and coarsely made, with singularly large and awkward extremities.

He constantly will see, among the country lasses, lovely complexions, fine eyes, and fine hair; but rarely, or never, slender waists, shapely limbs, small feet, or taper ankles.

Of this the reason, if we look for it, is not obscure. In the first place, the upper classes have a large mixture, when they are not wholly, of the Norman blood: a race famous, in all time, for straightness and height of stature, for symmetry of form and beauty of face, as much as for valor, energy, and daring. The lower classes, on the contrary, are purely Saxon to this day, and the Saxon race, though stout, robust, and sturdy, have been in all times short, square, sturdy, and ungraceful.

There was, then, something in her air, which would have indicated in a moment to a practised eye that this English girl—

for she had all the characteristics of the English blood—and indeed at that day there was little, if any other, in New England—was of a gentle race. Not perhaps of the high nobility, nor of pure old Norman blood, but at least of the gentry.

It was not in her manner only that this was apparent, although her attitude was very graceful, and every single movement easy, unstudied, and naturally beautiful; nor was it in her face, though that was indeed heavenly.

Her features were as regular as those of a Grecian statue, but neither features nor coloring gave the inexpressible charm to that sweet young face. Nor was it intellect or genius, for although these were not wanting, and although a physiognomist would have told you of latent poetry, and warm imagination, and deep thoughts, it was clear that they were as yet all latent—that her talents were as yet to her a sealed fountain, waiting perhaps the touch of passions, equally dormant, to call them into life.

It was the singular expression of purity, of truth, of artless, unsuspecting, unquestioning innocence, which beamed from every line of that sweet, joyous face, inflaming it with an air of angelic holiness and love, that made it so remarkable.

And it was this expression which gave to her that appearance of extreme youth which was contradicted by the maturer beauties of her delicate but rounded form; nor could you look upon her face, without seeing that the mind within must be pure and guileless, as that of a little child, without thinking of that beautiful text, which bids us believe in the Savior's words, "That in heaven their angels do always behold the face of my Father, which is in heaven."

If her appearance, however, the shapely slenderness of her tall, rounded figure, the fairy smallness of the white hands, the fine setting on of the head, the curvature of the swan-like neck, the falling arch of the shoulders—if all these, I say, would have betokened her of gentle birth, the simplicity, if not rudeness of her garb, would have gone nearly as far to disprove the inference.

She wore no cap or bonnet on her sunny hair, but a broad carsenet riband, of a pale, silvery gray, drawn tight around her temples, and tied in a close knot just above the left ear.

A handkerchief of spotless muslin covered her shoulders, and veiled, though it could not conceal the outlines of her beautifully-moulded bosom; and sleeves of the same material fell loosely down to her elbow in wide plaits, from beneath the shoulder-straps of a tight russet-colored jerkin, or corsage, as it would now be called, laced down the front from the bosom to the point of its long stomacher. A full, loose petticoat, of gray serge, nearly of the same shade with the riband which confined her hair, was not so long but that it displayed a clean ankle, and as pretty a foot as ever flitted noiseless over a Persian carpet, or dashed the dew-drop from a grassy lawn.

Such was the girl, who looked forth as the sun was setting with a long, wistful gaze over the beautiful bay which gave its name to the province of Massachusetts. And never was a rarer combination of physical and mental loveliness than that fair girl presented to the eye. And there was something almost strange in the union of a face so artless, innocent, and child-like, with a form so perfectly developed, so ripe in all the charms of young, lovely womanhood.

Long did she gaze and wearily, and as it seemed in vain. And an expression of gentle melancholy, chastened disappointment, came over her young face, as she turned away, convinced apparently that nothing was in sight, which she desired to see.

"I am afraid," she said to herself, half doubtfully; "though I know not at what, or wherefore. He said that he should not return until late—yet still I am afraid. I will go in, and pray—"

But she was interrupted here, by a soft, low, sad voice close beside her, though she had not perceived that any one had approached her, as she stood there under the declining sunbeams, absorbed in anxious thought.

"See, Ruth, see!" said the voice with a slightly foreign accent; "see there, under the sun. The master's boat is coming. You could not see it for the glitter of the waters in the wake."

The girl looked quickly, whither she was directed, turning with so little surprise as proved that the plaintive voice must be familiar to her ear.

"Yes! yes! I see, Patience," cried the girl eagerly, her cheek flushing slightly as she spoke. "I see, and I thank you. It is my father; God grant that he bring us good tidings."

And, with the words, she turned round to the person who had addressed her, stretching out her hand kindly. It was clasped instantly; but the fingers that clasped it were of the hue of burnished copper, and, as she turned her head, the full dark melancholy eyes of an Indian woman looked wistfully into her own.

"Why call her Patience, Ruth?" said the Indian, with an expression, glancing across her dark features, that showed how much the name was indeed misapplied—"why not call her own name? why not say, Tituba?"

"Well, then, thanks, Tituba," replied the girl, with a gentle smile. "But I think Patience a far prettier name; and it is good too. And then it angers my father; he says Indian names are devices of the evil one."

"And English names *lies!*" answered the bond-servant, for such was the condition of this wild, free-born child of nature —"Lies, every one! What for call Patience, when not patient? Just so old father called Merciful! what that but a great lie? He prays God to show mercy; shows not, himself, to Tituba. Flog! flog! what good in names! Call Patience, when not wish, not hope, not try, to be patient. Tituba hates patience. Never call her so, good Ruth, when alone."

The manner of the poor Indian woman was strange and sad to witness. It reminded one of a warhorse, had he ever seen one, debased into a carrier's drudge.

There was the wild, clear eye, but its free glance was dimmed and humbled. There was the finely-formed head, but it was lowered and depressed, by the accursed stamp of man's servitude on the brow that God made free, in his own image. There were the graceful, lithe, strong limbs, but they were listless and oppressed by the soul's bondage, moving, though loose, as if in fetters.

Ruth gazed upon her earnestly, and the tears rose unbidden to her soft, calm eyes. The words of the poor servant had performed their errand, straight to the heart. The truth of those words—their strong, disgraceful truth—smote her; and she could not deny, even to herself, that sternness rather than mercy was the attribute of that father's character, who yet was never stern to her, and whom she loved, even herself, half fearfully, half fondly.

"I will—I will call you Tituba," she answered quickly; "not when we are alone, however, for that would be deceit, but always; and when my father is in the milder mood, I will plead for you, poor Tituba, that he be gentle to you, as he is to me ever But now, go in. It is too likely he comes home bearing sorrow with him; and his sorrow is dark and wrathful toward men, though submissive toward Him who sendeth sorrow, as he sendeth joy, for the good of the creatures of his hand. Go thy ways now, poor girl. I hear his foot on the rocks below, and it sounds angrily. Go thy way, and for my sake, try not to hate, try, I would say, to love my father."

"No," answered the woman, sullenly. "How she love when he flogs all the time, and prays, and flogs again? No — not love father, not try to love! Tituba never try to love master. What made the white man the Indian's master? God made the master, merciful Whalley says! Did God make the *slave*, Ruth? No! Tituba will not try to love Merciful! Need not try to love Ruth!—loves Ruth already, without trying!"

The steps of the man, who had been seen, some time before, approaching from the westward across the fair bay, were now heard distinctly, as he ascended the isolated rock; and just as his head appeared above its rounded summit, Tituba turned away with a dogged air, and walked off with a slouching, listless gait toward the cottage.

Ruth sprang, with her whole soul anxiously flashing from her eyes, to meet her father.

CHAPTER III.

THE FANATIC.

Σε τὸν σοφωτὴν, τὸν πικρῶς ὑπέρπικρον.

SCARCE had the poor Indian girl made a few steps toward the cottage, before the man whose head they had seen above the rocks came into full view.

He was a tall, dark, athletic man, from forty-five to fifty years of age, and might have been termed handsome, both in figure and in face, but for the gauntness and emaciation of the former, which was so great as to convey an idea of monkish maceration to the mind of the beholder, and for the gloomy, grim, and austere expression which distorted features otherwise fine and noble. His eye was keen and piercing, but wild withal, and at times fierce and fiery. His nose was well shaped and aquiline, though too sharp and fleshless toward the extremity. It was the mouth, however, as is generally the case in strong and powerfully-defined characters, that gave the expression to the whole face.

The lips were thin, and rigidly compressed; and in them and all the surrounding lines, austerity, pride, dogged resolve, cruelty; in short, almost every evil passion might be read, with this exception only, that there was nothing sensual or animal to be discovered in their expression.

Indeed, whether in head, or face, or form, it was impossible to detect anything that was not almost purely spiritual, though it was much to be doubted if that spirit were not so far perverted as to be now almost wholly evil.

His hair, which had been in his youth as black as a raven's wing, was now thin and grizzled; and his dark face was marked with many an intricate and deeply furrowed line; but they were lines of thought and passion, not of age; nor, indeed, had time left many traces on his erect and iron power, or diminished anything of his hard sinewy strength.

His hands, though lean and wrinkled, showed cords and sinews that would not have disgraced a Samson; and his tread, though slow and deliberate, was firm, solid, and unyielding.

He was dressed in a close-fitting, straight-cut jerkin, of thick black woollen serge, buttoned up from a little way below the hips, where the skirtless and unseemly garment ended, to the throat, where it was relieved by a broad collar of clear, coarse linen turned squarely over it. Loose breeches of the same material, with a pair of huge fisherman's boots reaching to the mid thigh, completed his attire, except that he had a tall broad-brimmed and steeple-crowned hat on his head, and a large boat-cloak thrown across his left shoulder. A leather thong buckled about his waist contained a long, buck-handled knife, and in his right hand he carried a very heavy old-fashioned musket, with a barrel of five feet in length, altered from the antique fashion of the match, to the more modern, though scarcely more effective, fire-lock.

Such was the man who called Ruth Whalley daughter—the man for whom she was looking out with anxious expectation, with a solicitude so evident, that it would have told much of love, had it not seemed to participate, in some degree, of fear.

And could it be that this stern, fierce, proud, sneering fanatic—for such he must have been, or his looks wofully belied him—could be the father of a being so pure, so gentle, so affectionate, so lovely, and so artless, as beautiful Ruth Whalley.

It is an old, and for the most part a true saying, though not so refined as it is practical, that "like breeds like"—the wise Roman of old knew it, when he sang, in his deathless verse:—

"Fortes creantur fortibus et bonis;
Est in juvenis, est in equis patrum
Virtus; nec imbellum feroces
Progenerant aquila columbum."

The tawny Indian knew it, when he looked with suspicion even on the tried virtue of old chiefs, whose sons proved recreant in the field.

Yet, though no man has ever seen the noble racehorse spring from the loins of the coarse cart-drudge, or the sagacious hound from the low-blooded cur; yet are there cases, where the best and fairest of our race have sprung from rude and unsightly stocks, though not perhaps devoid of ancestral worth or virtue.

Of this, if it be so, as can, I think, be hardly doubted, Ruth Whalley was a singular example.

Never a harder sire gave life to a sweeter child. Yet little would it seem that he prized the bright young creature, on whom scarce any eye, save his, could have looked unloving, or undelighted.

Yet he did look unlovingly at her—ay, and unlovingly he spoke—as she sprang forward to cast her white arms about his neck, asking him fondly if he had brought good tidings.

"Minion, what dost thou here?" he asked harshly, in reply, "wasting the Lord's best gift of daylight in loitering thus, looking on the sea, which is not half so light or so wanton as thou art; and tuning, I dare well avouch it, the voice which was given thee for prayer and praise, to idle and lascivious minstrelsey. Tidings! what tidings should I bring, but of wrath in heaven, and on earth fear, and tyranny, and persecution? The Lord has hid his face—has hid his face, I say, from Israel—nor will he turn it on us any more until we have thrust out our sin, and cast away our abomination from us! Go in! go in! I say—what do you here? Go in! your mother is to blame, minion!—and that brown daughter of perdition with you, too! Take heed, lest one day she lead you to worship her God—which is Satan! Get thee in-doors, I say. Thou shalt hear more anon, that will, I trow, please thee less, even than this that I have spoken."

Ruth Whalley looked simply and innocently into the stern man's face, while he spoke; and, as he finished his harangue, turned quietly away, as she was commanded, and moved toward the cottage-door. Most girls, addressed, as she was, with such a volley of unmerited reproof, would have replied either with indignation, or with fear and sorrow. But Ruth was neither vexed nor tearful. Her fair face, it is true, grew somewhat paler, but shed no tear, nor expressed any wonder.

Her father's bearing was a matter too familiar, too much of every-day occurrence, to excite astonishment, or even to call forth active sorrow. He was, indeed, a hard man. One of those cold, bitter, avaricious, selfish natures, which owe it, perhaps, rather to the chillness of their blood and the lack of temptation or of opportunity, than to anything of principle or of humanity, that they fall not into the commission of great crimes.

This, Merciful Whalley had, it is true, avoided; he had kept his hands, it is true, incorrupt from stealth, unstained from blood-guiltiness. But his heart! his heart! oh, what a mass was there, of envy, selfishness, uncharitableness, malice, slander!—and if he set his hands, as he often boasted, to no evil work, assuredly he set neither his lips nor his mind to any good one.

Self-righteous, self-esteemed, self-arrogant, self-justified, he judged all men, himself excepted, and rarely judged but to condemn them.

It is probable that, from his childhood up, he had never done an act of charity or kindness, unless it were from selfish motives; or loved a human being, except for his own gratification.

Loud in the meeting-house or conventicle, loud in possessions of all virtue, loud in denunciation of all sinners, he was yet louder in his cold domestic tyranny. The very dog arose from the hearth, and shrunk away into the darkest corner, hearing its master's footstep at the door. Yet, for all this, without his own house, though feared rather than liked, Merciful Whalley was not ill-esteemed in the neighborhood.

For Merciful was well to do in the world; and in the opinion of the rich, wealth, in a neighbor, is a great coverer of sins.

Talk not of charity! Charity may win the poor man's love;

but is it not a tacit censure on the rich man, who is less charitable?

No! no! for the most part there is no saint in the rich man's calendar so worshipful as the richer and more avaricious men —and so it was with Whalley.

His deeds of benevolence and mercy were thorns in no neighbor miser's side—his kindness to his servants or dependants rebuked no man's severity. He was rich; and therefore most worthy the highest place in the synagogue, and the first seat at feasts.

It must be said, however, for all the man's cold selfishness, and lack of all milk of human kindness, that he was scrupulously just and honest in his dealings.

He never had oppressed the fatherless, or widows; he had removed no landmarks. If he assisted no man, he wronged none. If he forgave no failings on the part of others, he asked no forgiveness for his own. Perhaps he thought he had himself no failings.

He certainly would have been astonished to hear his griping avarice, which he denominated painstaking and God-fearing thrift, denounced as a vice; and there would have been no end to his marvelling, had it been insinuated to him that his austere and sour port, his disgust at all innocent amusements, his contempt of all gentle affections, his bitter hatred of all whom he chose to designate sinners—hatred to which he often gave a personal and persecuting character—were more akin to evil than to virtue.

Originally, he might perhaps have been a self-tormentor; he had now degenerated (this at least is certain) into a tormentor of others. With him, all love was lust; all Christian charity, a weak countenancing of sinners; all mirth, wantonness; all humanity, a tampering with the evil one.

He was one of those, in short, who deem a stern, morose

countenance, a cold and unfeeling heart, the surest signs of grace; who cherished his worst vices as the most fruitful virtues; who deemed himself superior to his fellow-men, for the very lack of those qualities which bring them nearest to the angels, and for the plenteousness of those which most assimilate them to the brutes that perish.

Merciful Whalley was, in one word, a man—such as whom there are, at all times, but too many in the world, but who in that age especially abounded—who bring virtue into more disrepute, and work more evil to the cause of righteousness, than the most scarlet sinners.

A man, who in all his practice converted the beauty of holiness into deformity—who would have changed the heart of man, destined by its Creator to be the shrine of all sweet and pure affections, into a temple consecrated to the twin fiends self and mammon; and the fair world, with all its beauty and its joy, into a very hell.

Such was the father, who scowled on his pure and lovely child; reproached her with rude and angry words; and half believed her to be a vessel of wrath, because she was, what the good God intended that we all should be, joyous herself, and a minister of joy to others.

He scowled upon her grimly, as she went her way obedient to his bidding; and felt more than a partial inclination to call her back, and reprove her for that very obedience and submission, as savoring of hypocrisy and scorning.

But he restrained his spite, to vent it upon other objects, strode after her, gloomy and grim, and entered the door of his own home, to stand before his family, a being dreaded and severed, rather than trusted or beloved, by all around him.

CHAPTER IV.

THE FIRESIDE.

"O quid solutis est beatius curis."

THERE is no happier scene on earth, none upon which good angels may be supposed to look with more complacency, than the assemblage round the evening fire, of a united, happy, loving family: when the overburdened mind throws off its load of cares and anxieties; when the exhausted body enjoys that respite, which itself is pleasure, from the labors of the day; when the heart, weary and faint with struggling against the coldness and selfishness of the outer-world, comes back, like a bird to its nest, to repose confidently on the affections and devotion of the tried and trusted few.

Of all the blessings, for which man should thank God, daily and for ever, and of which, alas! he is ever too regardless until their loss has taught him their true value, this is the choicest gift.

And if there be an error, which treads closer on the heel of sin than any other, it is that of the man, who by negligence, or selfishness, or hardness of heart, converts this blessing into a curse, steeps this light of humanity in cold and cheerless gloom.

There was no lack of comfort around the hearth or in the rustic kitchen of the "Cove cottage."

A blaze, almost like that of a furnace, went roaring up the wide open chimney; nor, though it was summer-time, was the warmth unpleasant, so freshly did the moist sea-breeze sweep in through the open lattices, from the broad Atlantic, and so cool did the overhanging rocks, and the sun-proof shelter of the pine-trees render that shady nook. There was no lack of wealth. In the midst of that cheerful blaze, hung a huge caldron, from which issued an incessant simmering song, and a rich, steamy odor, prophetic of a savory meal.

The kitchen was a long, low room, floored, roofed, and wainscotted with unpainted pine-wood; but every part of it was white, almost as snow, and reddent, if I may so express myself, of cleanliness. From the huge rafters overhead hung, in long rows, a goodly show of venison hams, and flitches of bears-meat, interspersed with strings of onions, and bunches of sage, and thyme, and other culinary herbs.

The ample meal-tub, in one corner of the room, the harness-cask of pork, and the barrel of salted haddock in another, attested the ample provision made for the creature comforts; while the bright range of pewter plates, glittering like silver on the shelves above the dresser, and the huge oaken chest, displaying by its open lid, large store of clean, coarse linen, perfumed with lavender, and rosemary, spoke volumes for the thrift and care of the females of the household.

Was not, then, Merciful Whalley a pre-eminently happy man?

The lord had increased his stores. He eat the labor of his hands; Oh! well was it to him.

His wife was as the fruitful vine upon the walls of his house.

His children like the olive-branches round his table. Wherefore, then, was he not blessed among men, and happy?

His wife the chosen of his bosom, she who had left friends, home, and country, to follow the enthusiast into the far and fearful wilderness—she, who had once shone forth the pride and beauty of a sweet English village—what was she now! did she look like one, who was in herself happy, or the participant of another's happiness?

Wan, faded prematurely, gray-haired, not certainly from the lapse of years, hollow-eyed, with a timid stealthy tread, an anxious glance, like that of a hunted animal, a weak apologetic smile, that was in itself unutterably sad, and painful!

And the children, the olive-branches round the righteous, the rich man's table!

Goodly in form and feature, excellent in stature, healthy and strong and handsome, were they as children should be; as happy children are!

Sweet Ruth, thou wert the first-born, and to a parent that appreciated duly that priceless gift of God, a dutiful and loving child, what a treasure wert thou!

Four others were assembled, on that evening, in the low kitchen—three stout, hearty boys, strong-limbed, ruddy complexioned, and not without a certain air of superiority, to the mere drudging rustic.

The eldest of the three might perhaps be sixteen or seventeen years of age, the youngest twelve; and all the three, as I have said, were comely to look upon, well clad, well conditioned. What was it then, that lent so strange and unnatural an aspect to those young faces, those bright eyes that should, to fulfil the ends of their all-kind Creator, have been alive with innocent and artless merriment.

There was no mirth in those eyes! no frankness, no ingenuous gleam of out-bursting native truth in those youthful features! no sunshine of the innocent and fearless soul on those faces!

There was no thought in those smooth, patient brows.

Instead of thinking, active, energetic, and impulsive creatures, obedient to the fresh, noble impulses of heart and nature—they were mere passive, listless, senseless, almost soulless, agents of a will to which they bowed, not in the least that they understood or loved it, but that it was stern and superior, and enforced absolute submission.

Is such the stuff whereof to make free men, good citizens, and Christians, or slaves, rogues, and hypocrites?

The fifth was a little, little girl not above four years old—two intermediate children had died infants—and this was now the youngest, and would have been the pet of any other family. A lovely babe she was, with large, soft, hazel eyes, like her sister's, and a profusion of light-brown silky hair, falling in natural curls over her neck and shoulders. But even she, this tiny, prattling babe, that should thus far at least have been preserved aloof from fear—which to weak natures is so often the first cause of sin—that should have been all glee, and merriment, and love, she like the rest was grave and silent in her little plays, with an air of unnatural constraint pervading her whole manner, and a shy, sidelong look that seemed to be continually expectant of a chiding.

This little one sat on the sanded floor, between the table, which was spread for the evening meal, and the glowing hearth, holding in her lap a favorite kitten, and playing with it gently, but neither laughing aloud, nor crowing and shouting, as most children of her age would have done.

The boys lounged idly on the rude wooden chairs and benches, which surrounded the walls of the room; the day's work was finished; their hands were unoccupied. It would seem that their minds were as much so. Conversation they had none; books they had none; with the exception of the Bible—which, alas the day! had been rendered distasteful to them, by being forced upon them as a penance and a task, at an age when the intellect is too feeble to grasp its consolations, or comprehend its glorious promises—and a few tracts, so stern, so savage, and so unrelenting in their morality, so utterly uncharitable in their tendency, and so disgusting, not to say blasphemous, in their language, that it required no adventitious cause of dislike to deter the young men from opening their denunciatory pages.

The mother of this sad-eyed and gloomy family went to and fro, from one room to another, intent upon her household duties; but she performed them, as it were, mechanically, and with nothing of that joyous interest, that hope of pleasing, that certainty of meriting and meeting approbation, which renders even the most ungrateful toils in some sort agreeable, when undertaken in behalf of those whom we love.

There was one other person present in the room; and that one so remarkable, that he must not be lightly passed over, although he sat mute and motionless in the chimney corner, never turning his eyes toward any of the family—of his family, which was collected about him, or appearing to take the smallest notice of anything that was passing.

He was a tall, dark, stern old man, apparently near eighty years of age. But those years, though they had been spent in hardship, in warfare, in toil, and in exile, left many traces, on his marked face, and sinewy though lean and emaciated frame. He sat perfectly erect in his chair, with his arms resting squarely on its elbows, and his dark clear eyes fixed on vacancy. The muscles of his mouth, which were as hard as iron, and showed a will as indomitable, never relaxed into a smile. He seemed to live on memory only, and on the past; so little heed did he take of any sublunary matters.

Sometimes, if any of the children spoke louder than their custom, much more if they laughed aloud, or if the babe set up, as it would do at rare intervals forgetful, a shrill, childish laugh, he would look quickly at the offender, with an expression of eye that would alone have sufficed to awe him into silence, without the harshly intonated "Peace!" which was sure to follow that dark glance, in accents which were anything rather than pacific.

Sometimes, when no one spoke or moved, when not a sound was to be heard save the low whisper of the sea breeze in the pinetops, or the deep monotonous inrolling of the surf, he would start, as if at some fearful voice in his ear, and gaze around him wildly, almost fearfully, and clutch at the left side of his girdle, with his thin, bony hands, as if to find a weapon.

Then, in a moment, as if recovering from his trance, he would shake his head with a sort of angry and impatient sorrow, and relapse into his day-long musings.

Yet singular as was his manner, and dark as was the cloud which, it would seem, had settled down not only on his features, but on his secret soul, there was nothing morose, or mean, or cruel about the old man's features.

Stern indeed he was, but with the sternness that is severer upon himself than human nature. Hard, self-denying, and ascetical, yet full withal of high and noble purposes, enthusiastic, and a dreamer of great things, fanatical perhaps and wild, but zealous and sincere, and an appreciator of sincerity in others.

Such had that old man been, in his days of eminence and power—for he had been both eminent and powerful—before exile and persecution had thoroughly distorted a mind, perhaps erratic in its natural tendency, and almost quenched its wild and penetrating radiance in silent gloom and torpor.

His hair was as white as snow, as were his shaggy eyebrows, and the heavy mustache, and pointed beard, which still clothed his upper lip and chin.

His dress was a long-waisted and close-fitting jerkin of black serge, with a white linen band, loose, black trunk-hose, and coarse, gray, woollen stockings. He wore a broad, buff belt about his waist, and it might well be that the long basket-hilted tuck, or broadsword, which hung in its steel scabbard, besides a morion and horseman's musquetoon over the mantlepiece, had once swung from it on his thigh, and clashed on spur and stirrup amid the stormy rush of squadrons.

No weapon graced it now, however, but an oak staff with a brass ferrule leaned against the elbow-chair in which he sat unconscious, and a tall, steeple-crowned hat, lay with a large, black cloak, near at hand, in case of his choosing to go abroad.

Such was the aspect of the room, and such the looks and occupation of the company, when lifting the latch gently, and entering without any smile or greeting, Ruth Whalley joined, after her short conversation with the master of the house.

" Father is coming," she said quietly, " and I much fear he brings evil tidings ; for he seems anxious and disquieted."

At the word 'father,' instead of rising with alacrity and joy to meet him, the three boys moved in their chairs uneasily, and drew themselves up into erect and rigid attitudes, and then the elder reached the Bible from a desk, whereon it lay, and opening it at random, began to study it with diligence.

The child that was playing on the hearth, jumped up, and dropped her kitten, which took refuge, as soon as the heavy step of Merciful became audible without, under the chair whereon the old man was sitting.

A vague expression of distrust, almost of fear, crossed the babe's face ; and running to her mother's side, she clutched her grogram gown with both hands, as if she were flying from an enemy.

The mother spoke not, but looked up and interchanged a speaking glance with Ruth, lifted the little one in her arms, and pressed it to her bosom ; then heaving a long, painful sigh, pursued her household occupations.

The door opened abruptly; and, uttering no kindly word, unloving, and unwelcomed, the austere man crossed the threshold of that, to gracious hearts, the sweetest sanctuary, his own home.

CHAPTER V.

THE EVENING MEAL.

"Desideratoque tandem acquiescere lecto."

WITH a deliberate and searching glance, Merciful Whalley noted all that was passing, as he entered, ere he spoke; and when he did speak, it was with the cold authoritative manner which long habit had made now a part almost, of his nature.

"Gideon," he said, addressing the eldest of the boys, "take down the boat-locks, and the keys, and make all fast for the night. And, mark me, whose duty was it to see to the drying of the Seine?"

"Abner's, to-day, sir," answered the second, growing very red in the face. "I calked the seams of the 'Good Hope,' this morning—"

"And in the afternoon?" inquired his father, with a piercing glance.

"I was out on the reef with Gideon catching tautaugs," replied the boy timidly.

"Ha! couldst thou find naught to do, more pressing? Abner, thou wilt go supperless to bed; and think thyself dealt but too leniently withal, that I do not chastise thee soundly—the wind hath blown the new seine on the stakes, and torn a rent in it, of a yard long, and upward. Go fetch it up, and secure it on the upper railings. Enoch, go help thy brother."

Never did eastern slaves obey their master, with more prompt obedience; but it was all mechanical, eye-service all, done grudgingly, for fear, and not for love.

When they had left the room, he took off the high-crowned

hat, which he had not removed before, wiped his brow with the back of his broad hand, and setting his long musket down in the chimney-corner, threw himself into the chair, which Enoch had lately vacated, opposite to the old man, who had not altered his position, or seemed to be aware of his son's entrance.

And now, for the first time, did anything resembling a human expression cross the dark features of the Puritan. As he gazed on the old man, who sat there, all unconscious of the wild storm that was brewing, buried in his own wilder recollections, the muscles of the austere man's mouth worked visibly, and something like a drop of passing moisture twinkled upon the lashes of his cold, hard eye.

His beautiful child had been watching him with tender and almost compassionate solicitude. She alone pitied and loved, more than she feared, her father.

The wife of that stern man's bosom, who once would have laid down her life to soothe his slightest sorrow, was now so shy, so timid, and so spirit-broken, that she no longer dared so much as to intrude her consolation on one whose afflictions were for the most part of his own creating, and far beyond the sphere of any mortal comforter.

To his boys he was only the oppressive taskmaster, the rigid and unbending tyrant.

But to Ruth, exquisite Ruth, he was not only the revered father, but the unhappy, self-tormented man. She never asked, never considered, whence his sorrows ; she saw that they were sorrows, and, whether real or imaginary, it was enough for her to know that they did pierce his hard heart to the core, and wring from him groans of agony, which she had heard in the dead of night, when all save she were sleeping, and she watching in fear and sadness at the door of the conscience-stricken sufferer.

Perhaps, had he been milder in his mood, more human in

his affections, more accessible in his sorrow—perhaps, I say, she had then loved him less.

Now, as she saw him alienating all around him by his black mood, till she alone of all his family had any sympathy with him; compassion, the true woman's instinct, the tenderness which flows but the more abundantly the more exactingly it is demanded, attracted her to him irresistibly. And ere long she felt that, in some sort, he reposed on her, and rested the frailty of his disordered manhood on the immovable strength of her feminine affections.

From that day forth—from the hour and the minute in which she felt herself to be the staff and support of that unhappy and wrong-minded parent—no coldness could have frozen, no violence turned back, the warm tide of her sympathies, the depth of her devotion.

And, to do justice to the man, although he rarely smiled on her—for smiles were strangers to his gloomy nature—although to her, as to all the rest, he was indifferent, severe, and cold, yet to her, and to her alone, he was never violent, and rarely harsh or bitter.

He would gaze at her often with a softened eye, and as that eye would dwell on her pure face, right index of her spotless mind, his heart would expand, as far as it was capable of expansion; and he would smite his breast, and mourn over what he deemed her perilous and lost condition; even, he would himself have said, "as Rachel weeping for her children, and would not be comforted."

Sometimes, he would even listen to her voice, and give himself for a while to softer feelings, as her low, silvery tones warbled the precious songs of David; and he would liken her strains to the prophet-king's inspired minstrelsey, "when he took a harp and played with his hand, so Saul was refreshed, and was well, and the evil spirit departed from him."

And therefore she loved him; and if her love was mixed with fear, it was not lessened by it. And what mortal feeling is there so pure, that it has not some touch of evil in it, whenever the true Christian's love for his Lord and teacher can not divest itself entirely of some sordid thoughts of self?

As pure, however, as any human sentiment can be, was sweet Ruth Whalley's tenderness toward that cold-hearted and uninteresting man. And now, as she observed the anguish of his soul, while he gazed silently in his own father's face, she was the more convinced, of what she had been led to suspect by his unusual sharpness to herself, that some deep, real sorrow, some actual affliction, was at hand, which had disturbed him, almost beyond endurance.

Her heart yearned to him. Her beautiful brown eyes were filled to overflowing, with tears, which it cost her a mighty effort to repress, as she crossed the room gently, and seating herself on a low stool by his side, took one of his large weather-beaten hands, and pressed it lovingly in her soft, slender fingers.

It almost seemed to burn her, as she took it; so hotly did the fever of his distempered spirit drive the blood through his veins, swollen well nigh to bursting.

"Father," she said in a soft, tremulous whisper, so low that it reached no ear but his, "dear, dearest father!"

The Puritan looked down upon her for a moment; and it may be that his spirit smote him for his unkindness. For the moisture, that had scarce gemmed his eyelash, swelled into a full tear, slid down his wrinkled cheek, and fell heavily upon his daughter's hand. Still he was not ashamed, but laid his broad palm on the soft, glossy curls that covered her fair head, and replied to her caress, saying, like her, in a low voice—

"Thou art a good child, Ruth; so far as one of us miserable sinners may be called good; and I believe thou lovest me. Would, O my child, would God! thou didst so love thy

Lord, and hatedst me, who am but as a worm, as a vile potsherd, to be trodden under foot, or dashed piecemeal in his day of indignation! While HE, wouldst thou but turn thy love to him, can save thy soul alive!"

"I can not prove how fervently I love HIM better, than by obedience to his word, by honoring, I mean, my father, and ministering, if he will permit me, to his sorrows."

"Alas! alas! for the false doctrine!" groaned the enthusiast aloud. "Knowest thou not, wretched child, that he taught, 'if any man come to me, and hate not his father and his mother, he can not be my disciple'?"

"And yet, my father," returned the gentle girl, nothing abashed or disconcerted by his perverse and blind adherence to the letter of one single text, "the Lord blessed Ruth, my namesake; who hated not her mother Naomi, but loved her, above all earthly things, and cherished her, and left for her, home, kindred, friends, and country; and went for her to glean in a far land, even in the fields of Boaz. And yet, my father, the Lord blessed Ruth, and gave to her prosperity, and peace, and happiness exceeding, upon earth. May he do so to this his servant likewise, and more also; not in this perishable world, but in his holy heavens!"

"Amen! Amen!" replied the hard man, for the moment, wholly subdued and conquered by the pure faith and humility of his fair child.

A momentary silence followed, for Merciful, as often happens with men of his moody temperament, was more ashamed of the bitter feelings he had displayed, than he had ever been, of the worst acts of his lifetime.

Ruth was too timid and too inexperienced to follow up the advantage she had gained: and the same cold and heart-chilling reserve, which had prevailed before her gentle effort, was again falling on the domestic circle, when the door opened, and the boys returned, their tasks performed, to the fireside, creating a momentary bustle by their entrance.

Almost at the same instant the mother came in from a different direction, followed by Tituba, the Indian girl, bringing with them, hot cakes, and bowls of milk, and butter, such as was set before Sisera of old, and all the preparations for an abundant evening meal.

The caldron was removed from the iron hook on which it hung, and its contents, which proved to be that standing dainty of New England, a rich chowder, were poured into a large tureen of Delft ware.

Then the pale mother stepped up to her lord, and announced to him, with bated breath and a downcast eye, that supper was ready, if he would please to partake of it.

Heaving a deep sigh, that was almost a groan, the Puritan rose from his seat reluctantly, as if he considered it the most unpleasant and sinful thing in the world to taste the bread for which we are taught to pray daily.

When he had risen to his feet, however, his conduct showed one of those strong redeeming points, the existence of which prevented his character from being altogether, and intolerably odious—his deep affection, namely, and respect for his old, impotent, and dreaming father.

It seemed as if in that one feeling toward that one person were absorbed all his capabilities of loving. As if the passion which he once had felt for the partner of his lot whether it should be good or evil, the paternal tenderness with which all men regard the offspring of their bed, the very patriotism which had once burned so fiercely in his bosom, were all merged and concentred in his devotion to his aged father.

To him, as Hector to Andromache, that old man stood in lieu of all other ties, all other kindred. He was to him as wife, and children, brethren, and home, and country.

And now, as timidly as a short time before his wife had stood before him, inviting him to the well-provided table, he stood before the white-haired elder, and begged him, with a voice as humble, to rise and come to supper.

Thrice was he compelled to renew his bidding, before his father comprehended him.

When he first spoke, the old man started as if aroused from sleep, and gazed with unmeaning eyes into his son's face. At the second invitation he drew his hand across his brow, as if to clear away the mists which time and powerful memories had gathered round him, and then shook his head half-wistfully, half-sorrowfully, as if conscious of his own infirmity.

Then, with a mighty effort, he seemed to collect his mind; and, at the third summons, arose calm and quiet, with the graceful ease of a gentleman, and simply saying—

"I crave your pardon, son Merciful; I was busy with old times," he moved steadily across the floor without assistance, and took his place in a high-backed arm-chair, at the head of the board.

Then Merciful drew near the table, and clasping his hands, uttered a long and vehement prayer, full of denunciations of that sinful and headstrong generation, of dark anticipations of the wrath to come, and of expostulatory and familiar arguments with the Almighty, such as to better-regulated minds would appear almost blasphemous. This strange grace ended, he took his seat, distributed the plenteous viands in silence to the members of his family; and that done, fed in silence, with an immoderate and wolfish appetite.

Scarcely a word was spoken during that gloomy and unsocial meal, unless it were a passing request to be helped to the contents of this or that dish, until toward the end of the repast, when a strange scene occurred, which led in the end to strange and fearful consequences.

CHAPTER VI.

THE INDIAN.

"With whom revenge is virtue."

During the progress of supper which was by no means hurried—for, although they divested their meals of all intellectual or social character by the austere silence in which they partook them, the Puritans were far from being averse to the pleasures of the table—during the progress of supper the Indian girl stood, with a sullen cloud overshadowing her comely features, through which there flashed at times a gleam of ungovernable hatred and ferocity, behind the chair of her master, Merciful. It seemed to be only by a great effort that she refrained from some display of violent temper, when she was called upon to assist him to any of the condiments or eatables which he required. And it was, perhaps, well for her that his mind was absorbed so completely in the consideration of the tidings that he had, that day, received in Boston, that he took no note of the Indian girl's changed and disrespectful demeanor.

It was not, however, destined that the evening should pass over, without an explosion; and, singular as it might seem, sweet Ruth was the immediate, though most involuntarily, cause of the outbreak.

She had, that very evening, promised the poor drudge that she would never address her by the name of Patience; rightly attaching small importance to a mere word, and deeming it of far greater consequence to conciliate the mind of the poor heathen, by kindness and judicious teaching, than to irritate and revolt her feelings by the continued application of a term, which she abhorred, and probably esteemed degrading.

It is true, when she made that promise, Ruth had not fully envisaged the anger, which her rejection of the Christian appellation he had chosen for the bondwoman, was likely to arouse in her father.

Perhaps she overrated her influence over his evil mood, and fancied that the milder temper he had exhibited for a little space that evening, would be of more endurance than it indeed was.

However this might be, when the supper was nearly at an end, she raised her eyes with a gentle smile to the bondwoman's face, and said in her musical and winning tones,

" Will you not give me a glass of fair, spring water, Tituba ?"

At the sound of the forbidden word, Enoch, the second of her brothers, started and let fall his knife upon the pewter platter, calling thereby his father's indignation on himself, no less than his attention to his sister's dereliction.

" Leave the board, Enoch," said the deep voice of Merciful, " since thou canst not behave decorously. And thou, Ruth, what meaneth this, that thou callest yon dark-skinned daughter of the evil race by the foul name which marks her out unto perdition ?"

" It is her own name, father," replied the gentle girl, " the name that recalls to her the wild home of her childhood, the mother who lulled her infancy, the little brethren who played around her. She loves her own name, father. It speaks to her of the days when she was free ; when her people were a great nation. — Oh ! suffer her, I pray you, to be called Tituba. She hates the name of Patience. I do not think that there can be so much in a mere name."

" Thou dost not think !" exclaimed the Puritan, his cold, black eyes dilating with astonishment, and his iron mouth distorted into a grim, sarcastic smile. " And who taught thee to think? Who made thee, if I be not overbold to ask it, a teacher in Israel? Wo! wo! rebellion and perversity of heart! Wo! wo! and alas! that, on this night of tribulation, when it has pleased the Lord to try this house in a hot furnace of affliction, alas! I say, that on this night, I should hear from the lips of child of mine, such blasphemy against the Lord's most holy ordinance of baptism, with water and the Spirit. Go! go! my wretched and misbelieving child, go to thy chamber, mortify thy soul with prayer and humiliation, and this pride of thy soul with fasting. And thou, swart child of sin, see what the evil of thy heart hath wrought of sorrow to thy young mistress. Beware, that I hear no more of this, or thou shalt rue it long and sorely. Pray to the Christian's God, pray that thou mayest believe; Patience thou art, and Patience—"

"Patience, I am not!" replied the Indian girl, haughtily, but not angrily; and it was remarkable, that, under the influence of pride and excited feeling, she no longer spoke in broken English, or expressed her thoughts with difficulty. "White man, my name is Tituba—my mother's brother was great Miantonomah, the war-chief of the mighty, the free, Narragansets!

"White man, my tribe were lords of all the land thy greedy eyes have looked upon, ages before thy big canoes crossed the great lake, to make them slaves, and wretched.

"White man, my people were the chiefs of that great tribe.

"And what is the white man that he should rob the Indian, not of the land only and the liberty, which the Great Spirit gave him, but of his very name and nature?

"The white man is a tyrant to his slave, a dog to his enemy!—The white man's God is a devil, if white men do *his* bidding!

"Hear my words, white man, Tituba will die when the Great Spirit wants her, but she will *not* be Patience, she will *not* bow down to the white man's God. No, white man! she will pray to the Indian's devil, rather!

"White man, my words are spoken."

It is, perhaps, surprising that the Puritan should have allowed the child of nature to conclude her powerful harangue uninterrupted; but, though he was a stern and at times a cruel man, he was not passionate, or quick to anger.

His errors, great or small, were those, not of impulse, but of deliberate and resolute opinion.

He rarely broke in upon the speech, or prevented the action of any one; but, the speech or action committed, he judged it uncharitably, and punished it unmercifully.

Moreover, in the present instance, he was surprised; first, that his daughter, the meek, gentle, humble-spirited Ruth, should have presumed to think at all, and more, to think independently, and differently from himself; and lastly, that the Indian, the heathen, the slave, the poor, soulless, helpless, broken-hearted outcast, who, for the most part, scarcely could find words to express her submission, should break out into such a torrent of strong, fiery, and well-chosen language.

Balaam stood not more utterly aghast, for a moment, when his ass turned and rebuked him with a human utterance.

Not long, however, did the Puritan's astonishment endure; he arose to his feet with his brow black as night.

"The *masters* have eaten sour grapes," he said, "and the teeth of the *slaves* are set on edge! The Lord is angry with his people! Lo! we will seek the Lord in prayer. Perchance, he will vouchsafe to point us out a way to escape his wrath—peradventure, he will bear it in upon our spirits, with what chastisement we shall chastise this daughter of perdition. And thou," he added, turning with an unchanged brow to the Indian girl, "and thou, begone to the workshed, until I come to conjure this rebellious and accursed spirit out of thee."

But she moved not at all to go, nor quailed before his scowling eye; but stood, with her arms folded on her breast, as if defying him.

"Will the white man flog Tituba?" she said, in tones of the most tranquil resolution.

"Ay! peradventure. If so the Lord"—

But ere he could utter another word, she interrupted him, in a shrill, high-pitched cry, tremulous with passion—

"Never again!—never again, white man, shall you lay lash on Tituba! Scourge your own base white flesh! Lash your own children, like dogs, and yet viler brutes! Shed your own coward English blood! But never again! never, never, strike an Indian, and a woman!"

And, with the last word of her rapid and broken exclamation, she bounded upon him, her eyes flashing fire, like the panther of her own native wilderness upon her prey.

A long two-edged and sharp-pointed cook's knife, which she had snatched unperceived from the dresser, gleamed in her lifted hand, as she sprang upon her tyrant.

Down! down it came, flashing in the sunbeams, swift as the lightning's thought executing fire!

Aimed full and surely at his neck, above the collar-bone, had that blow fallen undiverted, Merciful Whalley had indeed, as she said, never struck blow again, nor moved hand or foot, in this world.

And so completely was he taken by surprise, that he made no effort to avoid or parry it.

His miserable wife sank down into her chair, clasping her hands over her eyes, that she might not at least see the death-blow.

The old man had withdrawn from the table, during the loud discussion, entirely unconscious of all that was passing; and coiled up, as before, in the chimney-corner, was watching the smoke, as it rolled up the chimney in thick wreaths, with an eye that scarce knew what it noted.

Gideon, the eldest son, bounded forward, but too late; the other boys had been banished the room almost an hour before.

But Ruth, brave Ruth, who had arisen at her father's command, and was retreating to her own chamber, emboldened by the peril of that ruthless parent, leaped in between them, with a loud piercing cry—

"Tituba! Tituba! he is *my* father!"

The eyes of the Indian girl glared fearfully, but it was all too late. She could not check the blow.

It fell!

But the cry, and the attempt Ruth had made to arrest her arm, diverted the aim; and striking on the clavicle, the point of the knife was turned against the bone, and glanced off, inflicting only a superficial wound in the muscles of the shoulder.

In the next moment Gideon had seized and disarmed her; for, the brief passion over, she subsided instantly into the crest-fallen, spirit-broken drudge, she had been before her unpremeditated effort.

The Puritan staggered beneath the weight of the blow, so vigorously was it dealt; but in an instant he rallied, as calm, as inscrutable, as dark, and impassive, as his wont.

"'The Lord is the strength of my life, of whom shall I be afraid?' But thou, child of iniquity, murderess, devil-worshipper, surely of thee, and such as thee, it was written, 'Thou shalt not suffer, one of them to live!' no; not one!" cried the Puritan.

"Father, dear father, thou art wounded; but, the Lord's name be praised, for ever and for ever, I have preserved thee!"

"Not thou, my daughter, but the Lord, even the Lord of Hosts!" replied the enthusiast, with his eye glaring wildly;

for he was under the excitement of that fierce, overmastering spirit, which he believed to be inspiration. He put her aside gently, as she threw herself into his arms—

" The wound," he said, " is nothing; thou, Ruth, shall see to it anon, when I have taken order with this *witch*."

He turned to the Indian girl, who stood now motionless as a statue, her head bowed, her arms listlessly hanging by her side, expectant, as it seemed, and careless of her doom.

" Go!" he said—" Go! I have spoken! Pray to your God, if you believe in any! Go! I follow!"

Without a word, a glance, a gesture, in that calm dignity of submission, so characteristic of the Indian who never resists, when resistance is evidently unavailing, she passed with noiseless steps out of the kitchen.

And heedless of the tears, the sobs, the supplications of his daughter, who had so lately saved his life, at imminent peril of her own, he strode out doggedly behind the Indian.

He closed the door—locked—double-locked it after him.

There was a long pause—breathless, frightful!

Then came a thrilling, quavering scream—a scream that made the blood curdle in the veins of all who heard it.

And then—silence.

CHAPTER VII.

THE VETERAN.

"Quæ fuerint juvenili incorpore vires."

SEVERAL seconds elapsed after that frightful cry had arisen and subsided, before any of those present could collect their faculties sufficiently to take any action.

The wife of Merciful, a delicate and tender-hearted creature, never from her youth upward endowed with much energy or spirit, had long ago been so utterly subdued and crushed by the commanding will and rigid authority of her husband, that she would scarcely have ventured a remonstrance, had she seen him applying the brand to the house in which she was dwelling.

The tears, it is true, flowed in streams down her pale, meager cheeks, and trickled through her thin fingers, and her words were half lost amid convulsive sobs, as she cried—

"Oh! he will slay her! he will slay her! Merciful God, spare him the burthen of blood-guiltiness!"

But she did not arise from her chair, or make any effort at interference.

Gideon, than whom a hardier or braver boy never spread canvass to the wind, so far as natural perils were concerned, was so unfortunately impressed by his father's tyranny—for by no milder name can the domestic despot's iron rule be characterized—that he would rather have faced a hunted bear, naked-handed, than stood between that parent and the victim of his wrath.

It seemed, for a moment, that the stern Puritan would be permitted to work his vengeful will on the unhappy girl, without a single effort in her favor.

The face of Ruth was as white, and almost as cold, as statuary marble; her beautiful eyes were fixed and dilated so unnaturally, that a circle of white was visible around each glaring iris; her hands were clasped in an agony of suspense; her lips apart; and her whole frame motionless and rigid.

She stood, arrested by that awful sound—that yet more awful silence—in the very act of springing forward. A breathing, living statue, petrified, as it were, in the very ecstacy of terror.

Again that fearful scream rose clear and piercing; again, again, filling every corner and cranny of the house with its terrific volume.

And through it, and over it, were heard a succession of heavy, sullen sounds, the reverberation of the accursed thong plied on a helpless woman. Then was the spell broken instantly that had held Ruth Whalley motionless.

She had believed that all was over—that the fell deed of vengeance was completed—that the wild scream of agony, which had so frozen up her heart's blood, proclaimed that miserable man a murderer.

Tremendous as it was, the second scream fell on her ear like tidings of joy and hope.

The blood rushed to her face, her fixed eye flashed lightly. At one spring she reached the door, beat violently with her delicate hands on the hard pannels, and cried in accents that spoke, as clearly as her words, her unstained and holy purpose.

"Hear what the Lord sayeth, 'Thou shalt do no murder!'"

But her weak mother, terrified rather by the wrath of her husband than by the sufferings of the slave, and abject in the selfishness of that most selfish of all feelings, personal apprehension, said,

"Peace, oh! peace, Ruth Whalley, you will but irritate him."

"Irritate him!" exclaimed the noble girl; "Listen! do you hear that? Irritate him! Gideon, brother, if you have one spark in your soul of manhood or of courage, bring yon axe hither;—strike one blow, and save your father's soul from the guilt of murder."

But the boy stirred not; so utterly had the tyrannous domestic sway, and the heart-chilling puritanic rule quelled and subdued the nobler portions of his nature.

Still the wild shrieks pealed heavenward imploring; still the atrocious scourge clanged in the hands of the tormentor.

But now at every blow the long-drawn screams were feebler, hoarser, fuller of agony than of fear or indignation. They sunk gradually into low, shivering moans.

"Great God!" cried Ruth, "will you hear these things, and stand cowardly inactive? Give me the axe!"

And, as she spoke, she seized the ponderous implement, which at another time she scarcely could have lifted, and, moved by the tremendous excitement, wielded it like a feather.

One heavy blow fell on the lock, and half drove it from its fastenings, and the stout, oaken panels groaned and quivered.

Again she was upheaving it; and the next moment would have beheld the door battered from its hinges, when from the farther end of the room a voice was heard, that arrested her on the instant.

That which it has occupied pages to relate, had occurred almost in as many seconds. A minute certainly had not elapsed between the utterance of Tituba's first cry of anguish, and Ruth's assault upon the door.

And during that minute, which seemed almost a lifetime to

the actors, every one had been occupied so completely by the terrors of the scene, that not a thought, not an eye was directed to the old man, who, had he entered their minds at all, they would have supposed to be dozing, as usual, unmoved and abstracted in his chimney-corner.

Far from it. When the first cry fell upon his ear, whether it acted as the key to some treasured hoard of memories, which it unlocked and poured out upon his darkened spirit, or merely caused his nerves to thrill with a keener sensibility, his aspect changed upon the moment.

It was like the uplifting of a heavy curtain from a fine picture. The scattering of a thick mist from a sunny landscape.

His eye which, a moment before, had no "speculation in't," was now filled with a strange, deep meaning. His features, which had been blank and rayless, as those of an idiot, betraying no play of the intellect, no working of the godlike mind, were in an instant preternaturally sharpened—alive and quick with a keen, eager, vigorous expression.

Yet was neither the light and meaning of the eye that of calm, evenly-balanced reason, nor the sharp expression of the features such a one as is often seen, where the intellect is clear, and its operation regular and healthful.

Still, it was not the wild glare of insanity that flashed from the speaking eye.

It was not the unnatural shrewdness of the crafty lunatic that informed those high features.

He arose to his feet instantly, drew his hand once across his brow with an air of uncertainty, perhaps of weakness. Then, as the second shriek smote his ear, he looked abroad keenly with an inquisitive and eager gaze, which yet seemed to be at a loss, and hardly to recognise the objects around him.

On one thing, however, it fell with a quick glance of recog

nition—the long, steel-hilted tuck, which hung in its steel scabbard, above the mantelpiece.

He grasped it without a moment's hesitation; unsheathed it with a steady hand, gazed on its clear and polished blade with an air of exultation, tried its point and edge with his finger, proved the elastic temper of the steel by bending it against the floor and suffering it to spring back to its length, and then fitting its chain about his wrist, strode forward with a firm step and an erect and steady bearing, as if to confront a foeman!

"What, ho!" he cried aloud, in tones trumpet-like and spirit-stirring—tones that displayed nothing of the tremulous debility of years. "To arms! to arms! Ring out the city-bells! Strike drums!—sound trumpets! The bloody Girgashites are upon us. The savage Rupert and his rake-hell cavaliers! To arms! to arms! They are within the walls already!"

Ruth dropped the axe, which she had lifted for another blow, at those strange words. Her mother, startled by this new terror, rose with a faint cry from her chair and staggered forward to meet the veteran Roundhead; as, feebly vigorous, he strode on bearing aloft the bright rapier, which had done service in its day, whether for good or evil, toward the fated door.

Gideon himself, aroused to something like spirit, by this strange resurrection of his grandfather's mind from the dull and deathlike sleep in which it had so long lain dormant, appeared to nerve himself by a struggle for action.

But nothing did the old man heed them. He shook back the long, thin, silvery locks from his brow, and with a flushed, hectic cheek, and fire in his eye, rushed forward, his whole mind evidently full of some painful and vivid recollections.

"Are ye men?" he cried aloud once again. "Are ye men, that ye suffer them to deal thus with your wives, your children? Ho! Rally! rally! Hear ye not how the women shriek, and will ye not make in? Lo! where yon love-locked cavalier hales the fair maiden in his licentious arms! Lo! where yon fierce Alsatian tosses the infant on his pike!—Make in, I say, make in! Strike for your children's safety—strike for the honor of your women! Tarry not, but make in!"

As he spoke, he attained the door, which Ruth had already half-beaten from its hinges; but, ere this, the long shrieks had subsided into those deep and shuddering moans, which were if possible more awful and appalling. His hand was on the latch, and he had shaken it once stoutly, when roused again to ecstacy by some more cruel stripe the miserable girl set up another cry, more terrible than any she had uttered.

"God of my fathers!" shouted the old man, turning ashy pale, the transitory flush passing from his wan cheek like the last sunset hue. "God of my fathers! it is she! Ho! Rachel, Rachel! wife of my soul, I come! I! I!—it is not, it can not, shall not be—it *is not*, too late!"

And, with the words, raising his foot with all the energetic strength of young and robust manhood, he put his whole force into one crashing blow, and split the heavy door asunder.

The room was already growing very dark, for the lustre of day had died out from the western sky; and the wood-fire upon the hearth threw wavering and uncertain gleams over the strange and agitating scene.

At the loud crash of the broken door, the cries ceased, and the clang of the scourge; and the harsh, stern voice of the Puritan, deepened by the echoes of the vaulted cellar and staircase, into a sort of hollow roar, was heard, asking angrily,

"Who dares intrude upon me? Hence! begone, or fear mine heaviest indignation!"

"Tush! tell me not of fear!" returned the old man. "Come forth, I say, if you be'est prince, or peer, or base and mercenary stabber; come forth, I say, and thou shalt meet a man!—A man who has braved thy betters, who has not held his hand nor refrained from the shedding of high blood—even the blood of crowned and anointed kings! Come forth, I say, leave torturing, helpless women, and meet a man, indeed—meet me, even Edward Whalley!"

"My father!" exclaimed the Puritan, in a voice now tinctured somewhat by superstitious awe; and leaving his barbarous occupation, he hurried up the steps from the cellar, to ascertain what was passing.

The fire-light was rising and falling; now flashing out for a few seconds and filling the whole room with clear lustre; now fading utterly away, and leaving the place steeped in glimmering and uncertain twilight.

But just as Merciful Whalley reached the head of the staircase, pallid, and grim, and suffering under the effects of that exhaustion, which not unfrequently succeeds to the indulgence of any overmastering passion, one of the brightest of those flickering gleams rose from the hearth, and fell directly on his haggard face and features.

There was a gory spot upon his forehead; his hands were dyed with the same odious hue, and in his right he held a knotted cord, whence there fell gouts of blood upon the clean washed floor.

As the figure of the Puritan became visible ascending, the old man rushed at first to meet him with his sword uplifted, almost in act to strike.

But as his eyes fell upon the bloody brow, the bloody hands, the bloody cord which they grasped, old recollection seemed again to overpower him.

He dropped the rapier, clanging upon the ground, staggered two or three paces backward, clasping his white, emaciated hands over his eyes, and uttering with a doleful cry the words:

"Too late! too late!—O Rachel, Rachel, Rachel!" He would have fallen to the ground but that Ruth and her brother caught him in their arms, and supported him to a chair; whereon he fell back, for the moment, completely exhausted and overpowered by that strong excitement.

"What is all this ado?" said the hard father, looking around him very gloomily, but yet more angrily. "What have you done with him?"

"Nay!" replied Ruth, meeting his eye, as she had never done before, calmly, but firmly, inspired by womanly resolution, womanly indignation. "Nay! rather, what have *you* done, father?"

"Punished a murderess and a witch!" he answered almost fiercely, "and so robbed the gallows of its due."

And his angry eye glared upon his own fair child, as if yet but half satiated with revenge, he would have wreaked his fury on her likewise.

But to Ruth Whalley his frown had lost all its terrors; and she gazed on him with a sort of abhorrent compassion.

"Speak, father," she said, in a voice full of deep feeling. "For your soul's sake, I conjure you, speak! Have you, an elder, and judge of your people, broken God's sixth commandment?"

"See thou to that," he answered her, moodily, going in great perturbation toward the chair of his father, on whom it would appear that all his thoughts were centred, even in that dread moment.

"By the Lord's grace, I will," she replied steadily, although she turned deathly pale, for she supposed from his manner that all was indeed over. "And may he, of his infinite mercy, grant, that you be not called to answer it, beyond all hope, all endurance!"

And lighting a lamp, she went down stairs, horror-stricken, but fearless, alone to the place of torture.

CHAPTER VIII.

THE CHANGE.

"My heart is in the coffin, there, with Cæsar,
And I must pause till it come back to me."

As soon as Ruth left the kitchen, in search of the poor victim of her father's anger, Merciful Whalley occupied himself actively and efficiently about the old man, who had fainted, after the violent agitation of his mind.

Directing his wife to apply cloths steeped in cold water to his temples, he produced himself, from a cupboard of which he kept the key, a flask of some powerful cordial, which evidently had not been disturbed for many a year, since it was mantled over with thick cobwebs.

A few drops of this applied to the old man's lips resuscitated him almost immediately. He heaved a deep sigh, opened his eyes, and again closed them, and then, after a sort of tremulous struggle, sat up erect, and looked around him.

But his mind still wandered, nor did he seem to recognise any of those by whom he was surrounded. Yet it was not the apathetic dullness of his usual mood that was now apparent in his manner, but an uncertain wavering, as it were, of his mind between the past and present.

"Where am I?" he exclaimed. "Where is Rachel?—I thought I heard her voice but now; and yet," he continued, gazing around him with a bewildered eye, "and yet this looks not like the townhall of Bristol—nor hear I any longer the cries of our women in extremity, the shouts and the trumpets of the terrible malignants!"

"Peace, father! peace!" said Merciful, in tones as gentle as he could shape his mouth to utter—"This is not Bristol; nor are we any more at all in England. The days of the war are long since ended; the son of the 'man of blood' sits once more eminent upon the throne, from which his father fell; and we are here, leagues aloof, in New England, whither our people came to seek that liberty of conscience they might not have at home."

"Wherefore tellest thou this me, son Merciful?" said the old man recovering his memory at once, and not relapsing any more into the mental lethargy which had so long possessed him. "Dost thou believe me so old already, so frail-witted, that I know not this? Am I not in thy house, within the limits of the good Bay Province, and are not these thy wife, and thy children, whom I see around me? But—but—" and again his eye assumed a troubled aspect, "I see not—where is *my* wife—where is *my* Rachel! Ah! I remember, I remember!" and, as the full illumination of memory and reason returned to his shaken intellect, he bowed his head between his knees, and wept as bitterly as if long years had not elapsed since she whom he deplored fell in her innocence and youthful love a sacrifice to the accursed fiend of civil discord. "Alas!" he repeated, as he raised his head, after a long and silent pause, "I remember. But what were those cries, son Merciful—those cries which aroused me from my meditations? Surely they were not fancy—they were not the mere coinage of distempered memory. No, no! I did hear a woman's pitiful scream, and that it was which awakened me. How long—how long have I been a dreamer in the life-long day?"

And he shook his head not doubtfully any longer, but in a sort of sorrowful compassion at his own frailty. It was strange, but it seemed that the shock, which those screams of Tituba had given to his nervous system, had aroused and renewed his intellect altogether.

He spoke calmly, pertinently; the fickle and unstable fire had died from his eye, the hectic flush had faded from his cheek. There was no symptom now of undue excitement in his air or manner, no sign of weakness in his firm and serene countenance, in his erect, unbending posture.

Merciful Whalley paused, ere he replied. Almost he hoped that his father's mind would again wander, so he might be spared the disgrace of confessing what he had done—for now that the deed was over—that the stern heat of cruelty, which prompted it, had passed in some sort away—he felt that his conduct had indeed been both sinful and disgraceful.

Yet it was not shame that he felt, but bitter, burning mortification; it was not sorrow or repentance, much less compassion for his victim, but a hatred toward her ten times more deeply seated than before, for that she was the involuntary and unhappy cause of his degradation.

But the mind of the old regicide did not again wander; and, seeing that his son replied not, he inquired again, and this time not without some sterness in his manner.

"What were those woman's screams, son Merciful?"

"Nothing—a trifle—a vile Indian squaw, a *slave*, whom I had need to correct," answered the Puritan, greatly embarrassed. "Let us not speak of her at present. I have tidings to give you of far deeper importance—"

"Nothing!—a trifle!" interrupted the old man, repeating his words indignantly; "the outcries of a woman nothing! the sufferings of a woman a trifle! Go to, go to, sir! I know nothing of deeper importance! I must hear more of this—an Indian and a *slave!* Who art thou, and what God made thee, that thou shouldst hold thy fellow-worms, the work of that same God's right hand, in bondage? Was that the lash I heard? Art thou, as the Egyptian, a taskmaster, a persecutor?"

"A bond-servant, I should have said," replied his son, "and not a slave. Assigned to me was Patience by the selectmen of the town, for her advancement in the culture of the Christians, her indoctrination in the pure faith of the—"

"And thou hast beaten her—beaten her like a dog?" asked the old man reproachfully.

"She would have slain me with the knife on mine own hearth," returned the son. "See; the blood is yet wet on my doublet, where she smote!"

"There is blood likewise on thy brow! on thy cruel hands! —on that twisted and knotted cord! Is that *thy* blood, Merciful?"

Convicted, writhing with smothered rage, the dusk man was silent.

"And thou—thou a Whalley, and *my* son, hast scourged the image of thy Maker, a weak miserable, wailing woman, until the blood rushed out of her tortured limbs to bear witness of thy brutal fury!"

Still he was silent; but that speechless mood was more eloquent than all the words an orator could utter.

"Ichabod! Ichabod!" cried the old man, in accents of the deepest, the most agonizing grief, "now, indeed, hath the glory of my house departed! Son Merciful, be no more son of mine. Begone! nay, answer me nothing now! Go to thy chamber; go, commune with the Lord in prayer; go, commune with thine own soul in silence! It may be, when thou hast repented thee of this dread crime, that I will hear thee farther."

"Hear me, at least, to-night," replied the hard and ruthless man, bowing at the same time to his father's will, with the same absolute obedience which he exacted of his children — "or your own life will be the sacrifice."

"When have I valued my own life at all," answered the regicide, "save as a trust which Thou," he added, turning his eyes reverently upward, "hast committed to my keeping, and which it behooves me, therefore, not to resign, save at thy bidding? Go, my son; seek the Lord in prayer; sin no more in this wise; and it may be, peradventure, he shall forgive thy sin! Go! I will speak with thee anon."

Crestfallen and humiliated, the cold, iron-hearted Puritan departed, gnawing his heart with deep and secret spite.

In a sweet mood for prayer, verily. When his whole soul was hardened and rebellious, and in arms against all merciful and tender feelings. When so far was he from repenting of his cruelty to the hapless Indian, that the sentiment which was uppermost in his mind was rage and resentment against her. When he was almost pondering, even as he knelt down himself to ask for mercy, how he could best avenge himself on that innocent and hapless being.

For a moment or two after he quitted the room, the veteran walked to and fro buried in deep thought, and at times heaving long and painful sighs.

No member of the family had seen him for years display so much intelligence or activity.

And in the midst of their wonder they expected every moment to see him relapse into his accustomed stupor.

But he did not relapse. On the contrary, it seemed as if the exertion of his faculties called forth fresh powers; for he paused suddenly in his walk, and said, addressing himself to the pale and agitated wife of Merciful —

"My daughter, this is very terrible, very disgraceful. Thou shouldst have hindered this!"

She hinder it? As well might a weak mortal undertake to

control Heaven's thunder, as she to withstand her husband's energetic and domineering will.

It may be, that after he had spoken, something to this effect crossed his mind, for he looked at her mildly, and a smile, half-sorrowful, half-pitiful, fleeted across his high features; and he spoke again without waiting her reply—

"Ay! ay! thou wouldst, if an thou couldst; I will avouch it. But, come—we must see to amend the evil he hath done. Light me a lamp, boy. Where is this Indian girl. Heaven forefend, he hath slain her."

"No! no! It is not so bad as that," cried Ruth, who came bounding up the stairs, and who seemed less surprised than any of the others at this resuscitation of her grandfather. "Though it is very bad, indeed, and terrible! She had fainted; but she is better now, and I want help; to carry her to her bed only—but I must have help."

"And *shall*," replied the veteran. "Gideon shall help you, my good Ruth: and I will go likewise. I had of yore some skill in the art of healing, and, it may be, it shall be yet not all unprofitable. Bring the light, boy, and the flask of cordial," and he waved his hand toward the bottle which Merciful had left upon the table.

But his wife fearful yet, and more apprehensive of her husband's anger, than desirons of ministering to the poor household drudge, cried anxiously—

"Oh! no, no, no! Do not take that; Merciful prizes it beyond its weight in gold. He never will forgive me."

"And if he valued it beyond his heart's best life-blood, he should do well to lavish it now freely, if so he may repair his cruelty—his crime!"

"But what shall shelter me," cried the weak, selfish woman, "from his anger?"

"And what shall shelter thee, I fain would ask," returned

the independent, scornfully, "from HIS wrath, which is as a consuming fire, who brooks not that his creatures should be feared and obeyed, to the neglect of his most holy law? Woman, go to! your weakness is akin to thine husband's wickedness, and scarce, if anything, less sinful. Wouldst thou, for fear of a passing gust of passion, suffer a mortal life, perhaps an immortal soul, to perish; and suffer, too, the guilt of that perdition to rest upon your husband? For shame! for shame! Is this charity?—But mark me, I will shield you from his anger, should it be roused against you; which, I believe and trust it will not!" and, without any farther words, followed by the boy bearing the light, and conducted by the sweet maiden, the old man descended the stairs to the scene of that cruel punishment.

That scene was too terrible, too disgusting, for description; nor will I harrow up the feelings of my readers, as I perchance might do, by a picture so horrible and odious.

It is enough that the wretched girl had fainted under the merciless castigation of her enraged master; and, though she had already recovered some degree of animation under the tender cares of Ruth, the shock which her nervous system had sustained was still clearly perceptible in the strong convulsive rigors which shook her dusky limbs.

The sovereign cordial was given to her freely by the old man, whose sternness seemed all to have melted away into the genuine charity of the good Samaritan; and this, with other remedies, speedily brought her so far to herself, that it was no longer difficult to remove her to the small closet in which she slept.

Her wild eyes glared with a savage expression of astonishment, almost of awe, as she beheld that strange old man, whom she had ever regarded with that superstitious veneration which the North American tribes extend ever to those whose intellects are alienated—busied so actively, so practically, and so skilfully, about her treatment.

It was plain to see that she marvelled mightily; but with the usual self-control of an Indian, she restrained her wonder, as she did also her fierce indignation, at the brutality of which she had been the victim.

She spoke no word, even in reply to her favorite Ruth; and, when she had been made as comfortable as circumstances would admit, they left her to her own swelling and passionate thoughts.

When the old man returned to the kitchen, he resumed his place in the chimney-corner silently, and sat for a few moments buried in deep thought.

Then looking up, he said abruptly to the others, "Leave me awhile. I would speak with Ruth alone. You, woman, go to your hushand, and essay if you may not soften his hard mood; you, boy, to bed—I will talk with you to-morrow."

"Now, Ruth," he said, when the others had left the room, "tell me how this befell; and if there be many scenes like unto this, in this household, the Lord forgive me, for I too have much to answer, in that I have so given up my soul to memories of the past—so suffered my heart to dwell with her who hath no more any home on earth, save in this bosom—that all my sense hath been benumbed and paralyzed these many days—these many years, I should say rather—for I have taken little note of time. Tell me, my gentle daughter, all, and fear nothing."

And she did tell him all, and fearlessly and freely; and they conversed long together, nor had Ruth ever cause to repent that she dealt honestly and openly with the old regicide.

The night was far spent when they parted; and when they did so, as she arose from her seat, the old man opened his arms slowly, and clasped her to his aged heart, and kissed her forehead tenderly; a bright tear twinkled for a moment in his eyes, long unused to soft emotions; and he whispered, in husky and interrupted accents—

"Bless thee! bless thee, my daughter. Thou art a sweet, and gentle woman, and affectionate and artless. Be steadfast in the right; and it may well be that thy true and loving virtues shall reconcile this sinful house to its offended Lord and Savior.

CHAPTER IX.

THE PERIL.

"The sheriff, with a monstrous watch, is at the door."

The night was far advanced ere the old man, who had for hours been debating with his son hard points of knotty doctrine, and gravely reprobating the course and conduct of his life, which had, it would seem, been suddenly revealed to him by the events of that night, would suffer Merciful to speak on any other topic.

At last, however, when it was nearly midnight—after the younger Puritan had made confession of his error; and, after they had prayed together long and solemnly, the regicide with genuine and enthusiastic fervor, his son with a strange mixture of sincerity and hypocritic canting—the father expressed his willingness to hear the tidings, to which Merciful had so many times, and so anxiously, alluded.

"You should have known them sooner," he said eagerly, as soon as he received license to speak, "for truly they are pressing; and there is no time to spare. My father, loath as I am to say it, even this very night thou must quit this dwelling, which can no longer shield thee from the persecutor."

The old man looked him steadfastly in the face, with a piercing and penetrating glance; as if he would have read, in his soul, whether this were not a mere excuse for removing him from the superintendence of family matters, now that he had discovered the tyrannous conduct of the master.

It would seem, however, that he was convinced of his son's sincerity, at least in the present instance, for without removing his eagle eye from his face, he asked—

"Wherefore, and whither, must I go?"

"The wherefore can not be answered in a word," replied his son.

"Answer it, then, in ten, or in fifty."

"I need not tell you," he replied, "that the son of the 'Man of Blood' sits once more on the throne of England, nor that all parties humble themselves in the dust at the tyrant's feet."

"Alas, for the good cause! I know it."

"But this you know not yet; that, after you escaped from England hither, and so shunned the fate of Hugh Peters, Cooke, and the rest, noble victims who perished on the scaffold, so bitter has waxed the vengeance of the malignant king, that not death itself has availed to shelter our friends from his brute fury. The corpses of Cromwell, Bradshaw, Ireton, have been torn from their violated tombs, dragged through the streets of London upon hurdles, yea, gibbetted at Tyburn, and beheaded amid the ribald exultation of Alsatian bravoes, pages, and pandars of Whitehall!"

"God of my fathers!" cried the old man, in tones that spoke more than horror, "and didst thou witness these things, and was thy thunder silent? Verily, verily, thy people have sinned deeply in thy sight, that thou hast turned thus thy face away from us!"

"Sir Harry Vane, moreover, honest and true Sir Harry Vane, hath shed his blood likewise on the block; and his soul lies among the saints and martyrs, who, like him, died rejoicing for the sake of their conscience and their God."

"Inscrutable are thy ways, O thou most Highest!" returned the regicide. "Yet are thy judgments true and righteous altogether."

"Now hear me, father, how instantly and urgently these things touch you. I have feared long, and with me many of our people, since we have got this new and furious governor, this painted scarlet kingsman, this persecutor of the saints, and scoffer at the word of God, even this petty tyrant, of a great tyrant's making, Sir Edmund Andross, to rule over us — we have feared, I say, long, that the judges of the man, even the late man Charles, who have fled hitherward, as David fled from Saul into the wilderness En-gedi, would not be suffered to dwell quietly even beyond the sea. And therefore have we kept watch narrowly. A while ago, it was made kuown to us how three, who had escaped to Holland, and were abiding, as they believed, peaceful and secure under the rule, and within the limits of a free, independent nation, were seized there, surrendered by the states, and have since died on the gallows-tree in England. Therefore, we had our spies more closely on the watch than before; especially when, three days since, the Rose frigate entered the port from England, and cast anchor nigh the fortress. Yesterday, I got word that there was peril in the wind, and straight I set forth to the city. This morning, it was avouched to me by a true hand, one who is near the governor in place, but his heart yet is with us, that warrants have come over in the Rose for your apprehension, as well as for that of Goffe and Dixwell. They two fled instantly across the country to New Haven. For thee, there is no time to do so, seeing that now the passes are all guarded;

and with to-morrow's sun the governor and his satellites come hither to arrest thee!"

"My race, then, is run," said the old man calmly. "I fancied that when so long a time had passed, I should have been permitted to linger out my days, until their natural ending. But the Lord he determineth all things, and all things for the best. Let them come, Merciful, let them come with their swords and staves; they shall not find the old man fearful, or unready; and for the small drop of thin blood, which they shall find in these frail veins, verily they are welcome to it."

"No! father, no!" cried his son eagerly, and in truth much affected; "this must not, need not, be; I can conceal thee nigh this place, where thou mayest lie hid in safety, until this tyranny be overpast."

"Verily, if thou canst, be it so. Our lives are not our own, to do with them as we list, but His who gave them to us for good ends. Where is it thou proposest to bestow me?"

"We must steal forth like thieves by night," replied the son, "not suffering one of these to suspect, even, whither we are going. Should that dark-skinned child of perdition discover it, she would betray us straightway."

"And wherefore, Merciful?" asked the old man, severely. "Wherefore? She has eaten of thy bread, and drunken of thy cup; — wherefore, then, shouldst thou say 'she will betray us straightway,' but that thou knowest she has grievances so bitter, wrongs so intolerable, that she were justified in betraying her tormentor? See, my son, see how our own sins are turned in against our own bosoms, and become scourges to afflict us. But say on."

"We must steal forth, I say, this very night. Here is a cave, or cranny, rather, in the rocks midway between this ledge, whereon the house standeth, and the summit of the cliffs. Many years since I climbed to it by chance seeking to rob a fish-hawk's eyry; and, wherefore I know not, I have told no man of its whereabout, nor can the eyes of any man discern it from below. The head of one of our tall pine-trees, which I have spared therefore, leans over and conceals its mouth. It is by the tree that I climbed up thither."

"You forget, Merciful," replied the old man with a faint, sad smile, "the limbs that could have borne me once to the crags, where the wild-goat pastures her tameless young secure from man's intrusion, are now bent, and weak, and well-nigh useless; your plan is naught, my son. My climbing days are ended. And if the Lord, in his infinite and wondrous wisdom, has given back to me this night the mind which has for years been sunk in feebleness and stupor, he has not given back, nor will give back the elastic tread, and the vigorous grasp of manhood."

"For all that I have taken thought," replied the other. "Night after night, since I foresaw the coming of this peril, have I climbed to the cave, and stored it with whatever I deemed needful for your safety and well-being. Good store of carpeting and blankets have I piled there already; and hoards of dried fish, and salted meats, and biscuit; and matches and charcoal, likewise, have I placed there; and in the cave itself there is a source of bright and never-failing water. I have rigged, too, a block and pulley at the entrance, with a strong rope, by means of which I can raise you up thither easily. As often, as I can do so safely, I will visit you. Meanwhile, you must tarry there, with as much patience as you can exert. Truly it will be tedious, and a most lamentable sojourning; but we must pray that the Lord in his good time will shorten it, and, when the strictness of the watch shall have overpast a little, I will convey you hence by sea unto New Haven, where you may be in safety."

"We will go!" said the old man, firmly. "Give me my

cloak and hat—my Bible and my broadsword—defence against the foes of both the spiritual and the carnal world! We will go! I am ready."

These things were soon collected, and Merciful's hand was on the latch of the door already, when he paused in the act of opening it, turned to his father, and said, "Tarry yet awhile. I will go see, lest they are peradventure waking."

He drew off his fisherman's boots carefully, and stole with a silent step, and a heart the throbbings of which appeared to him to sound audiby from door to door of his house, listening long and earnestly to hear some stir or breath which should indicate whether the inmates slept, or were yet waking, after the agitation and excitement of the evening.

He did not listen long, ere the regular and heavy aspirations, which came to his ear from every door but one, assured him that the inmates were buried in the deepest and most quiet slumber.

But the one door, of all the number, was that which the most disturbed him.

It was that of the little closet, wherein lay Tituba. There he paused long, stilling the very beatings of his heart, to collect the slightest sound, the faintest murmur, which might betoken the presence of any living creature.

But no sound or murmur rewarded his assiduous watch—no breath, no whisper. After he had stood there, not less than half an hour, he was compelled to retire, unsatisfied; certain indeed that the girl was within the cell, for how should she have escaped thence unseen, but doubtful, very doubtful, whether she was awake or sleeping.

That any one should sleep so breathlessly, so silently, appeared indeed scarce credible; yet it was hardly possible that awake, any one should retain one posture, so immoveably, so pertinaciously, that nothing should occur to produce even the rustling of a garment.

Frustrated, he stole back at length to his father, and whispered to him the result of his observation.

"I fear she may again have swooned," said the old man, forgetful of himself and his own peril; "let us go see to her."

"I had not thought of that," replied the son. "It may be so, indeed. I will look to it when I have bestowed you safely! Come, father, come; there is no time to tarry."

And snatching up his own gun and cloak, and carrying his heavy boots in his hand, he stole out into the dark and moonless midnight, supporting the aged man with solicitous and tender care.

He closed the door after they were without, and again stood awhile to listen. Not a breath, not a stir within. It was clear that his purpose was effected; that their exit had been effected, thus far at least, unheard and unsuspected.

CHAPTER X.

THE CAVERN.

"In that dark chasm, where even sound
Seemed dark—so sullenly around
The goblin echoes of the cave,
Muttered it o'er the long black wave."

THE night was as dark, as a cloudless night can be, in which there are millions of bright, twinkling stars, and steady burning planets, gemming the deep expanse of azure.

The moon had not yet risen, although there was a faint glimmer on the verge of the horizon which showed where she might be expected.

The overhanging rocks, the black shadow of the giant pines, the dun coloring of all surrounding objects, even to the everlasting sea, which uncurled and unruffled showed no white crests of angry foam, but rose and fell in long monotonous cerulean ridges, contributed to render everything indistinct to the eye, and almost invisible at ten paces' distance.

The silence, in so far at least as human sounds are concerned, was absolute; the dull, low moaning of the sea as it rolled in unbroken to the shore; the whispering sigh of the west wind among the vocal branches of the pines; the slight rustling of the herbage wet with the heavy dews of summer; and the continuous chirrip of the cricket; such were the only things that spoke to the ear, in that tranquil midnight.

"All is safe," whispered Merciful. "Tread on the grass, father; it will give no sound under your footsteps. Steadily; that is well. We shall reach the spot instantly."

And indeed many seconds had not elapsed, before they stood under the canopy of two of those huge pines, which grew close to the seaward front of the platform, yet so near to the crags, which walled it on all sides, that their evergreen boughs covered their gray and rifted faces; while their heads towered to within a few feet of their summit.

"The cavern's mouth is directly over us," said Merciful, "some eighty feet above the spot whereon we are now standing. It is so mere a crevice in the cliff's face, though it expands within, that, even were the pine boughs not so thick-set before it, no human eye could discover what it is. As they now shroud it, the tower of London is not a safer fortress. Tarry you here. I will go up, and lower down the rope by which to raise you; but move not, I beseech you, till such time as I return."

Without waiting a reply, he threw down his cloak upon the grass, and placed his gun against the trunk of the tree. Then grasping the bolt firmly with his arms and knees, he swarmed up it easily, until he reached the fork of the first branch, to which he swung himself with a vigorous effort, and was lost to sight utterly in the dense umbrage. He had not been absent many seconds, before the rustling of the boughs, as they were displaced by some weight descending from above, announced the hook and rope which the Puritan sent down; and scarcely had it touched the greensward before Merciful followed it, and again stood beside his father.

"You have heard nothing?" he whispered, as he drew near to the old man—"nothing that should excite suspicion?"

"I know not," answered his father, whose senses, purblind and dim before, appeared to have been almost supernaturally sharpened. "I am not very sure that I did not hear a footstep here, close beside me. But I can see nothing."

"A lynx could see nothing, nor an owl even, in this black

hole," returned his son. "The ears are the only sure guide; let us listen!"

And they did listen, as men will do, whose lives are dependent on the clearness of their senses. But if there had been any sound before, it was not repeated; and Merciful said, after a pause,

"There is nothing. It must have been fancy only. Come, father, let me make you ready; there is no danger."

"And if there be," said the old man firmly, "this will not be, I think, the first time I have faced it."

His son then secured about his waist, over his cloak which he belted close about his limbs, a broad belt of stout buff leather fastened in front by three buckles, and having at the back a stout iron ring into which he inserted the hook, which he had lowered from above; two loops were next passed over the veteran's arms, and made fast to the rope, and his flapped hat bound down with a kerchief to protect his face against the branches, through which he must be drawn up. Then, having proved the strength of the whole apparatus by a strong jerk, Merciful climbed the tree a second time, entered the cavern's mouth, and in a moment swayed away upon the line, and raised the old man without material difficulty to the entrance of the narrow crevice.

Another moment, and he was safely landed upon the ledge of the rock, after his swift ascent.

Another yet, and he was disentangled from the ropes and bandages, which were coiled away instantly in readiness for the next occasion.

"Give me your hand now, father," said the Puritan: "the cave grows wider, in a moment, and loftier; here you must stoop your head low, and move carefully and slowly."

He led him forward a few yards; then paused. "We are

arrived," he said, "at our journey's end. Stand still an instant, and I will strike a light."

Then after groping about for a few moments, in the interior of the place, with which he was so well acquainted, that he required no light to find what he wanted, he produced a tinder-box and matches; dropped a thick curtain of carpeting, which he had provided, over the low and narrow entrance; and then, secured against any prying eye, lighted a large, thick candle made from the wax of the wild bee.

The clear lustre filled the small space with a radiance, which in another place would have been cheerful, even here it went far to dispel the gloom of that melancholy and wild asylum.

The cavern was a small, nearly circular apartment, about twelve feet in diameter, and as many in height; its floor was dry white sand, and its walls were naturally free from any kind of humidity; which was the more remarkable, that in the inmost corner there was a small, round basin, about three feet in circumference, full to the brim of bright, sparkling water, with a fountain of silvery bubbles gushing perpetually up from the bottom, and showing how lively and strongly aerated must be the limpid spring which fed it.

A crevice in the rock just below the brink of the basin carried off the superfluous waters, by some hidden outlet; and never one drop overflowed the lip, or moistened the white sandy carpet.

As much as could be done, secretly and by watches, to render such an abode comfortable, Merciful had indeed done already, foreseeing the contingency which had arrived.

A good bed was strewn in one corner, with warm coverlets, and good store of English blankets, purloined from his wife's hoards; and around this the rocky walls had been tapestried with pieces of rag-carpet, nailed by strong pegs of wood to their rude crevices.

"A shelf or two, secured in the same fashion, displayed a few pewter plates, a knife or two, and similar utensils, tin cups and bowls, and a pile of coarse linen towels. A small furnace, with a little caldron over it, two or three kegs containing biscuit and provisions, a very rude table and yet ruder stool of unplaned timber, with two or three books, a flask of brandy, and a brass candlestick, completed the furniture of this strange habitation.

"And now, my father," asked Merciful, tenderly, as soon as he had seen him seated on the stool, "think you that you can exist awhile, in this wretched hole, until I can provide for your escape?"

"Wherefore not, Merciful? Wherefore not, I beseech you?" replied the veteran cheerfully. "I shall be well fed, and well warmed; I shall be safe from foes without; and I have here my bible — what else doth man require?"

"And yet," answered his son — "and yet I fear me much —" and he hesitated, fearful of offending.

But the old man took up the word —

"Thou fearest," he said, "lest my mind should again wander. Believe it not, my son. It was not the infirmity so much of nature, as the indulgence of a morbid melancholy trick of musing, that so dethroned my reason. It hath pleased the Lord to arouse me from this stupor, perchance that I might be the better fitted to endure this trial. Now, therefore, I entreat thee, think no more of that, for I am strong in mind, as I have ever been since my boyhood, and stronger in my body than thou thinkest. Good faith! he should be a bold man that would essay to scale this citadel in my despite, with this good rapier in my hand, that did its work at Naseby."

"To-morrow night," added Merciful, "I will bring up your

petronels; I have them in the large oak chest, clean, oiled, and fit for service. I ran some bullets for them, too, the other day, when I was casting balls for my own boat-gun; and I will fetch up hither the small horn of powder. And if there be aught else that you require, you can tell me when I return, and I will have it here as soon as may be. Remember only, never to strike a light, save with the carpet lowered before the entrance, else might the glare betray you. Now, I will light the charcoal in the furnace. There is enough draft through the door, if we so may call it, and yon cleft in the roof, that there shall be no danger from its fumes."

It was not long before this was accomplished, and the warm, ruddy glow, which arose from the little furnace, rendered the cavern's aspect almost pleasant.

This done, the stern, grim Puritan approached his father, and it was strange to mark the play of tender and affectionate anxiety on those dark, iron lineaments, as he bowed his head humbly before the regicide, and said in an eager, interrupted voice—

"Bless me, my father. Bless me before I leave you."

Verily, man is a strange mass of contradictions—none so good or so pure, in whom there is not much of evil—none so degraded or so evil, in whom there is not much of good.

"Bless thee, my son—my own son, Merciful!—I do bless thee! For thou hast been to me a good son, ever, and an affectionate and dutiful. I do bless thee! and may God bless thee likewise!—the God of Abraham, of Isaac, and of Jacob; may he bless thee, my son, with an exceeding blessing! May he cover thy head in the day of peril, and prosper thy incomings, and thy outgoings! Yea, may he give thee, in this life, happiness and peace; and, in the world to come, life everlasting! But be thou Merciful, my son, as in name, so in deed also. Be charitable, and long-suffering, and slow to anger, and not over hot as thou wert this last evening; eaten up with distempered zeal, pitiless and cruel! Do so, my son, and God shall bless thee, even as I bless thee, and thou shalt be blessed, now and for evermore. Amen! Amen! Selah!"

And as he spoke, he fell on his son's neck, and clasped him to his withered breast, and wept warm tears of affection over him.

And Merciful was moved also, for the moment—moved even to tears; and it may be, that, for the first time then, his heart smote him, for he replied in the beautiful words of Holy Writ—

"I have sinned against Heaven, and before thee, and am no more worthy to be called thy son."

And it is probable that this once he spoke sincerely. The old man answered—

"Go, then, my son, and sin no more."

And with those exquisite and touching words they parted.

Merciful carefully raised a little portion of the carpet that concealed the entrance, and stole out so warily that no stray gleam of light flashed forth into the darkness to betray his treasured secret.

Then, throwing himself with a bold vault into the centre of the dense mass of evergreen foliage which feathered the cliff's face, he gained, by a slight exertion, the trunk of the huge tree; and lowered himself rapidly along it, until he stood, unperceived, as he trusted, by any mortal eye, under the leafy canopy.

After standing a moment or two there, silently listening, he raised his cloak from the ground whereon he had cast it, and felt about in the darkness for his gun, where he had left it propped against the pine-tree.

It was gone!—

He started aghast, as if he had received a blow—surely it

was here he had left it—he could not be mistaken. He felt for it again and again, but there it was not; he groped along the grass under the tree, in case it might have fallen, still he found it not. It was gone. It must have been removed; and by whom?

Madness was in the thought, and utter ruin.

He struck his hand upon his brow, and groaned aloud in the silence of the night; and straightway it seemed to him that a low, guttural, mocking laugh responded, exulting to his stifled cry of anguish.

"Ha! who is there?" he cried aloud, and sprang forward in the direction of the fancied sound; but no voice answered him, nor any rustling noise of garments, or flight of quickening footsteps on the greensward.

His rapid movement, however, brought him in contact with the stem of the second pine-tree; and, as he brushed it, something fell to the ground with a sharp metallic clatter.

It was the gun, for which he had been searching.

He stooped and raised it from the wet grass yet more disturbed, if possible, than he had been before.

He paused, reflected, harassed his memory with circumstantial questions.

No! he was certain, the longer he reflected the more certain, that it was leaning on the other tree, when he left it. What then could have removed it?

He listened long and vainly; he stole round and round, among the trees, to and fro, over the whole platform, but could descry no trace of any human being.

At length he made up his mind that he had been mistaken, and took his way to the rustic bridge which led seaward; for it was his plan to break one of the boat-chains, and put off to sea during the night, in order to mislead the members of his own family into the belief that he had carried the old man off by water, and so to divert all search from the neighborhood of this homestead.

This was soon done ; a heavy stone afforded him the means of shattering a weak link in the chain which moored his pinnace, fast-locked, as he had directed, not unadvisedly, by his son before supper-time.

The tide was up, and it cost him but a small effort to launch her ; he sprang in, shoved her twenty yards or better through the surf, stepped her mast, spread her canvass to the light western gale ; and, leading the sheets aft, seated himself at the tiller, just as the broad disk of the moon raised its upper limb above the line of the sea horizon, and poured a long sheet of tremulous lustre over the ridgy waves, a broad flood of glory over the starry heavens.

In order to gain an offing, he was compelled to tack once or twice, for the wind headed him ; and, in the first, he stood directly across the front of the platform and the bridge.

Just as he did so, a sudden splash in the water, as if a stone had fallen from the cliff, attracted his eyes upward.

Did they see truly ?—was there a dusky form watching his motions from the isolated rock ?

The light was quivering and uncertain ; yet was his eye true and almost unerring.

He saw it, as he thought, palpably — distinctly.

He stooped, caught up his long gun, from the thwarts on which it lay.

The form, or what his fancy shaped into a human form, still stood there ; he could not be so much in error.

He raised the gun coolly to his face—levelled it steadily—his finger was already on the trigger, when a cloud obscured the moon for an instant. It passed, and again she shone forth resplendent, far brighter than before, for she had now entirely emerged above the undulations of the ocean.

His eye was still riveted upon the spot, which it had never quitted.

But there was nothing there!

Could he — could he, indeed, twice in one night, be so strangely mistaken?

It might be so, truly; for his spirit was disturbed, and he was both anxious and full of vague imaginations.

He put about, and steered the boat twice, three times, to and fro, before his sleeping home, but nothing more did he hear or see to awaken his distrust.

The breeze freshened, and filled his sail, and drove his boat, with a hoarse rippling laughter, through the long swelling waves, as they began to roll in heavier, and longer, and more ridgy, from the wide Atlantic.

But he seemed to enjoy the quickening motion, and the fast rising breeze; for he spread yet more, yet more, canvass, and steered his little boat as near the wind as she could lay her course; and had there been, indeed, an eye watching him, it would not have been long ere its espial would be useless, so rapidly did he run seaward, and so soon was his white sail lost in the silver wake of the moonbeams.

CHAPTER XI.

DAYBREAK AT SEA.

"Here's the smell of blood still."

The hours of the summer night fleeted away. The stars rose, ran their courses, and set in their appointed places. The moon poured her soft splendor over the smiling waves, and in her turn waxed dim and pale before the advent of a greater and more glorious luminary.

And, dancing over the silver-crested ridges of the deep, with the gay wind singing in the cordage, and the divided waters laughing around his prow, Merciful Whalley passed that night alone, alone on the azure ocean, alone under the starry sky.

But as in mightiest revolutions, when they occur in their own days, men perceive little that is new, or wonderful, or strange, but labor at their daily toil, and eat their daily food, and sleep their nightly slumbers, careless and unconcerned, amid the shock of nations and the fall of dynasties. So in the centre of those grandest and most sublime phenomena of nature, those everlasting witnesses of order, of design, of providence, of an eternal, infinite, and all-wise God, Merciful Whalley sat in the stern of his pinnace, seeing indeed the silver moonlight, and rejoicing in its lustre; riding the waves and exulting in their tumultuous music; yet scarcely conscious of their agency, and altogether careless of their deep meaning.

His mind was, in truth, too much absorbed by his own interests, his own earthly fears and hopes, to give much heed to the vastness, the sublimity, the truth of nature's teachings.

He was disturbed and anxious about the welfare and the safety of his father, and this was the least selfish and most generous point, to which his thoughts were turned.

He was disturbed and anxious about his conduct to the poor Indian girl; not, indeed, that he repented his cruelty, but that he feared its consequences—not that his heart was penetrated with sorrow, and shame, and grief, at his own fall from manhood, virtue, honor, and humanity; but that his pride was galled at the scorn manifested by his sweet daughter, at the open reproof of his father.

He was disturbed and anxious about the state of affairs in the province generally; about the tyranny and oppression of the new governor; the destruction of individual freedom and of the privileges of the community; not indeed from any sense of patriotism, not from any broad principle, or any noble impulse, but from feelings the most personal and narrow.

He feared, in fact, for his wealth—for mammon, his soul's idol! He dreaded sequestration, perhaps confiscation; he dreaded, in truth, everything, except direct danger to his person.

For he was, at least, physically brave; free from that lowest and most degrading baseness, the fear of bodily pain—perhaps the only baseness from which he was free.

During that whole night, he sat still and pensive at the helm of his boat. He was in deep, abstracted thought all the time; and yet it would have been difficult, perhaps impossible, for him to say of what he was thinking.

Continually flitting from one small, narrow topic to another; at no time, pausing long on any one—at no time, grasping any wide or general view; at no time, blazing up with any high or godlike aspiration—at no time, soaring above the mists of time and place, or envisaging the infinite and eternal; the action of his intellect was, like all else of the man's character, earthy and earthward.

It would appear strange to any one, who had not studied character, who did not know something of the human heart, beyond the mere surface, to assert that this man, whose whole life was apparently devoted to religion, who had forsaken his native land, with all its ties and endearments, to seek in the wilderness "freedom to worship God," had yet no true sense of religion at all—no appreciation of its truths, no hold on its comforts. Yet such was the truth—he had some devotion, but no piety. Some feeling of the necessity of worship; some faith, or at least what stood in lieu of it; some fervor and excitement of imagination; and yet, in truth, no religion.

He believed, as he had heard that other men of his own caste and sect believed. He prayed, as he had been taught to pray, in his childhood, and as he had seen his father pray before him. And this belief, such as it was; this prayer—not gushing from the soul nor warm with gratitude and love, but cold yet at the same time fierce, barren of works, fruitless unto amendment, stood with him in the place of all essentials.

And all who believed not, prayed not, as he believed and prayed, were consigned, by his obstinate and narrow prejudices, to the wrath to come.

He was one of that class of whom, alas! that they should be so numerous, a sweet poetess has written in these latter days, and oh, how truly—

"Their lips say, 'God be pitiful,'
That ne'er said, 'God be praised!'"

—of that class, who call upon the name of the Lord, nightly and in the morning, yet never strive to do his bidding, never think of him, save when they would ask something, never uplift their souls in gratitude from the created unto the Creator.

The whole of this night, while he bounded onward, faster

and faster, on the wings of the freshening breeze, he thought of almost everything, save of Him who is all in all.

And the night waned; and the far east was dappled with gray streaks, that heralded the coming dawn; and he started as he perceived that another day was at hand; yet he thought of no thanksgiving, no penitence, for the past. During the hours of darkness, he had run far across the bay, eating continually into the wind, which had hauled gradually round from the west southwardly; had passed the harbor of Cohasset, and was fast heading down toward Plymouth, and Barnstaple bay, when the daylight began to glimmer in the east.

Then, arousing himself from his vague and unprofitable meditations, he looked around him earnestly, and noted every headlarrd and indenture of the iron-bound coast, until at length he was completely satisfied of his whereabout.

Then he looked to the sky, and was engaged for a few seconds in calculation, by which to ascertain what hour it might be of the morning, and how long he had been afloat.

Just as he had settled this point to his satisfaction, he became aware that he was very cold and chilly; for, to say the truth, he had been too much excited before that moment by his own musings to give much attention to his personal comforts or ailments.

But now he shivered; and as he did so, he stooped down, and gathering up his boat-cloak from the bench upon which he had thrown it, wrapped himself in it warmly.

Then, lashing the tiller fast, so that the boat should still hold its course, he went forward; opened the hatch of a small forecastle; and, after rummaging among its contents for a few seconds, produced a large, stone jug, or graybeard, as it was then called, such as was ordinarily used to contain distilled waters.

Extracting with his teeth the broken corn-cob, which wrapped in a hank of tow, had served as a stopper, he raised it to his nostrils, as if to make sure of its contents before suffering his lips to encounter them, smiled a grim smile of satisfaction, and, after a very sufficient draught, recorked it, returned it to the hatch, and stalked back, greatly refreshed, as he would have said, in spirit to his seat at the helm.

Meanwhile, it was rapidly growing light. A rosy flush had usurped the place of the dappled gray on the horizon; and the fleecy clouds, hundreds of which were hanging suspended in the calm, clear atmosphere, assumed the same tell-tale coloring.

Then a broad amber glow shot upward, and streamed longitudinally, over the flickering wavelets; and then, as it were with a bound, the great sun leaped forth, indeed 'like a bridegroom from his chamber,' to run his course of glory.

And it was broad, rejoicing day.

Then, then, did the dark man's soul awake! Then did his spirit arise yearning, as will do that at such a sight of the merest worldling, to make its morning sacrifice—to burst forth into praise and rapturous thanksgiving!

He saw that it was light; he knew that the sun had risen, because it was light—not because his eye, much less his breathless heart, had turned to contemplate that most immortal and divine of this world's perishable splendors.

He saw that it was light, I say; he knew that the sun had risen, and, it is probable, had any one expressed wonder at his apathy in presence of that sublime wonder, that he would have replied, that he "had very often seen it grow light before, and that the sun rose every morning."

How many are there not, now around us, who feel in the like manner, who would, perhaps, make answer in words of like indifference!

But was that all he felt—all he saw in the brightening daylight?

Reader, it was not all!

He saw that, as the day-star to which he had not deemed it worth while to turn eye or thought, dispersed the glooming twilight, he saw that which made him feel—made him shudder to the heart's core.

Since he had wrapped his cloak about him, and resumed his seat at the tiller, his eye had been riveted on his own knee, on a strange spot, which he could perceive indistinctly on the black frieze mantle.

He could not tear his eye away from it, and if he closed the lids, striving to banish the idea, the spot was there, palpably, *more* palpably before him, and now sanguine-hued.

The sun rushed up, and it was clear, broad day; and in the daylight—there was now no room for fantasy or error—clear and distinct that fatal spot assumed its true proportions—its true color.

It was the plain print of a human foot—a small, slender, shapely, human foot—the foot evidently of a female.

That print was stamped upon the cloak in clotted blood.

The truth, the whole truth, dawned on his soul in an instant. All his precautions had been taken vainly.

The Indian girl had heard him quit the house; had risen from her bed of torture; had hung upon his track; followed him to the shadow of the pine-trees beneath which he had dropped his mantle; had trodden on it casually, and left her accusing mark, in the clotted gore, which had been liquefied again by contact with the dewy herbage.

He did not *think* of this. It arrived in his mind by no slow process. It flashed on him like lightning. It was true. At once he knew it.

"Devil! devil!" he muttered savagely. "She has seen

all!—she will betray all!" He paused, and broke forth again, "No, no, though hell itself yawned for me!—I say no! she she shall not!"

And he put up his helm, the sail shivered, the lively boat fell off, and was full on the other tack in an instant.

Away! before the wind bellying the broad canvass, away! homeward!

Within an hour he was abreast of the city and the fort, when a fresh sound and a fresh sight again turned him from his track.

It was the clear and piercing danger of a well-blown trumpet.

It was a gallant sloop, the tender of the Rose frigate, with the cross-pennant of St. George flaring out from her topmast, with bright cuirasses and rich scarlet doublets flashing along her decks, as she stood full across his course, from the mouth of Boston harbor.

Again he went about—again with a gloomy, bitter malediction—and, taking in at once three fourths or more of his wide-spread canvass, he stood sullenly and slowy seaward.

CHAPTER XII.

DAYBREAK AT HOME.

"The morn is up again, the laughing morn."

THE commencement of a new day generally is, and it seems as if it should be always, a new source of joy and contentment.

And it is very sad when this beneficent order of nature is so far altered and reversed, that each "new morn" but brings to the poor sufferer "new sorrows."

Yet it is thus but too often. Many, many are those, who, after wearing out sad nights on sleepless pillows, or, at the best, sinking at last into that painful and unrefreshing slumber, which is not sleep, but worn-out nature's trance, find nothing in the coming of another day, but the return of thoughts too painful to be borne, of memories of that irrevocable past, which, in its time, most blissful, is now the arch-anguish—remorse, regret, repentance, but no hope—no hope for anything in this world, save its last gift—the grave.

And if there are—as indeed there are—many of the free, the rich, the great, those whom the foolish crowd envy as if pre-eminently blessed who feel thus, what must it be with the poor, the low, the starving pauper—what must it be with the *slave?*

The same gorgeous daybreak, which aroused the dark Puritan from his unquiet and unholy musings, aroused the hapless Tituba from her painful and restless slumber. For, after she had espied all with the keen eye, treasured all in the unforgetful mind, of wakeful vengeance, she had crept back to her miserable pallet; and, after wrestling long and tossing to and fro, in the anguish of her lacerated body, in the fever of her burning mind, she had fallen into a heavy, dreamless stupor.

Now she arose, and looked forth upon the morning. The same glittering sea was outspread before her eyes, the same gorgeous heaven o'erhung her, with the same golden orb, charioting light, and life, and glory upward, on which Merciful Whalley was looking unconcerned and careless.

And she, the poor, half-instructed savage—she, who had heard of God, only to find his worshippers her tyrants and tormentors—she, who had learned servitude, and anguish, and Christianity, as at one and the same lesson—she, to whom, indeed, a new day was but another word for a new period of toil and torture—how did she gaze upon the miracle of light, and in what spirit?

There was—there was, more of the true, the lowly, and the grateful spirit of the Christian, in that poor, overtasked, despised, scourged heathen, than in her haughty master, who like the pharisee blessed God that he was not as other men are.

Poor creature! she distinguished, and how few of mankind do so, between the falsehood of a creed, and the error of its would-be believers.

She could see that all Christians were not evil, austere, bitter, gloomy, cruel; although the most of her experience had lain among those who were so. She knew Ruth Whalley, as well as her father, misstyled Merciful.

She loved the one, as much as she loathed the other.

Loathed? Ay! loathed, and despised—for she could read his paltry soul—even more than she hated.

For she was born an Indian; and if, in some things, she had learned to be *almost* a Christian, she had not yet learned the Christian's last and hardest lesson—the lesson to forgive

Hers had been once a high, proud, daring soul — a soul worthy of her lineage! But suffering had broken the audacious pride — weakness had tamed the elastic, haughty heart — sorrow had fitted her to the meek Christian's creed.

And she had listened to the sweet voice of Ruth, bringing her heavenly tidings. And, with the native poetry of a free, wild imagination, nursed in the beautiful and boundless wilderness, she met half-way the teachings which declared to her the God whom she had ignorantly worshipped — in the roar of the cataract, in the music of the treetops, in the still majesty of solemn night, in the exulting splendor of the happy day.

And now, as she gazed out over the sea, and into the unfathomable sky, her soul expanded with great vague indescribable imaginings. Her heart was softened with poetry and love; imbued with a sense of dim, undefined religion, that made her breath come thick, and fluttering, and faint — that filled her eyes with tears, but not of sorrow.

At this moment, there was a stir in the cottage behind her — a hurrying of feet to and fro — a flapping of doors — a hum of eager and anxious voices.

Then a quick light came up into her dark eye, and the teardrop was dried, in a second, as if that fiery light had been pregnant with fierce heat. And a red burning flush mounted into her dusky cheeks, and sat there permanent — a glaring spot, telling of terrible excitement.

She clasped her small hand tight, so tight that the nails pierced the palm.

She drew a long, sonorous breath, which sounded almost like a sigh, but was none — a wild inspiration, full of revengeful triumph.

"I have them!" she cried aloud, casting her eloquent eyes up to heaven. "I have them! They are mine! mine! mine! Tituba's soul shall bleed no more with the white man's torture

—his tears, his groans shall comfort it! Tituba's back shall burn no more with the stripes of the white man's scourge, his father's blood shall heal it."

"Tituba, Tituba," cried the soft voice of Ruth, from within; "are you abroad, poor Tituba? Have you seen the old man? Have you seen my father?"

Her fiery glance sank, instantly subdued.

"He is her father," she said gently. "Her heart would bleed likewise—Tituba is athirst; her heart is very hot within her! She loves Ruth—she hates Merciful!—well! she will wait—she will see!—"

And then, raising her voice, she replied, without answering directly to the question—

"Merciful is gone—old man gone."

"Gone, whither?—whither have they gone? good God! tell me; tell me; what new misery is this?"

"Merciful is gone," she replied, waving her hand seaward. "Ruth, come with Tituba, and she will show her."

And taking her young mistress by the hand, she led her swiftly down the little path toward the bridge, the three boys following eagerly behind her. When they reached the fence of gnarled roots and branches which guarded the platform's brink, she pointed downward, and all saw at once that the pinnace was absent.

Gideon thrust his hand instantly into the pocket of his doublet, to ascertain if the keys were gone, with which his father had intrusted him at supper-time. They were still there. He drew them forth, and said doubtfully—

"I locked them all fast, with my own hand, last night; this is strange, Sister Ruth."

"White man no eyes!" said the Indian girl, scornfully. "See, there, chain broken; there, large stone chipped and cracked—that broke chain! Boat gone, too. Merciful gone, old man gone! That speaks clear as so many words. Merciful in a hurry, broke chain, took boat—why white boy ask? why not look, see, understand?"

"But, good Heaven! Tituba, did he take grandfather along?" cried Ruth, anxiously and much alarmed.

"Tituba not see anything—not say anything about grandfather," was the reply. "Merciful took gun, powder, shot-pouch, fishing-lines, net, too—they are all gone—no one else taken them! Old grandfather has got legs, arms, of his own—hits, too, when he like to use them! Why he not go away himself?"

But as she spoke, there was a glance in her eye that told Ruth that she knew more than she chose to say. She soon dismissed the boys, on some pretence or other, and when they were gone, turned to the Indian girl, and said, "Now tell me."

But Tituba shook her head only, and then in her turn asked—

"Tell, Tituba?—why old grandfather, old Edward Whalley, not use his wits? Tituba thought he had no wits. But he has many; great, quick, wise, very wise. Why he not use them?"

"I can not tell you, Tituba, for I know not," replied Ruth.

"Tituba will not tell you where old Edward gone," was the answer. "Better for you to say, when any one come to ask, when *soldier* come to ask where Edward Whalley—better for you to say, 'I can not tell you, for I know not.' Tituba knows—but *will* not."

"And will you not tell any one—will you not tell the soldier, Tituba?" asked Ruth, beginning now to understand or suspect something of the matter.

"Don't know," said the girl, very doggedly. "Merciful love old Edward—Tituba loves not Merciful—*hates* Merciful! Merciful made Tituba's back bleed! How he like it, if

Tituba make old Edward's head bleed—Merciful's heart bleed! Don't know now—know better some time."

"See! see! Ruth, Ruth!" cried the the three boys, rushing hastily down from the house, Gideon carrying a telescope in his hand—"See, there is a sloop, with the royal flag, steering straight hitherward. She is full of men, too!—soldiers in scarlet cassocks, and bright armor!"

Ruth looked up hastily; and there, almost within a pistol-shot, lay the Rose's tender, her head veering slowly to the wind, and her white sails coming down with a run, as she dropped her anchor.

"Perhaps, know better *soon!*" said Tituba, with emphasis. "Know *all*, why he not use his wits; why he gone—perhaps *where*."

"But do you know why he did not use his senses—why he has gone?" exclaimed Ruth, in amazement.

"Perhaps!" answered the quick-witted girl—"perhaps he lose his wits, so to save his head—perhaps gone for the same reason! Perhaps, soldier come to take it."

"Do you love me, Tituba?"

"Yes! yes!" she replied eagerly; "much, very much!—why ask, Ruth, when you know I love you?"

"If you *do* love me, Tituba; you will not tell these men."

"Don't know," she again answered doggedly; "hate Merciful, love Ruth! Love revenge, too! Revenge very sweet, perhaps love revenge better."

And, with the words, she turned away, and walked off, with a dogged and angry air, that showed it would be useless to address her farther.

Then there came from the ship the clear, sharp clangor of the trumpet, and a hoarse voice—

"What, ho! there: house, ahoy!"

"Ahoy!" replied the elder of the sons.

"Send a boat instantly," answered the voice.

"Ay! ay!" cried Gideon; and sprang hastily down the steps, calling his second brother to accompany him, prompt to obey the unfriendly summons.

CHAPTER XIII.

THE ROYAL GOVERNOR.

"Come guard the door without; let him not pass,
But kill him rather."

But a few minutes had elapsed, since Gideon had crossed the gangway of the English pinnace, when the alarmed spectators, who numbered by this time all the household of the Cove cottage, beheld a larger boat lowered from the stern of the man-of-war. A dozen persons entered her; four of them ordinary sailors, two men, as it appeared of superior rank, and five armed soldiers, having Gideon, now seemingly a prisoner, in the midst of them.

No long time was, however, given them for speculation or surmise. Six or eight strokes of the oars brought the boat to the little dock, at which she was made fast; and then, leaving one man as boat-keeper, and posting another as a sentinel with his match lighted on the round-headed rock, the party landed.

The first who crossed the bridge was a tall, dark-complexioned man, of a fine figure and stately bearing, who might, perhaps, have numbered some forty-six or forty-seven years. He was attired magnificently in the costume worn at the court of the second James, a loose coat of crimson velvet, splendidly laced with gold above a glittering steel breast-plate which shone like silver in the dazzling sunbeams. Full breeches of the same material with his coat, and heavy horseman's boots, adorned with the gilt spurs of knighthood, a huge black wig, falling quite down to his shoulders, and reeking with the most exquisite perfumes, and a low-crowned beaver decorated by a hat-band of white feathers, completed the attire of this proud dignitary. The only weapon which he carried, was the ordinary walking rapier of the day, suspended by a broad, blue silk scarf, crossing his cuirass under the velvet coat; but he held in his hand a handsome clouded cane with a crutch head of solid gold.

The demeanor of this gentleman was stately, perhaps even haughty; and, although he was by no means void of that quietude and easy grace which arise from a consciousness of high station and gentle birth, his carriage and the superciliousness of his glance seemed to betoken both arrogance and presumption.

His face was such as many persons would term handsome, for the features were all well formed and regular, the eye was clear and piercing, and the coloring fine and harmonious. Nor was there wanting a strong intellectual expression on the brow, an air of indomitable resolution about the mouth. Yet was the whole expression of the face of Sir Edmund Andross—for the unwelcome visiter was no other than the new governor of the Bay Province—unpleading, nay almost repulsive.

It was impossible to look twice at that countenance, without reading in its strong lines a dark tale of indulged and pandered passions, of fierce licentiousness, unbridled insolence, and all the evil habits of the mind, which are so apt to be the fruits of an unchecked career, whether of public or of private despotism.

Never, perhaps, were two men more alike, and at the same moment more different, than Sir Edmund Andross, the royal governor, and Merciful Whalley, the rebellious Puritan.

Both of these men were fanatics — Andross of loyalty and aristocracy — Whalley of bigotry and independence.

In both did the fanaticism, which was visible in every action of their lives, subserve to one end — self-glory, self-gratification.

Both men were self-deceivers; the one served Mammon only, believing that he served his God — the other, while professing to be the creature only of his king, was the slave of his own power, pleasure, and lust.

Neither would have paused one moment to consider how many tears or how much agony his own gratification would cost any man; or hesitated, at all risks, to obey his own impulses. But Andross would have trampled under foot openly the law which restrained him. Whalley would have violated it as readily, professing all the while his veneration for its authority, and proving by hypocritic cant that to violate was to obey it.

Such were the two men, whom the policy of others, no less than their own passions, were soon about to bring into collision. They were both keen-witted, bold, daring, and unscrupulous; both equally subservient to self-interest; equally reckless of the rights of others.

But, although Andross was armed with all the authority which a despotic king can delegate to his most trusted minister, the Puritan was the stronger — the more dangerous. The stronger, because, while in truth, scorning utterly all the opinions of all men, he professed to obey the public voice implicitly — because, while acting wholly in obedience to the basest of earthly passions, he successfully presented an exterior of austere and self-denying virtue — because, in one word, he concentrated all his energies upon one point, and led the people with him, as surely as by chains of iron, through their own flattered prejudices.

Sir Edmund, on the contrary, sought for no golden opinions

from any sort of people — he bore his vices on as bold a front as if they had been virtues ; and cared not a rush which they were esteemed. He was continually shocking the scruples and wounding the prejudices of men, on matters of no moment, offending to no purpose when, with a little management, he might as well have been conciliated; and thus laying up against himself hoards of enmity and resistance to be brought forth, and perhaps to turn the struggle, in times of real emergency, efforts of real moment.

Such was the man, who now, for the first time in his life, set foot upon the green sward of that secluded cove — set his foot there, unconscious that in so doing, he was taking the step, which of all others involved most deeply the fortunes, the fate of his whole career.

Yet so it is, but too often, with us all — the wisest as the weakest!

We strive with ceaseless toil, with multifarious turmoil, to rear some mighty scheme, which is to build our fortune as high as the rash edifice on Shinar's plain! The bubble bursts — and lo, thin wind, and an unsavory odor!

We go about some trivial thing, some careless task, perhaps some lightsome pleasure, thinking of no result beyond the present; and thence, by no effort, no thought even of your own advancement, greatness, glory.

The combination, which we most strenuously guard against, as the most ruinous, will work together in the despite of all our efforts, and works at last not ruin but unheard-of prosperity.

The plan, which we have laid most craftily to win us glory, succeeds beyond our wishes, and we are crushed by its success.

What is this? Fortune? Accident? Fate?

Fortune is nothing, save in the chances of a die! Accidents, there are none in this vast universe, from the fall of the sparrow to the death of the hero!

Fate is —— What? a weak — I had nearly said *wicked* — word to express the ways of God, which are in themselves all wise, though in our small, presumptuous blindness we discern not, and miscall their wisdom.

Sir Edmund Andross landed that morning from his gay pinnace upon the wild and lonely coast, thinking to find a regicide, a captive — he found instead his fate!

To him, that morning was the beginning of the end.

And in his train there was another, who, very different in all respects from his chief, had cause, for many a day, to call to mind that fruitless mission, that rude cottage and its tenants.

To Henry Cecil, also, that morning was the unsuspected cause of many and strange things. The captain of Sir Edmund's body-guard, the scion of one, among the noblest of England's old patrician houses, he had applied for the appointment, more in a gay and romantic spirit of adventure, more in the heat of a young poetical imagination, prompting him with the wish to see the marvels of the great Western World, than in any desire of gaining advancement, or of achieving glory.

Too young, and, to speak the truth, too gay and thoughtless, to have reflected much or deeply on politics, or on the art of government, he was, in the true spirit of the fearless, faithful cavalier, a firm believer in the church, a stanch supporter of the king. His whole soul full of the high aristocratic creed, the high aristocratic virtues, he could no more imagine a true religion, apart from the one, than a consistent or sound liberty, without the other.

Yet never did a young heart thrill more quickly to the republican renown of a Brutus, a Timoleon, or a Cato, than did that enthusiastic royalist's. Never did tenderest heart of woman sympathize more compassionately with the sufferings, or fieriest heart of the patriot blaze more indignantly at the wrongs, of the poor or unprotected.

And yet this youth was linked as a comrade and supporter, nay, in some sort connected as a friend to the contemner of all virtue, the scorner of all glory, the grinder of the poor, the oppressor of the weak — the despot Andross.

In form and appearance also, Sir Henry Cecil was as strongly contrasted with his superior, as in the qualities of intellect and heart.

Not above six-and-twenty years of age, he at this time presented as perfect a model as can well be imagined of complete youthful manhood. Somewhat above the middle stature, his slender yet symmetrical frame gave promise of great strength in future, while it was evident even now that it possessed that springy, vigorous, and active elasticity, which in the young supplies admirably the want of that tempered and hard robustness, which comes only with maturer manhood.

His face was eminently handsome, not regular indeed or perfect in feature, but what is much better, full of fine feeling, deeply fraught with social, alive with the flashing light of, intellect. A broad fair forehead, not very high, but singularly firm and thoughtful; large gray eyes clear as steel, and quick as the ray that flashes from its polished surface when sudden light enkindles it; dark eyebrows, and long lashes; a nose somewhat too prominent perhaps for beauty; and a mouth, the lines of which were rich with every good and gentle expression, at times arch and humorous, yet lacking not their share of firmness and even pride, and a well-cut, bold chin, completed the contour of his singularly winning and attractive countenance.

His hair of a light sunny brown, for he was both too handsome and too high-born, and yet more too free of spirit, to be trammelled by the hideous fashions of the day, fell in a profusion of long wavy curls over the collar of his doublet, like those of the gallant cavaliers of the first King Charles, unpolluted by the disfigurement of hair-powder, and undistorted by the barber's irons.

His mustaches, and the long-pointed beard which he wore on his chin, were many shades darker than his hair, and gave a military and manly expression to a face, which its fair complexion and air of extreme youth would otherwise have rendered somewhat effeminate for one who had, for years already, commanded veteran soldiers.

He wore the scarlet uniform which had already been adopted as the uniform of England — though not at all, as some writers have asserted falsely as the *livery* of the king; it being Cromwell who first brought it into use — but of a widely different fashion from that of the present day. There was the scarlet indeed and the glittering lace; but the long shoulder-knots of riband with aiguilettes of bullion were as different from the modern epaulette, as the long cambric cravat trimmed with rich valenciennes from the black stock, or the bright plates of polished steel guarding the neck and shoulders from the small moon-shaped gorget, which bears its name, with neither its utility nor its splendor. Ruffles of Brussels lace at the wrists of the coat, and at the knees of the breeches, a fluttering scarf of silk and gold crossing the left breast and wound afterward about the waist, supporting the long horseman's sword, huge boots, and the hat, with its cincture of snowy plumes, made a gay show, indeed; and the free line and graceful flow of all the decorations formed a picture far more attractive, though scarce so practical or soldierly a display, as the closer and more angular lines of the modern costume.

The rest of the party consisted of a lancepersade or corporal, with four private troopers of Andross' body-guard, all splendidly equipped and heavily armed, with long broad-swords clanking on their heels, pistols in their girdles, and carabines or musquetoons, with lighted matches, in their hands.

Behind these men, came Gideon, in charge, as it seemed, of the two sailors, who had landed; and one of whom walked on each side of him, with a cocked pistol in his hand.

Deep consternation fell on the hearts of all the tenants of the little cottage, as that proud pomp ascended the rugged staircase and crossed the rustic bridge. They knew not, indeed, nor could they in any wise imagine, the object of this visit. They were unconscious even of the persons, who thus broke in upon their privacy.

But they perceived at once they were men high in authority; and that they came thither, as the soldiers proved, with no intent of peace or friendship.

Ruth's eye fell first upon the pleasant face and gentle lineaments of Cecil; but ere it dwelt there a moment, or gained confidence from what it read therein, the baleful features and sinister expression of Sir Edmund flashed upon her, and she beheld Cecil no longer.

It was strange with how stern a fascination that evil visage and dark lurid eye riveted the glance of the fair girl in anxious agony.

The sight gave her pain, exquisite pain. Yet, had it been to preserve her life, she could not have withdrawn her eyes.

She shuddered, and a wild terror crept into her soul — was it a prescient sense of that which was to come?

She struggled with that vague, dismal terror — but she could not dispel it; and, while she was yet gazing, he caught her as it were in the fact, and smiled with a fierce and almost fiendish glee, rejoicing in the mastery which he felt that his mere aspect had exerted over her.

Andross had met his fate! —

CHAPTER XIV.

THE SEARCH.

"Dressed in a little brief authority."

ALTHOUGH no person of those present suspected the object of this strange arrival, all were alarmed and apprehensive of some evil.

Nor were their fears diminished by the first words of the leader of the party —

"Hah!" he said, in harsh and haughty tone, that corresponded well with his port and the expression of his features, "ha! what is this — what is this he tells me? Merciful Whalley absent — where is he? Ha! when went he forth? Whither hath he gone? Speak out, I say, or by St. George, ye shall rue it."

His words were addressed apparently to the mother of the family, although his licentious gaze never left the fair features of the daughter.

"Nay, noble sir," faltered the timid woman, "we know not when he went, nor whither, nor can we tell you where he is; for —"

"God's life!" returned the other, "dost think I am a fool to be put off with such lies as this; or one of your drivelling beggars of town elders, to lack the means to extort truth. Know, woman, that your husband is accused, under heavy circumstances, of high treason, in harboring and helping an excommunicate and outlawed knave and felon, one Edward Whalley; truly a parricide; one of the bloody and accursed murderers of that most holy martyr, King Charles I., of —"

"My grandfather!" exclaimed Ruth, clasping her hands, in an ecstacy of terror, and for a moment losing her wonted self-control—"this, then, is the fearful secret!"

"Ha! didst thou know it, too? Wert thou, too, aiding and abetting in this crime?" said the governor, turning with a triumphant smile toward the maiden.

"If crime it be to cherish a weak, old, distraught and helpless man—yes!" replied Ruth, firmly.

"If it be a crime to shelter the king's traitor! If—into a pestilent nest of rebels we seem to have fallen! Now, mark me, little one, were I disposed to severity, I might arrest thee instantly, as guilty on thine own confession of misprision of this heinous treason—the forfeiture of which is death!* Knowest thou that, ha?"

"I knew it not," she answered mournfully, but steadily. "I only know that the law of God commands us to 'honor our father and our mother that our days may be long in the land.' Other law know I none, nor have heard of it. Nevertheless, God's will be done!"

"Oh! noble sir, dear sir," exclaimed her mother, casting herself at his feet, "she knew it not—she knew it not! So surely as the Lord liveth, she knew not that her grandsire was one of the appointed judges of the late man!"

And in the extremity of her terror for her daughter's safety, she used the words, which, often heard on the lips of the fierce Puritan, were in themselves almost enough to have convicted her, in those days, of treason.

"'Appointed judges of THE LATE MAN!' Ha! by the spirit of rebellion!" shouted Sir Edmund furiously, and no longer

* The punishment for misprision of treason was not death by the law, but this period of English history is peculiar for the subjection of the law to the royal will; and the crime for which Lord William Russell suffered was, at the worst, but misprision of treason.

with feigned anger, for, in despite of all his inconsistencies and vices, he had at least this merit, that he was faithful and sincere in his creed of loyalty, however ultra it might be. "Appointed judges! Mark that, Sir Henry Cecil, the godless, hypocritical, blood-thirsty, low-born butchers of his most sacred majesty, she dares to designate 'appointed judges!' The king by right divine, the Lord's anointed, she blasphemously terms 'the late man.' I know not wherefore we should tarry for any further proof. I know not wherefore I should not order all these into instant custody, to be dealt with thereafter as the law directs, and this den of thieves and traitors to be levelled forthwith to the ground!"

Cecil, thus called upon, approached the governor, not without some expression of dissatisfaction upon his noble features, and spoke to him for a few seconds in a low voice, so that no words of his reached the ears of any other than Sir Edmund. Yet was it plain enough, that they were unpalatable to the great man. His brows were contracted into so dark a frown that they almost met. His eyes flashed with a lurid and fierce light. His nether lip quivered with impatience, and he repeatedly clutched the hilt of his sword with a rapid gesture, while his lieutenant was speaking. At length, however, his quick temper mastered him, and he broke out with a fierce oath,

"Ignorant! ignorant! No! by the life of Him that made me! here is no ignorance, but most rank rebellion, as I shall show you presently! Hark you, girl, answer me what I shall ask of you; and see that you answer truly."

"If at all of a surety," replied Ruth, "I shall answer truly."

"If—mark me that *if*, Sir Henry! Well, mistress, you did not know, you tell me, that this grandfather of yours was one of the king's murderers; is this so?"

"I profess, as the Lord liveth, that she knew not the king was slain at all!" replied her mother.

But taking no heed of the interruption, and keeping his eyes fixed on the girl's ingenuous features, Andross exclaimed sharply,

"Answer me, mistress, yea or nay!"

"I knew *not* that he was one of the king's judges!" answered the maiden; "but my mother errs, I *did* know that the king was judged to death and slain by his people!"

"Ha! thou didst know that—of a truth thou art learned, lass, already; and yet, I trow, thou shalt be taught a thing or two thou knowest not, ere I have done with thee. Now, tell me, beautiful precision that thou art, didst thou not know that this grandfather of thine was a proscribed and outlawed traitor?"

"I knew it not!" she replied firmly.

"Nor that, by the king's proclamation it was made treason, under penalty of death, to rest or harbor him."

"Nor that, sir, either; but, natheless—" She was about to add something further; but, as she was on the point of speaking, a quick glance from Sir Henry Cecil, who stood a little way behind the governor, and his finger laid on his lip, gave her timely warning, and she stopped short and was silent.

"But, natheless," repeated the governor, mocking her, "natheless what, sweet one?"

"I have already replied, noble sir," she made answer, calmly, "that I knew not, nor had ever heard of the proclamation which you named."

"But you began to say something more—what was it? Palter not with me, minion?"

"I believe, sir, that you have not the right to ask me that," replied the young girl.

"I think not, indeed," said Sir Henry Cecil, gravely, although his face was somewhat flushed, and his eye keen and angry.

The governor, irritated already by the demeanor of Ruth, turned furiously on the young baronet, whose well-intended interruption, perhaps, did no real service to the maiden.

"I believe, sir," he said in accents of the most imperious and galling scorn, "that you hold a commission as captain in the king's horse regiment, maintained as my body-guard; but I am yet to be informed that you are associated with me either as an expounder of hard points of law, or as the keeper of my conscience. For you, minion, if you answer not, and that instantly, you shall know, ere you are six hours older, that I have the right to do whatever I think proper in this stiff-necked and insolent Bay-Province. It were a fine thing, truly, if the immunities and privileges which belong to the free-born Englishman alone should follow such a sort of runagates as ye are to the world's end, and pass down to generations. Speak, I say, wench, or we will take means that shall make you find your tongue!"

"Natheless, had I heard the king's proclamation, or any other human law, commanding me to do that which God's law prohibits, or prohibiting that which God's law commands, I should have surely disregarded it."

"I thought so," answered the governor, with a sneer. "Now, are you satisfied, Sir Henry. Proper wise heads are yours to judge the legality of laws. Any excuse for rebellion is enough, it seems. So, I suppose, as a corollary from this loyal axiom, you have hid the old traitor from us likewise."

"It needeth not," answered Ruth. "For he, too, is gone, and we know not whither."

"Gone! Jade, thou liest!" cried the despot in a furious rage, grasping her by the slender wrist and shaking her violently. "Gone!—whither?—when?—but, surely I am mad to ask, for this is palpably a lie! Take two of the men, Sir Henry, and search every nook and corner of the hut, and arrest the old knave and dotard who is concealed doubtless in some cunning place. He is too old and feeble to be removed far."

The brave and generous-minded young man obeyed silently, not perhaps displeased at being sent from the immediate spot, where he was likely to witness so much that made his blood boil, which yet he dared not as a soldier under his legitimate superior object to, or resist.

As Cecil moved away, however, with the men, taking one of the younger boys along with them to open the doors, Sir Edmund, who was no mean judge of character, no unskilled reader of the human heart, was pretty well convinced that the woman had spoken the truth, and that his victims had, indeed, escaped him; for their demeanor was so quiet and fearless, that it betokened their consciousness, that there was little or no danger to be apprehended from the search.

"You say that they are both gone, and that you know not whither? How is this, or how can it be? Woman, didst thou not ask thy husband, nor thou, girl, thy father, whither he was bound, when he would return?"

"We knew not," they both answered in a breath, "that he was going hence at all. When we retired to bed last night, *they* were together communing and praying in the kitchen, nor till we fell asleep, did we lose the sound of their voices. When we arose this morning early, the chain of the boat was broken, and they were both gone hence."

"Ha! that may be indeed. Is it your husband's wont thus to go often forth by night?"

"Well-nigh nightly," answered the woman, either to fish or to fowl, which are a part of his occupation; nor does he ever tell us what he intends to do, or whither he is going. He is a silent man and very secret. Nor do I dare to ask him what he tells me not of his own free will."

"And goes the old man with him oftentimes?"

"Never before since we have dwelt here."

"Nor has he gone hence now, I fancy," said the tyrant coldly, "but we will soon see. Ha! how now, Cecil," he continued, as his officer reappeared from the cottage—"have you found him?"

"We have searched thoroughly from the roof to the cellar, and there is no one in the place," answered the young soldier. "It must be as they say; they must have escaped by sea."

"I fancy not. There is no cause to make it likely. They could not have heard aught of our intentions. No, no! they are hidden somewhere. Some secret closet in the walls! Some cunning hole, I doubt not; but we will have them out ere long, I warrant me. Here, lance-pesade, take two of your men and set fire to the house in a dozen places, with the matches of your pieces. The rats shall be smoked out, or roasted in their holes!"

"No! no! you will not, you can not, you *dare* not be so cruel!" exclaimed the mother of the family, half frantic from terror and despair. But Ruth spoke not, for she judged, and judged rightly, that to speak were but a waste of words.

"Will I not? *dare* I not?" answered the tyrant, looking her full in the eye, with cold insolence, "that you shall soon see. And you, sirrah!" he added, turning short to the subaltern, who was hesitating, scarcely able to believe that the governor was in earnest, "to your duty! Set it on fire!"

The man moved away, reluctantly, to do the bidding of his commander, with that stern obedience to discipline, which has in all ages been so especially characteristic of the English soldier. But, as he did so, Sir Henry Cecil took two steps forward, and addressed Andross firmly, but at the same time respectfully.

"May I ask you, Sir Edmund, have you commission to do this? Martial law has not been proclaimed, I think, in the province."

"You may ask, Sir Henry Cecil, any absurd and useless question you may think fit; but it does not follow that I will answer them. To this, however, I will reply thus—ample commission!"

"And may I ask to see it?"

"It is *this*," replied the governor, striking his hand on the hilt of his sword, "will you question it, Sir Henry?"

"No, sir," replied Cecil, "but I will no longer wear *this*," and, as he spoke, he unsheathed his own sword, kissed the bright blade, and then snapping it across his knee, flung the fragments over the cliff into the rolling surf. Then, without a moment's hesitation, he unbuckled the bright scarf, which distinguished the governor's guardmen, and, before Sir Edmund had time to speak, flung it with the empty scabbard on the green sward at his feet, saying, "I resign my commission, sir—the king has lost a soldier."

"And gained, I suppose, a rebel!" retorted the other, with a sneer. "Your resignation is accepted, sir. The privy council shall be informed of this."

"They shall, upon my honor!" answered the gallant young man. "And now, Sir Edmund, I will request you to remember that I am no longer your inferior; but your equal, as an English gentleman, of rank higher than your own."

The governor doffed his plumed hat and bowed with ironical humility.

"I bow," he said, "to the higher rank! which, however, I suspect will be abridged a little, when the king hears of this. But enough! I will brook no insolence, hear no remonstrance.

Now, sirrah, lance-pesade, bestir yourself. That hut is not afire, and by the God who made me! I stir not one step hence until its roof-tree lie upon its hearth-stone in one heap of ashes. Bestir yourselves, knaves, or you shall taste the pickets, or take a ride upon the wooden-horse! Fire it, I say, fire it, at each of the four corners! It shall house no more rebels."

CHAPTER XV.

THE WRONG.

"Why flames the far summit?"

Authority is a strange touch-stone whereby to test man's equanimity; a marvellous changer of man's heart. Many a one, who in an humble sphere has earned and merited opinions, has given promise of great things in future, has proved himself kind, noble, equal minded, when tried in the furnace of acquired rank, and power over his fellows, has turned out in the end to be but of base metal after all. Many a nobler, deeper spirit, which, for a while depressed by low circumstances, may have caught some stain from the base things around it, have condescended to some acts unworthy of its natural tendencies, when suddenly uplifted to its proper sphere, has cast away all the toils on the instant, has emerged from all the unworthiness, and shown the intrinsic difference between the "dust that is a little gilt," and the true "gilt o'erdusted."

But this, the latter change is, as I said, peculiar to the greater, the nobler, and the purer minds of men; and is perhaps as rare, as the former alteration is of frequent occurrence. It would seem very wonderful, could anything seem wonderful which we see almost daily, that the possession of power to afflict, to oppress, to torment others, should beget the desire to do so. Yet, from the petty pelting Dogberry of some small village, to the mighty Kaisar on his imperial throne, how often do we see this truth, how seldom the converse exemplified.

Again it would seem strange, did not its commonness make it familiar, that greatness should sit more lightly upon him who has inherited it all untoiled for, and should by him be wielded with far less oppressiveness toward the inferior; than by the lowly born, who has struggled upward painfully, and at length won unwonted power. The task-master, who was a slave of old himself, is the most merciless oppressor of the class from which he was emancipated yesterday. The plebeian magistrate is he, who has the least compassion for the sorrows, the least indulgence for the offences of the poor plebeian. The rich burgher, who once raked the kennels for a base meal, is he who least frequently unbuckles his fat purse to aid his starving neighbor. The baseness, that is native to their souls, is but the more apparent in the altered circumstances. It is not that the soul is changed for the worse within, but that the shell without is unduly elevated.

The heart and nature of the beggar is there still; clad in the garb of the noble it is true, yet still beggarly and base. And it may be regarded as almost a universal rule, that he who tramples the most heavily on his inferior, crouches the most abjectly before the superior.

Sir Edmund Andross had achieved greatness.

Sir Henry Cecil was born wealthy, powerful, and noble.

Sir Edmund Andross had known want, scorn, suffering, humiliation. By dint of some great qualities, assisted—alas! that I should say, *assisted*—by some very base ones, he had emerged from the slough to glitter in the sunshine. But he had carried up with him the rank odor of the mire, to fester and become more offensive in the noonday lustre.

Sir Henry Cecil had been lapped in luxury from his cradle upward; he had known from his infancy nothing but care and kindness, pleasure, and wealth, and prosperity. Nothing mean had come near to him; no small degrading wants, no spirit-galling scorn, no soul-degrading humiliations. All his associations had been with the good, the beautiful, the noble, and the true. And of these two men the weak world would judge, that he who had suffered most, would most sympathize with the suffering; that he whose lot had been ever raised above the storms of adversity, would pitilessly see these storms burst on the heads of others; that he who had known humiliation would be humble—he who had known power and pride only, would by his very power be made proud.

The world would assert that this is truth and nature. I say that it is neither natural nor true!

The humblest man, who ever trod the earth, was he who had laid aside the infinite might, and majesty, and glory of the godhead in order to become "the man of sorrows." Is there in that brief recollection, no strong lesson? I can conceive no spectacle more pleasing to the eyes of angels, those blessed ministers who watch ever fondly over man's changeful course, hailing his least good deed with smiles of heavenly radiance, washing his darkest acts with tears of celestial sorrow—I can conceive, I say, no spectacle so pleasing to the eyes of those pure beings, as the great man bearing his greatness meekly; using his delegated powers only to mitigate the sorrows which he has never known; spreading his wealth about him, only to bless the poor and needy; and yet cheering their hearts more by his kindly voice and gentle air, than by the bounty of his hand.

I can conceive none more detestable than that of the self-made, low-born magnate, revelling in his brief authority, using his greatness only to wound, his wealth only to tantalize, his power only to trample under foot the wretched worms, of whom but yesterday he was the brother. And such, in many respects, as the latter picture, was Sir Edmund Andross. In almost all, such as the former, Sir Henry Cecil.

And yet, alas! for poor human nature that it is ever so, the virtues of the one were no more without their alloy of selfishness, than the vices of the other without their palliation. A gentle nature, and the pleasure which it gave him to do good, were perhaps greater inducements to the virtues of Henry Cecil, than any settled principle, or determined sense of duty. And a quick temper, and a rebellious pride toward his superiors, marred something of the loveliness of his demeanor toward those below him.

Of Andross too it must be said, that his oppressive temper, his crushing and tyrannic pride, were not so much the results of a malicious or unfeeling heart, still less of any deliberate intention to be cruel, as of a nature hardened and embittered by wrongs endured early, when the soul is as plastic to evil as to good; and of a false black estimate of the lower classes, drawn from the baseness of the tools whom he had found occasion to employ, and the base uses to which he had stooped himself, in winning his way to eminence. Bad as he was therefore, and cruel as he showed himself in this instance, neither the baseness nor the cruelty was deliberate or committed from the love of cruelty; though it would be too much to say that either was accidental.

A stanch and thorough-going loyalist, both from sincere opinion and from gratitude to the king his patron, a bitter hater from conviction, of that independent democratic spirit, which having burned itself out in England during the great civil war of 1642, had taken firm root in the soil of America; and as bitter a hater of the canting puritanical spirit, which accompanied it, Andross believed it really to be his duty to spare no means of crushing and eradicating both the latter wherever he should find them.

The character and principles of the man, whom he had that day gone out to arrest, were well known to him ; and he looked upon Merciful Whalley, and looked upon him justly, as a dark bad man, and a dangerous subject. His object in striking at this man was not merely the seizure of a regicide, and the punishment of those who resetted him. Had it been nothing more, he would have left the execution of the task to the ordinary servants of justice.

But the truth is, that he was well-informed of the existence, in the Bay Province, of a strong and growing party opposed to the extension of the royal prerogatives, and devoted to the propagation and establishment of civil liberty—that he suspected a direct conspiracy to be in progress, for the overthrow of the constituted government; and more than suspected Merciful Whalley to be at the bottom of it. In this view of the subject, he had determined, by seizing the father and the son, to strike a deep blow at the roots of the conspiracy, to make a terrible example ; to deprive the plot of its most formidable leader; and to spread terror far and wide through the hearts of the disaffected.

Frustrated utterly in this intention by the flight of the Puritans, perceiving that there must be treason at his own council board, and that his designs were made known to the conspirators, and anticipated by them, his anger knew no bounds. But it was a cool, calculating, and politic anger, aiming as much at future ends, as at the gratification of present vengeance. While this feeling was at work in his brain, instigating him to the perpetration of some great act of cruelty, which he would have called a great example, two other furious passions were added to that which was already strong within him unto evil. An ardent admirer of beauty in the other sex, a fierce dissolute licentious man, accustomed to gratify every taste how illicit soever, and owing to his position, having been hitherto seldom thwarted, he had cast almost instantly the eyes of unholy and impure admiration, on the beautiful face and voluptuous form of Ruth Whalley. The very calmness of her unaffected modesty, the unquestionable innocence of the fair young girl, joined to the freedom of her manner, and the frank artlessness of her speech, made the more vehement impression on his fancy or his senses, that he was little used to anything of female manners beyond the light license of the ladies who frequented the courts of the two last of the unhappy Stuarts. He had been turning it already over in his mind, while he was chiefly occupied with other matters, how he should gain possession of that sweet girl's affections, or, if that might not be, of her person; when the demeanor of Cecil, appearing to indicate some opposition to his will, perhaps some anticipation of his views, decided him; and he resolved at once upon his course of action.

"Fire it, I say! Fire it at each of the four corners!—It shall house no more rebels!"

And ruthlessly was that ruthless order obeyed.

Not a moment was given to the hapless women, not so much even as to bring out raiment, or food, or any of those little articles, the household gods of the affections which may be found in every household.

The domestic animals, the dog and the kittens were driven forth by the soldiers, more merciful than their commander; and then the work of destruction was commenced, and carried to a close with as little of delay as of mercy.

The doors were dashed off their hinges; and of these and the furniture a pile was made in the centre of the kitchen, with the addition of dry straw and light wood ; fire was set to this, and to the bark-covered roof, as well as to the pillars of the rustic porches, and to the wooden walls in a dozen different places. This done, the soldiers fell back, carrying their prisoners with them, close to the margin of the cliffs, and stood with their arms folded, leaning upon their matchlocks, and watching the progress of the conflagration.

It was a terrible and lamentable sight, rendered more lamentable yet by the pale faces and agonized demeanor of the wretched spectators, compelled to witness thus the destruction of their humble home.

The mother had fallen on her knees upon the greensward, and clasping her little daughter to her cold bosom, was gazing with tearless and stony eyes, speechless, breathless, and as it would appear from that fixed, stupid stare, nearly senseless, upon the progress of the ruin.

Ruth stood beside her, fearless indeed, and calm, but as pale as ashes ; her two younger brothers clinging, in terror of what should ensue, to the skirts of her dress. Once, her full, quiet eye met that of Andross with a reproachful, deep expression, which, dauntless as he was, he could not brook ; but, for the most part, it dwelt steadily upon the burning walls of the only home she remembered.

The face of Gideon was flushed fiery red with rage ; he had bit his lip till the blood trickled down his beardless chin ; his hands were clenched, and the quivering of all his limbs betrayed the violence of the passion, which he controlled in the dread only of calling down worse wrong upon the helpless women. The Indian girl, scarce comprehending all that had passed, gazed with round eyes of wonder from face to face ; until the flames burst forth from the roof, the door, the windows of that house, which had been to her only a prison and a place of torture

Then clasping her hands wildly, while a quick fire flashed from her eyes, she burst into a fit of loud, clear, thrilling laughter, so joyous and triumphant, that it struck terror to the hearts of the stout soldiers.

"Never more!" she exclaimed—"Never more to be a slave *there!* Never more to be bound and beaten like a dog!—never, never more!" and she leaped up from the ground, on which she had been sitting, and set up a long-drawn and savage yell of triumph.

Excited by this fearful outcry, and conscious as it seemed of the calamity, the house-dog raised his nose into the air, and after snuffing the atmosphere eagerly for a moment uttered a long-protracted howl, inexpressibly wild and melancholy, which was, however, brought to a quick conclusion by a blow from the sheathed broadsword of the lance-pesade, converting it into a sharp yelp of pain.

Just as this clamor ceased, there arose a fresh sound, stranger, and if it were possible, more awful.

It was a deep, hoarse, quavering groan, twice, thrice repeated—a harsh, guttural, hollow sound, full, as it seemed, of physical and mental anguish.

Every one started, and looked in his neighbor's face, and two or three of the soldiers threw up their matchlocks, and put themselves in readiness for action.

There was a minute of breathless silence; all listening in an agony of expectation to hear, if it might be repeated. But all was silence.

"In God's name, what was that?" cried Andross, at length, his lips white and trembling with dismay.

But none made answer to him.

"It came not from the burning building? Did it? Speak! speak, Sir Henry Cecil! There can be no one within!"

"Certainly it did not," replied the young man, forgetting his indignation at the late insolence of Andross, in sympathy with his remorseful terrors. "There is no one within; of that I am certain. It seemed to me, that it came from the summit of yon tall cliff to the seaward."

Again the Indian girl's eyes flashed in triumph, again she clapped her hands, and burst into her wild laugh.

"Tituba knows!" she cried. "Tituba knows! she has heard it before!" and again she concluded her sentence, with that long piercing yell.

As quick as thought Ruth Whalley turned the light of her gentle eye on the fierce savage, and her frame seemed to collapse beneath its influence, and she crouched down to the ground again with a low wailing murmur.

"What was it, then? speak, wench!" cried Sir Edmund, scarcely remarking then, in his eagerness, though afterward remembered, what Cecil had perceived, the gesture of the maiden and its effects on the child of the forest. "What was it, that strange sound?"

"The white man's devil!" answered the Indian. "If there be any devil worse than the white man."

At the first words, a shudder of superstitious awe ran through the rude soldiers; and the buts of their muskets clanged heavily on the rocky soil, as they grounded them by an involuntary impulse.

"Tush!" said the governor, coldly, recovering himself—"it was but the groaning of the timbers, as the flames started them," and he resumed his posture of unconcerned observation, awaiting with folded arms the result of the conflagration.

Meanwhile, the flames rushed up, blackening the face of the gray cliffs, and blighting the giant boughs of the green pines which overhung the cottage; and a vast pillar of white smoke soared slowly upward in the calm atmosphere, and stood there fixed and motionless, a ghastly and accusing monument of man's cruelty.

Fiercer they roared, and fiercer — and now beam after beam came crashing down; and the cottage was but a pile of smoking ashes with a light lambent flame wavering over it.

Then with a strange, heart-piercing cry the unhappy mother cast her child from her bosom, stretched her arms wide abroad, and fell, as if a bullet had pierced her heart, flat on her face, motionless, and it seemed lifeless.

The evil deeds of Merciful had recoiled on the heads of his unoffending family!

The scent of the innocent blood was purged from the guilty house by avenging fire!

And who shall say that it was not from Heaven?

CHAPTER XVI.

THE HOSTAGE.

"Be surety for his coming with thy life."

INTENSE was the disgust of Sir Henry Cecil at the illegal and barbarous actions of his late superior. That he would have resisted them is certain, could he have done so with any hope of success. But alone, and unarmed by his own hasty act, what could he think to do against seven powerful and well-weaponed men by active opposition.

Remonstrance he had tried, and that had proved worse than fruitless.

He remained silent, therefore, awaiting what should follow: intending at a future period to try what reparation might be obtained for wrongs, which he lacked the power to prevent.

So fierce was his concentrated indignation, that his fine face, from which the flush had now completely faded, was almost as pale as a corpse, even at the lips, which were compressed tightly over the clinched teeth.

His brows were bent into a dark frown, and beneath them his clear gray eyes shone with a bright, angry lustre. His arms were closely folded on his breast, and it was plain to see, by the convulsive tremor which caused his clinched fingers to work as if they were griping the hilt of sword or dagger, how violent was the mental effort by which he restrained himself from such fierce outbreak.

The others of the group stirred not, with the exception of sweet Ruth, who sprang forward to raise up and assist her mother, and Tituba, who caught the little girl in her arms, almost as quickly as the unhappy woman cast it from her, and soothed it on her bosom with one of those plaintive strains, half-sung, half-murmured, which are peculiar to the females of her race.

"Mother! look up! mother, dear, dearest mother," exclaimed Ruth, as she lifted her to a sitting posture, and wiped away the blood which was trickling from her nostrils in consequence of the heavy fall. "Mother, mother! my God! she is dead, she is dead! you have slain her!" and she looked up into the face of Andross, with an expression of reproach and pitiful despair that would have moved a fiend to mercy.

It did move Sir Edmund Andross.

He turned very pale, and took a quick step forward to the maiden's side, exclaiming —

"No! no! she is not dead — it is a fainting fit only; it is terror; she will revive directly. Here, Lambert, Martin, stir yourselves, run, fetch some fresh water, row back to the pinnace, and bring some wine and aqua vita."

His orders were obeyed; but Ruth who had shifted her

mother's head from her bosom to her lap, sat gazing steadfastly on the glazed eyes, and impassive features, and on the drop of congealed blood which had now ceased to flow.

She never had seen death before, yet now she knew it, by a sure instinct; surer far than the experience of the men who had so often witnessed it, so often, it may be, inflicted it, in broil or battle.

She held the inanimate and unresponsive fingers in her own, and felt the vital warmth fail gradually, and the flesh contract and stiffen.

"It is of no avail," she said calmly, but with that calmness which shows more agony of soul than the loudest grief. "She is dead! you have slain her! Mother! mother! poor, patient, unrepining, kind, dear mother! a sad life yours has been, and a sad end to it is this! Weary and toilsome has been your pilgrimage below, uncheered by much of human love, unrelieved by much sympathy or joy; but by the Christian's hope thou wert sustained, and in thy Savior's bosom thou art now happy. Wo! wo unto us who remain behind thee!" and, overcome at length, she bowed her head into her hands, and wept bitterly.

No further movement followed on the part of the bystanders, for all now saw that her words were indeed true; and that the shock and anguish of the moment had been too much for the shattered spirits and emaciated frame of the unhappy wife and mother.

Only Gideon stepped up to his sister's side with a more manly expression on his face than it had ever worn before, and manlier feelings in his heart.

It is events alone that ripen character; and one short hour will sometimes change us more from youth to manhood, or from strong manhood into the sere of life, than years of tranquillity and peace.

The younger boys crowded round the corpse of her who

bore them, with their young hearts, which had been checked and crushed for years by the stern rule of their iron father now overflowing with a torrent of strangely blended and tumultuous sympathies.

For a few moments Ruth wept silently, but then by a mighty effort mustering her heart, she laid the cold head down on the turf, knelt by it, stooped and kissed the pale brow and icy lips, and said in a steady voice —

"Farewell! farewell! poor mother, it will not be for long that I say fare you well!'

Then she arose to her full height, passionless and cold, and confronted Sir Edmund Andross.

"Man," she said slowly and impressively, "thou hast murdered her — her, who never wronged any living thing, by thought, word, or deed — the meekest, mildest, most affectionate of beings. As surely as if thou hadst stricken her with the sword's edge hast thou murdered her! Man may not call it murder — man may not judge nor avenge it! Therefore to man do I not appeal, but to God! He hath seen — he hath judged — and in his own good time he shall avenge! To this tribunal, therefore, I appeal! Before this awful judgment-seat I summon thee to meet the spirit of thy victim, and that right early!"

"Brothers," she added, catching Gideon's hand, with her right hand, and stretching out her left over the heads of the two younger, "brothers, look! there *she* lies, who bore, who nursed, who loved us all, with that love which none but a mother's heart can feel — there *she* lies, from whose poor, pale face we never have met aught but kind and gentle smiles — from whose dear lips, whatever we have merited, we never have heard aught but soft and loving words. That face will never smile on us again, those lips will never speak to us. She is lost to us here for ever. Look!" she continued, turning toward Andross, with a sterner manner, though still tranquil. "Look! there *he* stands who slew her. Look on him! Mark him narrowly! Observe him, that ye forget him not! Brothers, ye are now boys, but, with God's blessing, one day ye shall be men! I do not say avenge her, for vengeance is the Lord's; he shall repay! But I say, mark him, for He hath said that he will avenge the innocent blood, of whose sayings, it is written, that "Heaven and earth shall pass away, but my words shall not pass away!" Brothers, I have spoken. "The Lord gave, the Lord hath taken away, blessed be the name of the Lord!"

But as she ceased to speak, Gideon stretched out both hands over the body, and cried in a shrill, sad voice:—

"Hear me, Almighty! Hear me, thou spirit of the blessed dead! for here, henceforth for ever, I devote myself, body and soul; here I devote my brothers also, when they come to years of manhood, to be thy avengers! Man of blood! thou shalt think one day on these words that I have spoken; for when thou liest in thy blood, and a bloody death thou shalt die, I will stand by thy side and laugh at thy death-pang! I swear it by Him who liveth in the holy heavens, now and for ever!"

The face of Andross had expressed many deep and changeful emotions, while Ruth was speaking—for, to do him justice, he was both shocked and grieved at what had occurred; and felt no disposition to cavil at a woman's words in a moment so terrible, in the horrors of which he had moreover been himself an unwitting instrument. But now, at the threatening and audacious words of the boy, his cheek burned and his fierce temper resumed the ascendency.

"Somewhat too much of this," he said scornfully. "That which has happened, I regret as much as any one can do; but I am not answerable for it, even if it be caused by the performance of my duty. For the rest, I can make all allowance for the grief of a daughter, while I fear not the vengeance of Heaven, much less the impotent revenge of a puny boy, for acts in obedience to the orders of my king, and the laws of my country. But we must have no more of this. Now, my men, make the boat ready, we will return to the pinnace."

He paused uneasily, as if he had something more to say, and knew not how to say it; and, absorbed though she was in her great grief, Ruth perceived his embarrassment, and perhaps unwisely, unfortunately beyond a doubt, commented on it.

"What, is there more?" she said; for even in her sweet and gentle disposition tyranny and the agonies it had produced were awakening a spirit of rebellion. "What more of lawless cruelty, of heaven-daring outrage, is there yet to be done? Something it must be of appalling infamy, or of atrocity unheard, since it puts even thy bronzed tyranny to shame — what is there, I say, more? Is it not enough that you leave behind you poverty, anguish, ruin, where you found wealth, content-ment, peace? Is it not enough that you have left your foot-prints indelibly stamped in this once happy solitude, by death and devastation?"

"Peace! peace!" whispered Cecil, in a low kind of voice, drawing near to her; "oh, peace, poor maiden, for thine own sake — for the sake of those whom thou lovest."

"It is peace!" she replied, gazing at him with a pitiful look. "The peace of utter desolation! But once again, I must ask," she added, turning toward the governor, "hast thou more wrong to do us?"

"I wish that I could answer, 'No,'" returned Sir Edmund. His passion for the girl's beauty, which had been forgotten for the moment, and his resentment against Cecil, rekindling all the worst part of his nature at sight of his sympathy with her. "But duty must be done, painful or pleasant; and my duty it is, after all the treason which we have witnessed here, to remove you hence as a hostage, to be detained until such time as your father shall surrender himself into custody."

"Great God! it is impossible!" she cried, clasping her hands in agony—"it is impossible, that any man should be so barbarous! What! tear an orphan daughter from her dead mother's corpse—no! no! no!" she sobbed hysterically. "It is not so, it can not be—why, who shall bury her?—who shall feed these?"

And, as she spoke, she stretched one hand toward the dead mother, the other toward the youngest orphans.

"With that I have naught to do!" he replied; and, then hearing the brief, bitter curse which fell from the lips of Cecil, he added, "or rather, I should say to thee, quoting a text which thou knowest perchance already, 'Let the dead bury their dead!'"

"Thou art no man," she said, "but a devil!—almost, I believe, the arch-fiend himself!"

"Sir Edmund Andross," interposed Henry Cecil, bridling his wrath, and speaking as tranquilly as he could, "if you have both the right and the will to do this thing, which I can not believe; if you indeed think it your duty to secure this damsel, as a hostage, yet suffer her to remain here, and inter her dead; and I will pledge to you my word of honor, as a gentleman and soldier, and a knight-baronet, that I will be your warrant that, this sad duty done, she shall surrender herself up to you, within three days at farthest. We are not friends, Sir Edmund, we never shall be friends, but, on my honor, I would not see you do this thing for your own sake; for, though a stern and a proud man, I have never believed you base or cruel; and so surely as you do this, the world will deem you both."

"Have you done, sir?" asked Andross fiercely.

"I have not!" answered Cecil; "for, having told you that I am your enemy, it may gratify your pride to see your enemy a suppliant. I never bent my knee to a created thing; I would not bend it to preserve my life; yet I bend it to you now, and sue you humbly to accept the warrant of my honor, and let her tarry here!"

"Under Sir Henry Cecil's fatherly protection," he said, with a sneer.

The young baronet sprang from his knee to his feet; and grasped at the place where his sword should have hung—it was well for the governor that it hung there no longer.

Andross looked at him with a cool, galling smile, and said—

"It can not be, sir. I refuse even an enemy's request. If I could have granted it at all, I should have granted it to the girl's sorrow. Come, my men, lead her to the boat."

But at this moment one of the two seamen, who had accompanied him ashore, an old white-headed master's mate, but still strong and active, strode out, and faced the governor.

"By God!" he said, "Sir Edmund Andross, this will not go down here! On shore, you may be governor or captain, or whatever else you please, but on the deck of the Rosebud, no man is captain but Dick Foster," and here he swore an amazing nautical oath, "and while Dick Foster can stand up in his shoes, that poor thing shall not go aboard her!"

"*Shall* not?" exclaimed Andross, furiously.

"Yes! I said *shall* not, and I say it again, too, for all your toasting-forks, and pop-guns, and laced cassocks. Why, Lord deliver you, I have blue jackets enough yonder to spoil the hash of three times as many red-coats as you can count, even if the jollies would stand by you; and that I do n't believe they would; for so poor a devil as a jolly is, I never heard tell of one harming a helpless girl. Do you understand me now, Sir Edmund? I say she *shan't* come aboard the Rosebud. So you had better take Master Cecil's warrant for her, and let us be off. For I 'm sick o' this work," and he wound up his speech, as he had commenced it, with a tremendous oath, by way of peroration.

"Why, this is rank mutiny!" cried Andross, perceiving that it was doubtful whether he could reckon on the support of his soldiers.

"Rank mutiny be d—d!" the other replied. "I am no man of yours, Sir Edmund. "I know no superior here, but good Captain George of the Rose frigate, to which the Rosebud is a tender; and as for mutiny, I served black Jem when he licked the Mynheers in the narrow seas, when he was only Duke of York, and he knows old Dick Foster too well to believe your nonsense about mutiny. However," he continued, "mutiny or no mutiny, that lass don't go aboard the Rosebud this day, nor to-morrow neither. That's plain English!"—

"Plain English, sirrah! for which you shall answer one day," retorted Andross.

"Don't 'sirrah' me, Sir Edmund," answered the sturdy old man, laying his hand on the hilt of his cutlass, "or *you* shall answer for it *now*. For, if you do it again, I'll cut your crown before you are five minutes older."

Though sick and sad at heart, Cecil could not refrain from smiling at the total discomfiture of the governor.

"You laugh now, Sir Henry," said he sharply, as he saw the lip of the young man curl. "See if you laugh, when my turn shall come. Master Foster, you will repent of this.—But now, get your men to the boat; I will leave the girl under your pledge of honor, sir, that she shall be surrendered to the proper authority within three days at farthest."

"My word once spoken, sir," answered Cecil, gravely, "I can not recall it; otherwise, as things now stand, you should have no promise. Within three days she shall be given up in Boston, unless her father shall surrender himself in the meantime."

"Tu me la pagherai!"* said Andross, in Italian, with a half-scornful bow, which Cecil returned, saying, with a smile, "Wherever you please, Sir Edmund."

In ten minutes more, the men were all in the boat, which was pulled hastily back, bearing the governor, chafing like a hurt boar at the resistance and ill-concealed contempt which he had encountered, to the pinnace.

Scarcely were they on board before her sails were trimmed, her grapnels hauled in, and her canvass filled by the fresh merry breeze, which swept her speedily up into Boston harbor, ignorant of the misery she left behind her, and resembling rather some gay pleasure-boat, than a machine built by man for man's destruction.

CHAPTER XVII.

THE RETURN.

"And found his home a home no more."

It would be difficult to discover words, which should describe with accuracy the feelings of Sir Henry Cecil, at finding himself thus left alone in that remote and difficultly approached spot, in the midst of that bereaved and mourning family.

It must be remembered, that, until the preceding night he had scarce heard of the existence of these people, in whose behalf he had now thrown up his commission, and declared himself an enemy of the royal governor, perhaps, it might thereafter be assumed, of the government itself.

* "You shall pay me for this."

He therefore knew little or nothing of the habits, manners, or sentiments of the people to whom he now stood somewhat in the light of a protector; and it may be added further, that with what he knew of them he felt but little sympathy.

An ardent lover of constitutional English freedom, he had no common feelings with the advocates of democratical equality; he was no believer in the visionary schemes and ideal republics of Harrington and Vane. Earnest himself and sincere in his belief of the doctrines of the English church, yet at the same time an advocate of universal toleration, he could not but view with dislike and disgust the stern cold sectaries, who, flying from what they called persecution of their own sect at home, now persecuted every other creed with the bitterest and most cold-blooded rancor.

The very dialect of these people, their dragging the holiest names and most sacred things into association with the commonest and most familiar—their forcing the language of the church or conventicle into the domestic circle—their profane expostulations with the Deity—their contempt of all kind and endearing usages—their prohibition of all innocent amusements—all these things were to him odious and almost abominable.

He looked, moreover, on the trial and execution of King Charles I. as a great crime; and although he certainly did not believe in the propriety of dragging frail old men to the scaffold for a deed done, probably, in good faith, some forty years before, he yet felt not the least inclination to be brought into contact with men, whose manners were as distasteful to him, as their principles were hostile to his own.

As a soldier, obedient to discipline, he would scarcely have expressed, therefore, his disapprobation of the steps taken for the arrest of the elder Whalley, even if he had felt it more strongly than he did; and, as for the younger Puritan, he certainly had no doubt about the propriety of apprehending him, not on account of the shelter he had extended to his own father, but of the treason which he was believed to be plotting against the colonial government.

Cecil was, therefore, in many respects strangely situated. His own impulsive temper, joined to his natural dislike of all tyrannical and oppressive measures, had prompted him to stand forward as a righter of wrong, and a supporter of the oppressed, against legitimate authority. The subsequent violence of the governor had led farther than he would otherwise have gone; and now he found himself committed, as it were, to a line of conduct which might ultimately lead him he scarce knew whither; and that, too, in behalf of the people, concerning whom he had entertained many and grave doubts.

It is very true, that Cecil, as well as Sir Edmund Andross, had been deeply struck by the charms of the fair Puritan. For he, too, was an admirer of female beauty, though in a very different manner from the dissolute and licentious governor; and her loveliness was of an order to attract and fix the admiration of the coldest.

But in the difference of the dispositions and the principles of these two men, there lay the clew to what might almost make a history.

For as Andross, whose devotion to the sex was wholly sensual and physical, cared nothing for the mind, the accomplishments, the heart of the woman on whom he cast the eyes of passion; so Cecil, in whose estimation the beauteous body was but the casket of a soul, and to be loved and treasured, or despised and cast aside, according as that soul was beautiful or not, cast but a passing glance upon mere charms of the person, and was no more capable of falling, as it is called, in love with a fair complexion, bright eyes, fine hair, and a voluptuous figure, than of adoring a waxen puppet.

There was nothing, therefore, of love, even in its incipient stages, in the feeling which had induced him to step forward to the protection of Ruth Whalley. It was solely his hatred of all oppression, and his sympathy with all the oppressed, that had prompted him to the act, by which he had been apparently divorced from his countrymen.

And scarcely was the pinnace under way, before he began to envisage the extreme awkwardness of his position.

Alone, on an almost isolated rock, with no shelter from the weather, and, so far as he could see, no means of providing any ; surrounded by weak women, and children under age, with the exception of Gideon, who now, that the momentary excitement had passed away, appeared completely paralyzed by the terrible occurrences of the last hour, what was he to do, what to devise, even for the present ?

Then for the future : he had pledged his honor that this girl should be yielded up on the third day as a hostage. And now, that the enthusiasm and indignation which had urged him to give that pledge had faded, he could not but apprehend some difficulty in the performance of his promise.

Especially, in case the father should return, armed perhaps, and accompanied by his neighbors, to oppose her surrender.

While he was musing thus, gazing with vacant eyes over the rolling waves, across which the little bark was bounding with his comrades homeward, the young girl, who perhaps in some sort read his thoughts, drew near and addressed him timidly.

"You have saved us," she said in a low, soft voice ; "and now you regret it."

"Oh ! no !" he answered. "It is not that, indeed. I have done nothing but what, as a gentleman and a Christian, I was bound to do. I do not, therefore, in the least regret it. But surely, in all this, there is enough of difficulty to make me grave and thoughtful."

"Difficulty?" she replied, "difficulty—I do not understand you!" and then, as if a light broke suddenly upon her—"What!" she exclaimed, "can you imagine, for a moment, that I would break the promise you so nobly made for me?"

"Not you," he answered, looking into her soft dove-love eyes, with more of admiration than he had hitherto manifested, "Oh, no! not you; but perhaps—"

"My father!" she interrupted him. "Well; and even if he should oppose it, do you believe I would obey him, rather than the laws of truth, of gratitude, of honesty? Oh! no, sir; you do not know Ruth Whalley."

"I have scarce had time to do so," he answered, with a grave smile; "yet I think that I have not, at least, much misjudged you. But there are other things which disturbed me. We are alone on this rock, without house or any shelter, without food, drink, fuel, or change of raiment—without any means, in short, for the support of the living, or the—" and he paused abruptly, fearful of shocking her; but she took up the sentence where he broke off,

"The burial of the dead!—it is true! it is true! Mother, dear mother, and had I even for a moment forgotten you?" and, with the words, she threw herself at her full length on the greensward, beside the body, and clasping it with both her arms, buried her face in the cold bosom, and wept bitterly.

Cecil stood still, and looked on in silence, for he knew well, young as he was, that grief must have its course, and that it is neither wise nor kind to oppose its current.

But while she lay there, sobbing as if her heart would burst, the Indian girl crept up to Cecil's side, and pointing with a tremulous gesture, and a face almost distorted with terror, toward the sea, exclaimed,

"See, he comes! it is Merciful! Save Tituba, young soldier, save her from Merciful!"

Then, for the first time, it occurred to the young man, that he might himself stand in need of defence, in the first moments of the Puritan's despair and fury! He was not one, however, to take much thought of himself, when others called for assistance; and, though he might feel a passing regret that he had broken his good sword, and cast it from him, he still hastened to assure the poor Indian of his readiness to protect her.

"No one will injure you, he said, poor thing, while I am present;—but wherefore should you think he will harm you? and where is he? for I see him not."

"Merciful flogs Tituba," she replied, "always. Do good, or do evil, still flog! flog! If Tituba were a man, a chief, as her father was, she would ask no one to protect her. There, see, there! over the port of the bridge, his white sail rises and falls above the waters—so small, that it looks like a sea-gull's wing, but it is a broad, canvass sail—Merciful's sail! He will be here soon—then, young soldier, forget not, but save Tituba."

This further testimony to that, which he already more than suspected, the brutal harshness of the Puritan's disposition, went far to convince Cecil that he should have indeed no easy part to play, perhaps no safe one! Yet even in that moment of personal uneasiness the noble youth found time to think of the horrors which would meet the eyes of that stern man on his landing, and to consider how to palliate them.

He approached Ruth cautiously, as she still lay beside her mother's body, although the convulsive agonies of her first grief appeared in some sort to have abated, and stooping over her, said, very gently,

"Your father is approaching, my poor Ruth, will you not

rise and meet him? The shock will be terrible. It must not break thus upon him all at once."

She arose on the instant, and calmed herself, and restrained her tears, with a mighty effort. Nay! she stepped a few paces back to a spot, where a clear spring trickled from the rock, and washed away the traces of her weeping, and re-arranged her dishevelled hair.

Then walking steadily forward to the little esplanade before the bridge, she gazed sadly at the approaching boat, and said, loudly,

"Yes! it is he—poor father! This will be very grievous to him—all lost at one blow!—all lost, and she, too!—and it will shock him, too, the more, that he was not so kind to her always, as he should have been!"

But, as she spoke, she started as if remembering that those heard her, who should not; and then, recovering herself, looked anxiously around the little group, apparently in search of something. After a moment or two, however, she shook her head sorrowfully, saying, "Nothing—no! there is nothing left at all from the fire. I would we had wherewithal to cover her."

Sir Henry Cecil answered nothing, but he unbuckled from his shoulder the rich scarlet cloak adorned with a heavy fringe of gold, which was a part of the cavalier's costume of the day, and disengaging it from his person, laid it as gently and reverently over the senseless clay, as if he had apprehended that a ruder motion might yet disturb those dreamless slumbers.

Ruth gave him a deep glance of gratitude—one of those glances, which sink at once into the heart, and never are forgotten—and then rushed toward the bridge to meet her father; for the fresh breeze had swept his boat in rapidly, while they were speaking, and he was close at hand already.

A few minutes, and he stood upon the platform, haggard, and pale, and ghastly!

That single night of agony upon the deep, joined to the last three hours of terror and dark anticipation—for he had lain in his boat within a league's distance, his sail housed, and marked the movements of the royal pinnace, and the smoke hanging like a pall over his humble roof—had changed the man's appearance more than whole years of hardship.

What had been lines before in his dark face were now deep furrows, ploughed by the iron which had entered into his soul! The hair of his head was nearly as white as his father's.

Yet was his hard and indomitable spirit still untamed; and it was fury, rather, and the desire of vengeance, than grief or alarm, that contracted his stern features.

"Ha!" he exclaimed, as he reached the platform, and saw, as he supposed, the full extent of the desolation, "Father of Mercies! who hath done this?—and wherefore?"

"The royal governor," replied Ruth, taking his hand in her own. "But be not angry, father; for surely it is He, who can not err, that hath so ordered it."

"Wherefore?—I say, wherefore? On what pretext did he this villany, the bloody-minded tyrant and oppressor? I say, wherefore?"

"He came with soldiers to arrest you and my grandfather; and finding you not here, would not believe at all that the old man had gone hence, and so burned—"

But Merciful waited no further explanation. His eye fell upon the shrinking form of Tituba, who stood between himself and the body; and yet so stunned was he and bewildered by surprise and wrath, that he neither missed the presence of his wife, nor observed that of the young soldier.

At one bound he reached her, and before Cecil could interpose, exclaiming,

"Harlot and witch!—This is thy doing;—it is thou hast betrayed him!" he struck her a brutal blow on the bosom, with his clenched hand, felling her to the earth, ere she had time to cry aloud for succor.

But not content with this, he reared the heavy musket, which he still carried high above his head, grasping it by the muzzle, and brandished it to give full force to the blow, exclaiming, "As the Lord liveth, thou shalt work no more treason!"

Sir Henry Cecil, who, in his anxiety to conceal the body of his wife, had almost forgotten the words of the poor slave, stood too far aloof to reach him in time to arrest the stroke. Gideon was paralyzed with terror, Ruth overcome by so rapid a succession of horrors, and well-nigh fainting.

It seemed that no mortal help could save her; but Cecil, who never for a moment lost his quick wit, or readiness of mind, cried, in a piercing voice,

"Hold, madman! Do no murder in the presence of THE DEAD!"

"THE DEAD!" exclaimed the Puritan, aghast, starting, and holding back that felon blow.

But as Sir Henry spoke, he had stooped down and removed the covering from the pale face so calm, so fixed, so sorrowful in its last sleep.

"Great God! my wife! my wife!" and, dropping the murderous weapon, he fell upon his knees beside her, whom of late he had so little cherished, and a whole torrent of remorseful, and fond, and agonizing memories bursting at once upon his soul, he bowed his stern head on his hands, mute, convulsed, self-convicted, well-nigh choked with despairing anguish.

CHAPTER XVIII.

THE HUSBAND.

> "Now the friend's familiar step to greet
> With loving laughter, or the volume sweet
> Of those glad eyes."

Sir Henry Cecil had looked upon grief many times — had been familiar with mortal misery and mortal anguish in many a varied shape — yet never had he witnessed anything that could, in the least degree, bear comparison with the even tortures of the Puritan.

It was not grief alone at his bereavement; it was not the shock alone of seeing her, who had been wont to meet him, on his every return home, with silent looks of welcome — the only welcome that he would endure — outstretched cold, senseless lifeless, never to welcome him again.

No! had it been only this, he could have borne it. His resolute and iron spirit would stubbornly have struggled up against that torture.

No! no! it was the intolerable sense of wrong which might be repented, but never could be undone, nor requited to the deaf form which lay there unconscious of his present sorrow, as of his past unkindness.

He saw not the pale, wan, emaciated face of the dead wife, but the gay, lively, glowing features of the happy maiden, when he first beheld her, the star of the village company. It was not the ashy cheek of the cold corpse, but the bright blush of the warm, living bride, that was set before the eyes of his spirit. It was not the icy fingers that he felt, but the affectionate and twining pressure of that soft hand, that timidly encased his own before God's holy altar.

And then, as the vision faded from his soul, and he remembered that for years that face had been almost as much emaciated, that cheek almost as hueless, that once bright-speaking eye almost as dim, as now when the light of life had for ever left them ; as he reflected that for years the spirit, which informed that gentle frame, had been almost as dead as was the body that enshrined it now — wan, hueless, dim, and dead, through his own cold and gloomy despotism — his heart smote him — smote him, O God ! how heavily.

The many, many times, that he now felt, as all at once they rushed up, thronging unbidden, palpably upon his memory — the many, many times, when he had turned the happy smile upon that loving face into a bitter tear, by his cold carelessness. The many, many words, thoughts, deeds of fondness, which he had cast back upon that tender heart, ungratefully repulsed and cruelly requited.

And now he could no more blight her smlies with the chillness of his wintry eye, nor still her soft words with his gloomy brow — great Heaven ! what would he now have given to see her smile unchecked, to hear her speak unreproved, the promptings of her innocent soul !

What would he now have given to cast himself at her feet and cry, 'I have sinned, I have sinned against Heaven and against thee — pardon me, sweet and injured saint, and take me once more to thy broken heart, and let my future life be passed in one unceasing effort to heal the wounds made by my cruelty ; to requite, by a tranquil and serene old age, the sad youth, from which I have robbed the flower !"

But ever as he thought of this, the awful words, "IT IS TOO LATE !" seemed to roll over his head in immortal thunder.

God might forgive him, it is true, but she, whom he had wronged so deeply, could forgive him never!

Reader, if thou hast ever possessed a friend, now lost to thee — a friend, whom thou perchance hast loved as unselfishly as poor humanity can love — whom thou hast ever treated with as much kindness and consideration as the infirmities of the mortal will permit — thou knowest well how many little acts forgotten with the accident that caused them, thou wouldst give worlds, if it were possible, now to recall; how many things done which thou oughtest not to have done, how many left undone which thou oughtest to have done, crowd on thy soul, and cry aloud awakening remorse that must endure for ever. Reader, thou canst imagine what must have been the torture of that self-convicted man, as he knelt over the cold form of her, to whom he had been the tyrant in lieu of the protector; whom he had sworn to love, comfort, honor, and whom, instead, he had afflicted, harassed, treated as a slave.

He did not weep — tears are too genial visiters that they should come to those hard eyes — but the dark sweat-drops rolled as thick as rain in a thunder-storm from his knitted brow; and groans, as harrowing as ever disclosed the agonies of a most guilty soul, burst from his quivering lips; and he beat his breast with his clenched hands with violence, that showed how wholly and sincerely his mind was absorbed in its own terrible and gloomy recollections.

No one spoke to him — no one consoled him. For in truth his grief was of a nature too turbulent and stormy to render consolation possible. And, had it been possible, there was none present altogether capable of offering it.

Ruth Whalley, who had endured so much, and endured it so nobly during that dreadful morning, was at length wholly overcome by the mingled influence of her terror and her grief. Her habitual dread of her father's violence, although, as I have said, he was scarcely or never violent to her, had rendered her anxious and uneasy at the moment of his return; and, instead of looking forward to his presence, as to that of her best friend and surest comforter, she almost trembled at his coming.

Ignorant, however, of all that had passed on the previous night, little suspecting that her father was aware of Tituba's privity to his great secret, scarcely indeed suspecting, herself, how far the Indian girl was privy to it, or what the secret was, Ruth was far from anticipating the appalling burst of fury, which had made the unhappy man again almost a murderer.

When he struck Tituba to the earth, she had rushed to support and soothe her, and now while the old man was yielding to the agonies of his evil conscience, those two weak creatures sat weeping in each other's arms, half-paralyzed. For the high, gallant, and enduring spirit of sweet Ruth was for the moment weakened so far, by the successive horrors she had witnessed, that it was not much superior now to the poor Indian's frail and benighted intellect.

Gideon, ashamed to display the violence of his emotions, in a stranger's presence, and not entirely free from personal fear of his father, though he was conscious of no cause for fear, had withdrawn to a little distance from the scene of all these sad occurrences, and was sitting on a large stone at the foot of the pine-tree, the top of which concealed the hiding-place of his grandfather, with his face buried in his hands, and the tears trickling through his fingers, as fast as summer rain-drops.

The two younger boys sat motionless beside the corpse, crying themselves, but striving hard to smother their own sobs, and to hush the wild lamentations of their little sister.

And Cecil, with his arms folded over his great heart, stood silent, motionless; watching, with feelings singularly blended of disgust and compassion, the paroxysms of the Puritan's remorse and sorrow.

Not to compassionate such sorrow, in any human being, was utterly impossible to such a heart as Cecil's.

Not to feel something of contempt toward one so helplessly the slave of his own bad and selfish passions, and at the same time so fearfully blinded to his own failings by self-pride and the delusion of self-righteousness, was no less impossible.

Nor could one so clear-sighted, and so shrewd to read character from the smallest outward indications, as the young soldier, fail to perceive that nothing short of the consciousness of great real cruelty could call forth such bursts of remorseful self-accusal, such strange and almost blasphemous attempts at self-justification, as that dark sinner uttered; now toward the senseless corpse at his feet, now toward the All-Righteous and Eternal Lord, whom he addressed in terms the most awfully familiar.

Far be it from my pen to attempt even to record the crude extemporaneous raving of the fierce, ignorant sectarian. It is enough that they shocked the ears of Cecil more than the most profane oaths, and most licentious blasphemies, he had ever heard in the lascivious courts of the Stuarts, or in the turbulent camps of the Low Countries.

He was, indeed, on the point of interrupting the wild mourner with some words of advice, if not of comfort, when suddenly, as if at length his own violence had exhausted him, he became silent, stern, self-possessed.

He bowed down over the body, pressed his lips once to the cold brow, covered the face again reverently with the scarlet military mantle, which now, for the first time, appeared to attract his attention, prayed for a few moments in silence; and then, rising to his feet as quietly and firmly as if no storm of passion had ever convulsed his steady features, addressed the young soldier abruptly, though not perhaps uncourteously: —

"And now," he said, "it is time to ask who you may be, and what brought you hither?"

"I am one Henry Cecil," answered the other, "commonly called Sir Henry, late captain in the governor's life-guard, and with the governor, I came hither in the pinnace Rosebud."

"*Late*—captain!—ha!" returned the Puritan, apparently surprised at his reply. "And what —— but I will speak with you anon," he added, "my daughter must inform me of what has passed. Come, Ruth," he continued, perhaps unconsciously assuming a gentler tone, than he had used for many a year, "poor child, I am your only parent now, come with me that we may commune together in private of the past, and take council for the future. Come, my good Ruth, tears are now unavailing, and we have much to think of and to do—there will be time for grief hereafter."

At the kind words, the unhappy girl's tears flowed at first the faster; but restraining them she arose, and gave her hand to her father; who, with a gesture of cold salutation to Sir Henry, led her across the little bridge, and down the rugged stairway, to the sea-beach, and there for an hour and upward, they walked to and fro beside the trembling breakers, the hoarse roar of the surf drowning their words to all ears save their own, the deaf and pitiless sea the only witness of their sorrows.

CHAPTER XIX.

THE ARREST.

"Stand, ho! surrender—if ye stir, ye die."

It was near midnight, and the skies were black and starless. A huge and solid pall hung beneath the firmament, above the earth and sea, making the darkness almost palpable.

The funeral of Whalley's hapless wife was over.

"Dust unto dust, and ashes unto ashes," all that was mortal of her nature had been given unto earth; although the sublime words prescribed by the ritual of the English church, odious to those stern fanatics, had not been said or sung over the earthly tabernacle of the departed sister.

A long, colloquial, discussed rhapsody, half-preaching and half-prayer, had replaced that beautiful and soothing liturgy.

The feelings of the survivors had been harassed almost beyond their powers of endurance by many a home-thrust allusion to the qualities of the deceased, and to all her relations, mortal and immortal.

But, like all other earthly things, this torture also had its termination. Wild hymns were chanted full of austere denunciation of the godless, which term, in the meaning of the chanters, included all persons inimical to their peculiar doctrines.

And then, dark, stern, severe, and silent, the Calvinistic minister, and the few neighbors who had come to lend their aid to the bereaved and stricken family, went their way, cold and unsympathizing with those griefs of the heart, which were beyond their callous comprehension.

With the exception of Sir Henry Cecil, whom chance had domesticated in their circle, the mourning family were once again alone.

The aged regicide, whose hiding-place was now a secret no longer, had been for a few hours liberated from his cell, in order to participate in the funeral rites of the daughter of his house; and his had been the wildest, fiercest denunciation of the sons of Belial; the boldest and most earnest exhortation to resist the biddings of the man, who, like to Jeroboam, the son of Nebat, had made Israel to sin, and built high places to false gods, and hearkened unto priests — even the priests of Baal.

And great had been the delectation of the fanatical independent spirits who made it their especial boast, that they had founded in New England "a church without a bishop, a state without a king!"

But when nightfall approached, and the small band of armed neighbors returned to their homes along the iron-bound coast, each party in its barge or sail-boat, Merciful had insisted, as a measure of precaution, that his father should return for the hours of darkness to the seclusion of his cavern; it having been determined that, at an hour before daybreak, he should depart with his son and younger grandson, for a securer refuge on the shores of Connecticut.

Nor was this the sole step of precaution that the dark Puritan had taken.

One of the giant pine-trees had been cut down, and caused to fall in such a manner that its head rested against the crags, at about three fourths of their elevation above the little green, whereon once stood the humble dwelling of the rich fisherman and farmer.

The branches had been trimmed partially, so that the trunk, with their aid, presented to a bold foot a sort of rude, extemporaneous ladder, by which to arrive nearly at the top of the rocky wall, which fortified that narrow amphitheatre.

From the stump of a tree that had grown of old on the very brink of the precipice above, a stout, knotted rope had been lowered some twenty feet, swinging loosely in the air, so that an active man might reach it, when standing on the top of the felled pine-tree, and so, perhaps, perilously swing himself to the ledge above his head.

This rude arrangement had been made in a few hours; Gideon having attached the rope according to Merciful's instructions, during his visit to the farm on the main land, and the Puritan having felled and trimmed the pine with his own potent axe. Nor did he doubt at all that he might so be enabled to escape from any sudden onslaught of his enemies.

A large and tolerably comfortable tent had been pitched with the sails, masts, and cordage of the smaller boats. Bedding and food in profusion had been brought from the farm, a good fire had been lighted, and, so far as mere animal comforts were concerned, the family and their involuntary guest were well enough provided.

But the wants of the heart! the cravings, irrepressible and agonizing of the spirit! for them what care of mortal shall provide?

It was midnight—dark, silent, starless midnight—the heavens overclouded, the ocean moaning sullenly beneath its dark canopy of cloud and mustering storm.

All at the cove were buried in deep, heavy sleep—the child of sorrow and intense excitement. Sleep that exhausts rather than supports—sleep that, in very deed, was o'erwrought nature's agony.

The women and children slept in the tent, the men, Merciful, Gideon, and Sir Henry Cecil, lay in their cloaks around the wavering embers of what, some hours before, had been a cheerful watchfire, with their weapons ready beside them. The very dog had coiled himself away in some nook of the rocks, and slumbered before them.

And it was needed now—for, during an hour or more, there had been sounds and sights on the sea, and on the shore, which, had there been ears to hear, or eyes to behold them, would have created fear and apprehension.

First, the long roll of oars rattling in the rowlocks with that peculiar and regularly-marked cadence which tells the practised ear that the rowers are man-of-war's men, came swinging in from the seaward.

Then several hails were heard from boat to boat, checking the speed of this, and hurrying the loiterers in that, to the intent that all should come to land at the same time.

Soon afterward, lights might have been seen rising into sight, and lost again, moment after moment, as the bows of the boats which carried them, tossed on the ridgy billows.

Next came the crash of the keels, as they rode in upon the crests of the coming seas and were beached on the shingly coast; and then succeeded the suppressed hum of voices, and the sharp clash of arms, as the men landed, and fell into column, or file rather of two in front, in order to accommodate their movements to the rude rocky staircase, and the narrow bridge by which they were to gain the platform. The lights were now all extinguished, with the exception of a single torch, carried by a lance-pesade at the head of the file, and the matches of the musqueteers, which gleamed like a long row of glow-worms in the darkness.

Yet, for all this, the watch-dog had given out no warning bark—the sleepers slept, unconscious that the enemy was on their very threshold.

And now, the soldiery had scaled the steep ascent, and had begun to file across the wooden bridge—when, as their measured march sent out its regular and sullen sounds, the faithless guardian of the night sprang out from his lurking-place with a vociferous and useless clamor—and all were on their feet in an instant.

The first impulse of Merciful Whalley was to snatch up his wood-knife and his musket, thrusting the former into his leathern girdle, and cocking the other with a practised hand.

A moment's thought, however, convinced him of the folly of resistance; the rather as he saw the long line of matches deploying on the green, and attesting the presence of a strong company of regulars.

He turned, therefore, with a rapid step toward his temporary ladder, calling out to Cecil,

"Keep your troth, friend, and protect *her* in her peril, as you would that the Lord should protect you. Farewell, and God keep you!"

As his voice broke the silence, another voice was heard shouting to the soldiery—it was the voice of Clark.

"Hurrah! men, we have got the archfiend here. That was the voice of Whalley. Light up the torches, lads; and, ye surrender quietly—if ye are wise. Good treatment to all those who yield! Death to the man who stirs hand or foot in resistance!"

At these words, twenty or thirty torches were lighted, and a red, dusky glare was thrown across the narrow platform, touching the canvass of the white tent, and bringing into bold relief the little group of women and children, with the fine figure of Sir Henry Cecil standing conspicuous before them.

He held his hat in his hand, and had just snatched a musket from the grasp of Gideon, and cast it down upon the ground, setting his foot upon it, when his clear voice was heard, calm and sonorous,

"For God's sake, sir, whoever you be, use no violence;—

there are none here to resist you, and we surrender quietly to any show of authority, lawful, or unlawful;—there are none here but myself, and a few boys and women!"

"Sir Henry Cecil," he replied, "I pledge you my word there shall be no resistance, if you offer no violence."

"That is enough!—that is enough!" cried Nathaniel Clark, who had no relish for hard knocks, and entertained some salutary apprehensions of the Puritan. "Stand to your ranks, men, steady! Advance, lance-pesades, with the torches;—but, where is Merciful Whalley? I heard his voice, I am certain."

"He is gone," answered Cecil, quietly. "He fled so soon as he heard you coming."

"Gone!—fled!—impossible!" cried the other. "Quick!—quick!—bring up those torches. How should he have gone hence, or whither?"

The torches were brought forward rapidly, but their glare was insufficient to illuminate the dark corner under the shadow of the rocks, where Merciful was scrambling with such difficulty up the tree; and all might yet have been well, but at this moment a heap of dry torch-wood, which, in the first moment of alarm, Gideon had cast upon the embers of the watch-fire, kindled and burst out into a jet of clear, white flame, mounting high into the air, and rendering the whole scene as visible as if it had been broad daylight.

The Puritan had reached the head of the fallen tree, and was just grasping the rope. Another moment would have placed him in safety.

"There! there!" shouted Clark, "there he stands—away! follow him! fifty guineas to the man who takes him!"

Half a dozen of the soldiers darted away, and two began to climb with such activity and spirit, assisted by the light of the fire and the torches, and encouraged by the shouts of their comrades, that the foremost had reached the rope, and began to climb it, before Whalley, embarrassed by his long gun, which he had slung across his shoulder, had reached the summit of the cliffs.

It was a scene of terrible and painful interest. Even the gallant Cecil shook like a leaf with the strong excitement, while Ruth uttered a faint shriek, firm as she was in ordinary peril, and covered her eyes with both her hands, unable to look upon the catastrophe.

It was but a moment before Whalley stood unharmed on the summit, the soldier scaling the rope rapidly within six feet of him.

The stern Puritan looked down with a grim smile upon his pursuer; he drew his keen wood-knife, and knelt upon the precipice's edge.

"Back!" he cried to the man, in a deep, stern voice, "back! or I cut the rope!"

But the man's blood was up, and he replied only by a curse.

"Once more, I say, back, fool!" shouted the Puritan, "back, or you are but a dead man!" and he laid the edge of his knife to the cord.

Then Clark himself shouted from below to the daring soldier, "Come down, fool! it is all too late!"

But the man still persevered, and as the trenchant blade severed the hempen strands, he grasped the rocky ledge with both hands. Another second would have placed him on the summit beside Whalley; but, ready-witted in peril, the Puritan struck his fingers with the iron-bound butt of his musket; he relaxed his hold, and fell headlong.

A wild shriek burst from the spectators, and with a sharp metallic clang, the muskets of the soldiery rose to the aim unbidden.

It was well for the daring climber that he fell first upon the feathery branches of the pine-tree, which broke his fall, and thence upon the pile of boughs, which lay on the ground beneath it, else never had he moved limb any more! As it was, although stunned for the moment, and sore bruised, he escaped uninjured.

But, as he fell, the voice of Ravenscraft shouted to "fire," and a sharp running volley rattled immediately, waking strange echoes from the cliffs, and the balls fell pattering like hailstorm around him. Yet he stood on the brink, in the full light, unharmed and fearless.

But all were not so fortunate as he. The little group, composing his family, stood around the fire midway between the soldiers and their living target, and, although far beneath the line of fire, so rapid was the volley, and so bad the direction, that several balls struck about them.

One took effect fatally!

With a wild yell, poor Tituba fell headlong on her face among the embers of the watch-fire!—happy in this, at least, that she was dead before she struck the ground!

The victim of long years of violence fell by a violent and bloody death!

The feminine shriek reached Whalley's ears; the fall of the female figure met his eye.

"God of my fathers!" he exclaimed, in notes of the most piercing anguish, "is it—is it my child? my Ruth? my angel daughter?"

And, for a moment, Cecil feared that he would leap down from that fearful elevation.

"No, no!" shouted the youthful soldier, "it is the Indian girl—it is poor Tituba! Your daughter is quite safe—but, I fear, they have killed the other! Begone, for God's sake, Master Whalley, else shall more evil come of it! I will protect your daughter."

"I go; but, first, one shot to avenge Tituba!"

Almost as he spoke, a bright flash glanced from the muzzle of his piece, and, ere the full, round report had followed it, the officer, who gave the word to fire, lay gasping with a mortal wound upon the greensward.

That was the last act of that fatal night—of that dread domestic tragedy! The moment he had discharged that avenging shot, the Puritan retreated from the edge of the rocks, and, almost at the same moment, the wood which had blazed up so inauspiciously being consumed, the broad flaming light expired; and, save from the lurid glare of the smoky torches, the dismal scene, with its spectators, captives, and captors, would have been buried in utter darkness, as it was in dismay and dread.

CHAPTER XX.

THE DEPARTURE.

"Farewell, a long farewell."

UNDER whatever circumstances, there is always a feeling of melancholy, if not of bitter and painful regret, connected with departure from any place in which we have spent calm and happy days. How much more so, if that spot be the hallowed home of our childhood, the spot on which our eyes first opened to the daylight—how much more so, if our departure be compulsory, and its term indefinite, perhaps everlasting.

It would perhaps be difficult for fiction to invent a state of things more painful, than that under which Ruth Whalley was torn from that first home she had ever known, torn from it never probably to return thither.

The dwelling in which she had passed so many tranquil days,

a heap of smouldering ashes; the mother whom she had loved so tenderly, scarce cold in her untimely sepulchre; the father whom she revered and pitied with such reverence of filial affection, a proscribed fugitive, and outlaw; the Indian girl, whom she cherished the more that she felt almost as a mother toward her, so long had she soothed her sorrows and protected her, a bleeding corpse; her brothers, and, yet worst of all, her little sister, left by the mother's death and the father's outlawry, orphans on both sides! what could be more disastrous, more alarming? But, as if fate had determined that no particular should be wanting, this was not all, nor to herself personally was it even the most terrible.

She was a prisoner, about to be immured, as a hostage for her father's person — at the control, absolutely in the power, of a man, the most abhorred, the least scrupulous of means whereby to attain his ends, in all New England. Nor, with the woman's ready and instinctive intuition of all that regards the conditions of her sex, had she failed to decipher the atrocious meaning of the governor's wild, lawless glances, or to suspect the secret object of his persecution. Yet, upheld by the purity of an honest, innocent heart, confident of the justice of her cause, the rectitude of her intentions, she was so calm, so tranquil, so self-sustained, as she made the brief preparations for her forced departure, that Cecil scarcely knew whether to attribute the firmness of her demeanor to the highest grade of fortitude, or to insensibility of her position.

It was nearly low water, when the soldiers landed at the cove; and, as above three hours had elapsed during the terrible occurrences which signalized their coming, and the different preparations necessary ere they could re-embark, the tide was making rapidly; and a faint dappling of the east began to give token of the appearance of another day.

The officer, whom the avenging bullet of the Puritan had

stricken down in the midst of his triumph, wrestled long with his agony; and this had delayed the movement of the soldiers. It was too evident that he was wounded mortally, and that any attempt to remove him would be but to precipitate the fatal moment; anxious as he was, therefore, to return with the news of his success to his employer, Clark, to whom, though no soldier, the management of the expedition had been intrusted, could not attempt to enforce a re-embarkation. At length, however, the stout soldier breathed his last, sensible that he was cut down in the unjust quarrel of another; and bitterly complaining that obedience to orders that he might not dispute, had consigned him to a fate so untimely and ignoble.

" Had it been fighting with the enemies of my country," he gasped feebly with his choked voice, in faltering accents, " with the colors of my king above my head, and the broad day to witness gallant actions, I had not cared a rush—soldiers have but to die! but thus! thus! shot like a mad dog, in a night affray, by a lousy peasant—faugh!—is this the end—of—an—old—soldier!"—his words became more and more interrupted; his voice failed altogether; his head fell back; they thought that all was over.

But in a moment he raised himself erect with a convulsive motion, and cried aloud in clear accents, " Give me a soldier's grave! Farewell, old companions! Attention! England for ever! Hurrah! boys—hurrah!" And ere the words had well left his lips, he was dead!

And such, thought Cecil sadly within his secret soul, such is the veteran's end—a man like this lost to his country at a proud despot's bidding.

The brave man once departed, there was no more delay; his body was wrapped in his military cloak, and carried down by six of his men in silent sorrow to the barge. Short time was allowed to Ruth for her adieus to Gideon and the younger ones; short time for advice and exhortation. But she kissed each in turn, and pressed them to her bosom, and bade them be of good comfort, and not forget their God in the days of their sorrow. But when she came to the babe, her dead mother's darling, she wept bitterly, and placing her in the arms of her elder brother—

"Remember," she said, "Gabriel, that to this little one you are now all in all; to her you must be father, mother, sister, brother—God keep you—fare you well. Bury that poor thing, *there*—*beside*—you know—brother! God bless you, brother!"

Her words died in her throat; she could say no more; but she turned to Sir Edmund's emissary with air of true dignity—

"Now, sir," she said, "I am ready; lead on, I will follow."

And not daring to trust herself to take a last look at the ruined homestead, the fresh grave, or the sad group, whom she left behind her, she took the arm which Cecil tendered respectfully, and went her way in silent anguish.

In ten minutes more, the boats were darting toward the distant town as fast as the sturdy oarsmen could drive them through the water; and ere long, the breeze rising as the sun drew nigh to the horizon, and the gray dawn grew brighter, their sails were set, and they stood gallantly and gayly (as if they bore in them no breaking hearts, left none behind them) homeward before the wind that sent them over the ridgy waves with a sound as of a giant's laughter.

It was long ere the wailing of the younger boys and of the little girl, thus cruelly abandoned among scenes so fearful and heart-rending, was lulled into silence; but happily the sorrows of the very young are but, comparatively speaking, brief in duration; and, worn-out with fatigue and excitement, they sobbed themselves at length to sleep, and all was silent.

But Gideon slept not; the responsibility of his situation, and the strange calls upon his manhood within the last few hours, had made him a man, almost prematurely.

With a musket upon his shoulder, he was walking backward and forward, a sentinel over the living and the dead, when, scarce an hour after the departure of the boats, his father hailed him, from the top of the rocks.

"Gideon! what, ho! is all clear below?"

"All is clear, father. They have been gone this hour."

Merciful fastened a fresh rope to the stump aloft, and swinging himself boldly down, stood by his son's side in a moment.

"Let them sleep," said the stern father, melted now from all his sternness. "Let them sleep, Gideon, while they may. Now, mark me, there is no time to lose—the old man and I should have been out at sea ere this. The schooner is all ready, the tide up; we must get him on board, and then put off at once. Enoch shall go with me. But we will let him sleep, to the last minute. Now, for your own part; so soon as I am gone, get the two little ones into the pinnace, and carry them to neighbor Venty's house at Nahant. Martha will be a mother to them, for a while, for the sake of her who is gone. Get some of the lads to come and help you bury that poor thing. Then go to Boston, find Simon Bradstreet, tell him all that has fallen out, and do all that he bids you. Tarry in Boston till I come; and if in aught you may comfort Ruth, do so. Be quiet above all things; brawl not; nor complain loudly: nor resist the authorities in anything—the time is not yet fully come. Do you understand me, boy?"

"Perfectly, father," replied the young man, steadily and proudly. "And, with God's help, I will do all your bidding."

"Well spoken, boy," said his father, grasping his hand with a feeling akin to admiration. "Truly these are dark times, Gideon. But, remember, no hour of night so dark as that which is nighest to the blessed morning—and no night so black but the will of God can turn it into brightest day, yea, in the twinkling of an eye."

Then was a solemn pause of a few moments; and both mused deeply, and, perhaps, hopefully, until Merciful again broke silence—

"Come—we must go to work—there is no time for loitering."

Within a few minutes, the old man was on board, the moorings of the schooner, all save one, were cast off, the sails unfurled, and everything in readiness.

Then, for the last time, Merciful returned ashore. With Gideon's aid, he removed the corpse into the tent, and fastened the canvass closely to the ground with pegs and heavy stones, that neither beast nor bird should enter, until the return of his son with the men who should inter her.

Then Enoch was aroused, and sent on board the schooner, prond, in his boyish triumph, at being chosen by his father for an important duty; and then the hard man knelt and prayed over the grave of his unhappy wife; knelt and wept, almost tenderly, over his sleeping children.

Rising to his feet with a strong, silent effort, he grasped Gideon's hand, and went aboard his little vessel, without another word.

The last rope was cast of. In half an hour he was a league away to the westward, all his sails set and distended by a fresh favorable breeze.

Then Gideon awakened the little ones. He had victualled the pinnace for their short voyage, and stepped its light mast already; and now, with the old house-dog and the playful kitten, sole relics left of that large and well-ordered household he put them on board the last boat, rejoicing childlike in the thoughts of a merry sail over the sunny sea, and half forgetful of the mother they had lost, the sorrows they had felt, yestreen

—happy in that one faculty, the faculty of childhood only—that they could readily forget!

Save by the dead alone, the cove was now untenanted. The graves may be seen there yet: but human habitation was never raised again on that ill-omened spot.

CHAPTER XXII.

THE MOURNER.

"To breakfast, with what appetite you may."

It was already broad, rejoicing day, when the man-of-war boats, which had been despatched late on the previous evening, were descried coming up the beautiful bay, with their lug-sails set, dancing along before a brisk sea-breeze.

Nothing can be conceived more beautiful than the scene which was presented by Boston and its environ, even at that early day; when the dense verdure of the primitive forests had not receded wholly from the limits of cultivation, but was delightfully interspersed everywhere with the well-cultivated fields, and glowing gardens of the industrious and earnest settlers.

Some of the islands, with which the lovely bay is dotted, were still clothed in the untrimmed greenery of nature; some bolder and more sterile, were girt with incipient fortifications, and mounted with a few guns, under that meteor flag of England, which waved not then, as now, in every quarter of the habitable globe.

Boston which already at this time, with its neighboring villages, contained some ten thousand souls, was a beautiful and striking object; not clustered, like the compact and unventilated towns of the Old World, about some feudal turret, or hedged in by moat or rampart, but straggling over a large space of ground, with pleasant gardens and green groves between its happy homes, and the houses of God only lifting their modest and unsteepled heads above the breezy foliage.

The refined taste and poetical imagination of Ruth Whalley, at any other time, would have been kindled into rapture by the aspect of that fair city and the fertile hills around it, under the brilliant influences of the cloudless sky, and the sunny morning.

But there was no room now in her oppressed and sorrowful spirit, for any joyous or romantical impressions.

She had sat silent in the stern-sheets of the barge, and almost motionless, since she had left the cove. Insensible to the chilly dampness of the early morn and the fresh sea-breeze, so much more was she occupied by the intolerable weight of her inward sorrows, than by any consideration of her external sufferings, she was scarce conscious that some charitable hand had wrapped her closely in a warm boat-cloak.

How then should she think of the beauties of nature, how rejoice in the sun-lighted atmosphere, or in the rippling wavelets, azure with crests of gold, leaping and glancing in the morning's radiance, when she took no note of those bodily sensations to which at another time her every nerve would have thrilled painfully?

Between the sorrows of the past, and the anticipations of the future, it was all that poor Ruth could do to muster enough of resolution to face her position calmly, to refrain from vain tears and feminine lamentation.

How could she have done this, had she not been endowed happily with a character of no ordinary firmness; had not that character been formed by trials of no common or every-day occurrence; had not her whole soul been pervaded by love, and faith, and that true piety which hopes all, and confides all, to the wisdom and the mercy of the All-Wise, the All-Merciful.

Such love, such faith, such confidence, indeed, do much, and avail much—but they can not do all things, nor command entirely the course of human feelings. Mortality, alas! how trained soever to set its hopes on high, to lay its treasure up, "where neither moth nor rust doth corrupt, and where thieves do not break through nor steal," must still be mortality—must still feel the heart-ache, the fear, and the strife, which are part and parcel of its earthly nature; must droop and pine when bereaved of the loved, the lost; must shudder at the approach of trial and temptation; must wince beneath torture, whether it be of the body or the soul.

Thus was it now with Ruth Whalley. If ever heart was imbued with gratitude, and reverence, and love to the God whom she worshipped, in the singleness of her young spirit, it was hers. If ever soul was schooled and taught, by sad experience, to lay its burthens at the foot of the cross, and to count all earthly sorrows as everlasting gain, it was hers.

Yet there are moments, when the power of religion, however deeply it may penetrate the spirit, however much it may alleviate the griefs of those, who are not sorry as men without hope, can not control the anguish of the heart, or change melancholy to rejoicing.

Thus was it now with Ruth.

She knew, that it was well with the departed. She knew, that a life of suffering and sorrow, endured with exemplary resignation, a life of good-will and Christian benevolence toward all men, a life of faith, hope, and charity, must have won its exceeding great reward. She knew that the weak frame of her, whom she mourned, would be no more, was weary for everlasting—that the wounded heart would no more bleed, the o'erwrought brain ache no longer. She knew, in the holy, happy confidence of her strong faith, that the dear, dear mother, whom she had never seen on earth, but sad, sick at heart, unprized, ill-requited, was now enjoying bliss ineffable in heaven.

Yet she felt—she felt only, that the dear mother was gone hence, never again to beam affection on her from those deep, fond eyes; never again to smile welcome with those thin, pale lips, to smile with that mournful sweetness which made the wan face beautiful; never again to say "dearest" in that low, gentle voice, the very tone of which dwells in her ear, like unforgotten music. She only felt the void, the emptiness, the hollowness, which nothing in this world again should ever fill or satisfy.

How then should she take note of the white walls and the diamond lattices, laughing in the gay morning sunshine; or of the trees singing their joyous matins, with their breeze-shaken harps awake and vocal? How should she mark "the unnumbered laughter of the ocean waves," or enjoy the minstrelsey of the light summer gale murmuring gently over and around her?

No! no! There are griefs which overcome us like a summer-cloud; which pass not like the summer-cloud away. There are sorrows which fall with a weight so chilling on the heart, that we feel instantly, instinctively, that for us the glory of this world has indeed departed—that henceforth the sun may shine, but it will no more be *that* sunshine—that henceforth we may see, may love, the beauties of the fair earth and blessed heavens; but it will no more be *that* earth, or *those* heavens, on which we gazed so happily, so trustfully, through the charmed medium of a mutual soul.

Alas! for those with whom it is so. For them there is no future here; the past is their all on earth—their only object, in this life, must be thenceforth to forget the present—to dream of a futurity, beyond, incomprehensible, eternal.

It was not thus, however, that her grief smote the soul ol Ruth. The loss of the aged, how much beloved soever, is a thing so much in the ordinary course of nature, that though it may stun for the time, though it may even depress and sadden us, for days, months, perhaps years, rarely or never crushes us with that overwhelming weight of wo, which paralyzes all capacity for happiness thereafter.

Stunned she was, grievously, and oppressed, not by the past only, but by the darkest forebodings for the future—forebodings for herself, yet not selfish—forebodings for all whom she loved on earth.

She was alone, too. Alone in her sorrow—alone in her dread of coming trials.

There was no kindly voice to whisper comfort for the past, hope for the future.

The only friend, who could have consoled, was intentionally separated from her, in that dark hour. Her enemies were shrewd and deep-sighted in piercing the secrets of the heart—children of darkness, wiser in their generation than the children of light.

Intending to act on her mind wholly, it was their object to make her feel at once the utter loneliness, the isolation, the unfriended, hopeless position in which she was placed. And, with this end in view, Sir Henry Cecil, from whose gallant and daring spirit, coupled to his sincere hatred of all tyranny, Andross expected the only opposition he was like to meet in his infamous designs—Sir Henry Cecil had been purposely placed in a different boat from the fair Puritan; and that boat's crew had been instructed to lay somewhat behind the others, in order to prevent, if possible, the youthful knight from learning the fate of his fair fellow-captive.

It might have been about eight o'clock of the fine summer morning, when the three leading boats landed on the esplanade, under the guns of the frigate and the fort, on both of which the English flag was flying, over brave hearts and stout hands, as ever roamed the deep in pursuit of glory.

A company of musqueteers were exercising on the esplanade, with their bright gorgets and steel caps glittering gayly in the sunshine, and their red cassocks making a glorious show among the dark-colored cloaks and doublets and the steeple-crowned hats of the few artisans and shopkeepers, who had collected to witness the spectacle, with eyes half-admiring, half-abhorrent.

As the boats came to shore, the officer in command, detaching a small party to clear the mound of all idlers, marched his company down the beach, and formed it in close order, in a hollow column, open toward the sea.

Without a moment's delay, the soldiers who were in the boat with Ruth, a dozen perhaps in number, leaped ashore; and, Clark who had accompanied her, taking her by one arm and Foxcroft by the other, she was lifted to the dry ground, and instantly conveyed into the centre of that serried column, her guard marching after her into the hollow space, and filling the whole up, so as to render it a solid mass, of which she formed the centre, with six men on each side of her, and three times as many before and behind.

The word of command was given instantly; the drums and fifes struck up a march; and at a steady and quick step the column marched into the town, their several ranks and sloped fire-locks effectually concealing the sex and person of their prisoner, from any over-curious eyes.

The red-coats were not, at that time, at all more popular in Massachussetts, than they were at a later period; and, in some respects, it was perhaps unfortunate for Ruth that it was so.

For no persons followed the glittering procession, except a few idle boys; and no windows were raised in the streets through which they passed, no heads protruded to gaze upon the flaunting plumes and flashing weapons, or to listen to the exhilarating music.

The escort arrived, therefore, at the door of the government house, its purpose unsuspected; and, forming in the same order now as they had done before at the place of debarkation, the soldiers covered the entrance of Ruth into the house of her worst enemy, and she passed in unseen by any eye of friend or countryman.

Ignorant whither she had been conveyed, the innocent girl gazed around her with bewildered eyes, as she found herself instead of being within the precincts, as she had expected, of a dark and loathsome hall, with a circular staircase leading to a fair gallery above; adorned with arms, and standards, and emblazoned escutcheons, and tenanted by several lackeys, flaunting in royal liveries of scarlet and silver.

Nathaniel Clark alone entered the house with her, the heavy door closed after her, and by its sullen jar told her the fatal truth, that she was now as much a prisoner in that fair mansion, as she could have been in the darkest and most gloomy dungeon.

In total silence, her conductor led her up-stairs, traversed the corridor, entered a small ante-chamber richly furnished, and passing through it, flung open the door of a large and stately bed-chamber, and motioned her to enter.

"His excellency," he said, "feeling for your unpleasant situation, and desirous of alleviating, as much as in him lies, the sorrow and vexation it must cause you, has determined, as you are a prisoner for no crime, but a hostage only for your father's forthcoming, to detain you here for a while, in his own house, instead of committing you to a common prison. You will find food prepared for you, and change of raiment, and everything that is needful; a servant of your own sex will attend you; and it will not probably be very long ere you will be once more at liberty."

Ruth Whalley gazed at him wildly while he was speaking; and her lips moved as if she would have interrupted him; but, until he had ceased, no word came forth from them. Then she cried eagerly—

"His house!—did you say *his* house? His—the governor's?"

"I did," he replied, with a bland smile; "you will be lodged like the nobles of the land."

"Oh, no!" she answered, "oh, for Heaven's sake, no! Better the blackest, deepest dungeon! Oh, sir—kind, gentle sir," she continued, clasping her hands in an ecstasy of passion, "take me hence!—take me hence!—take me, for God's sake, to the common jail! Leave me among the foulest malefactors; but oh, do not, do not compel me to tarry here!"

"By my honor!" he answered coldly, "you do not know when you are well, methinks; nor have you much idea of what a dungeon is; or else you would not be so anxious to change your quarters. No! no! I have no power in the matter. I must obey orders. And you would not thank me to-morrow, if I broke them to do your bidding. No! you will not be of this way of thinking, long. You will be very well here—fine rooms, soft beds, rich fare. And, speaking of fare," he added, stepping up to a table sumptuously spread, "see what a morning meal is here—oysters in aspick jelly, a fat, larded capon, white rolls, and cates, such as women love—and champagne above all things. I commend you to the champagne especially. Sir Edmund is choice in his wines. And, seeing that you may be awkward at unwiring it, I will make the way plain for you." Then, suiting the action to the word, he uncorked the flask, poured himself out a pottering bumper, nodded familiarly to the poor girl, saying—"Come!

gayer thoughts to you, fair girl! and a good appetite!" and he quaffed it to the dregs.

Then, ere he left the room, he added, "you will be just as free here as at home, only you can't get out. The window is three stories high, and looks into a walled garden; the doors, I am grieved to say, I must lock behind me.—But don't, I prithee, look so disconsolate. Cheer up and take some breakfast; believe me now, you will feel much happier after breakfast. I am myself somewhat greasy of a morning, and fantastical, not to say melancholical; but after breakfast, it is a wonder to see how I brighten up again. Fare you well, and believe me, you will feel much happier after breakfast."

And, with a lamentable attempt at imitation of the light flippancy and licentious coxcombry of the young gallants whom he had admired in Sir Edmund's train, the vicious and base New-Englander liberated the poor girl, at least, from one odious thing, his own disgusting presence.

But she was unconscious even of that poor relief. She gazed around her for one instant, at the rich furniture, the gorgeous bed, the sumptuous meal, the splendid garments which were laid out as if for her use; and her heart sank almost hopelessly, as her worst fears were thus confirmed.

Her courage all gave way—she bowed her head upon her knees, and fell into a paroxysm of fierce agony, such as her calm and gentle nature never had known before.

CHAPTER XXII.

THE TEMPTATION.

For a short time after her odious persecutor had relieved her of his presence, the fair girl sat motionless, sick at heart, almost hopeless, and full of sad and terrible forebodings. It was some minutes before she could sufficiently collect her senses to understand or realize thoroughly her actual situation.

For so pure was her young and maiden spirit, so innocent, and so unconscious of all evil, that it was difficult, almost impossible, for her to comprehend the baseness and brutality of Edmund Andross.

Nor, indeed, until the visit of that vile pander to his foul will, had she surmised or apprehended any more formidable danger to herself than a few days of honorable durance. It was the cause only of that state of durance, in which she was held, and its probable consequences to her father, that had rendered her anxious and unhappy.

The sight, it is true, of the splendid repast under which groaned the rich table, and of the gorgeous dress prepared for her, had for a few seconds' space awakened some suspicions, but they were slight and transient; and until the vile agent of the governor's licentious and despotic pleasures had left her to her meditations, she had perceived no cause of seriousness or deep alarm.

But now, the whole dark truth broke on her soul at once—she saw, as we see objects, by the pervading glance of the electric flash, during the darkness of a stormy mind, all her own fearful perils, all her oppressor's schemes of infamy, all the woes that were gathering about her devoted family—all this she saw, more clearly, more palpably a hundred-fold, by aid of the spiritual flash which lighted momentarily up the darkness of her soul, than she had done by the steadiest light of reason.

All this she saw, but therewith she saw no way to escape from the toils, which were spread on every side of her, no strength whereby to resist the arm of actual violence if it should menace.

Long she revolved and pondered these things, but it was only to perceive the utter fruitlessness of any human intellect to plan, of any human force to effect her rescue.

At length, in obedience to the dictates of her warm, pious heart, and mindful of the customs of her father's house, she sank down upon her knees, and with clasped hands, and streaming eyes, prayed long and fervently to him who alone is a "present help in the time of trouble."

She prayed, not for the safety of her mother's soul, to do that the stern dictates of the puritanic rule forbade, as idolatrous and papistical; but that she might resemble her in patience, in long-suffering, in grace; that, like her, she might be preserved spotless from the foul stains of the world; that, like her, she might live in the faith, and die acceptable to the Lord. She prayed that the gray hairs of her father, and of her father's father, might be shielded by his hand, who alone can save, from any mortal peril; and that no shame might be brought upon them by any deed of hers, or wrong endured unconsenting. She prayed for her brothers, and for that hapless orphan sister, abandoned, in her tender infancy, to the precarious nurture of a stranger. She prayed also, though her voice faltered somewhat, and her heart fully smote her as she did so, for the young, gallant cavalier, who had so nobly and so gently striven to protect her; who had already, it might well be said, saved her from some outrage, and to whose aid, alone of earthly guardians, she looked with any confidence of hope.

Refreshed and strengthened she arose, as all must needs arise, who commune in sincerity and faith with Him who is in heaven; as all must needs arise who put hope where only safety can be found; and cast their burthen at the feet of him, who can alone relieve them.

Refreshed she rose, and strengthened; and then, neglecting the rich cates and dainties, which loaded the board, broke her fast frugally and sparingly, on a white wheaten roll, and a cup of pure water. This done, she turned to one of the tall mirrors which hung in several places on the walls, and arranged her disordered hair in neat and modest tresses; pinned her white kerchief closer across her sloping shoulders, and brought her simple yet becoming dress, which had been somewhat disarranged by the events and voyage of the past night, into its wonted state of graceful neatness.

When she had done this, she sat down quietly beside a window, which looked out upon the tops of the tall trees growing in the garden, and, having no other means of occupation or employment, was soon very busy with her own thoughts.

And about what should her thoughts have been busy, were it not with the wild and dark and terrible events which had rendered the last days the most strange and important of her whole life—how strange, and how important she as yet hardly knew herself, or doubted. And of whom should she have thought the most as connected with all those dark and terrible events, were it not of him, who had behaved throughout all those trying scenes with so much dignity and courage, so much respect and grace, and generous consideration—of whom, were it not of Sir Henry Cecil.

It is true, he was uppermost all the time in her mind—she strove to banish his image, she struggled to fix her thoughts upon other matters — she went so far as almost to reproach herself with light-mindedness and the lack of natural affection, that with her mother scarce yet cold in her untimely grave, with her grandfather a proscribed exile, her father in imminent peril of his life, her thoughts should be in this wise irresistibly attracted toward a stranger.

Yet it was all in vain. The words, the gestures, the graceful attitudes, the noble form of the young soldier would not be banished from the mirror of her soul by any exercise of her will, any upbraidings of her conscience. The clear, sonorous tones of his well-modulated voice rang in her ears incessantly — the soft light of his speaking eyes dwelt in her very soul.

And who shall wonder and upbraid. When it is fate, or nature — when it is licensed even by the words of Holy Writ — that they whom God hath joined together, shall not be sundered by any mortal arm, but shall leave father, mother, all things, for each other. And if they were not yet united in those hallowed ties which of two creatures make one being — if they had not yet fully admitted each one to his or her own soul, that they were as yet heart-united — still each had seen the other — and to each in that other was fate fixed for ever.

While she was buried yet in the strange, yet not unpleasing meditations, a footstep was heard approaching her door rapidly, when it had reached the very threshold it paused there, and no further sound was heard for several seconds.

Half-terrified, the fair girl listened, as if her very heart suspended on her sense of hearing. Her cheeks were suffused with a painful blush, her bosom throbbed as if its tenant would have burst the soft bonds which enclosed it.

Recovering herself, however, by an effort, she had arisen to her feet, and made two steps toward the door, as if to see who was the unexpected and unwelcome listener, when a hesitating knock was stricken on the stout oak pannel, and, ere she could reply, the key was turned in the lock, and the door opened from without, displaying, as it revolved on its hinges, the stately person of the governor.

"Ha! this is well, fair prisoner of mine," he said with a smile, as he beheld the preparations laid out for her morning meal. "It is partly for this that I came hither to see if my brave servants have ministered sufficiently to all your wants."

"Far more than sufficiently," answered the poor girl, "to one who hath never tasted of the wine-cup, nor known so much as the name of these foreign dainties. Slight fare is enough, and more than enough, for the poor captive, who pines for the free air of liberty."

"Do you so pine, my gentle maiden. Then I come, as I trust, a right welcome visiter; for I come to communicate with you now to the end that you shall be forthwith free!"

"Welcome, indeed! oh, more than welcome, noble and generous sir; shame, shame on me, if I have wronged you in my thoughts, and yet—"

"And dost thou indeed so pine to exchange this splendid chamber, this rich diet, a life of ease and luxury, for those wild rocks, that stormy sea, the toils and hardships among which I found you?"

"I do pine, noble sir, to return to the ruins of my childhood's home; I do pine to pray again beside my mother's nameless grave; to comfort my father's woes; to soothe my little sister's childish sorrow — oh, suffer me, suffer me to return, great sir, and I will bear you in mind ever at my prayers."

"And would you do much, maiden, to win your release, to win your father's pardon?"

"I would do anything," she answered clasping her hands together, "anything that I may do unreproved of Heaven."

He paused for a moment or two, as if to consider how he might the most easily approach his subject.

"Ruth," he said, "listen to me. I have dwelt for long years in the noblest court of Europe, of the world—among the loveliest, the most beautiful of women, yet, maiden, never have I loved until now. When first my eyes beheld you, they beheld their fate. I adore you. Without you I can not exist—be mine, and you are free to-morrow—be only mine, and your father, your grandfather, are pardoned."

The young girl looked at him steadfastly, as if she would peruse his soul. "Be yours," she answered slowly. "Be yours. Nobles of your degree wed not with girls of mine—how then shall I be yours?"

Even his cool effrontery was at fault, and he hesitated ere he made answer—

"Be mine," he said, "by the gentle bonds of love, not by the iron shackles of this world's hypocritic custom—"

"Silence!" she cried, interrupting him with an air of perfect majesty. "Silence! for shame! if not for charity or virtue! Rather die all—father, grandfather, sisters, brothers—rather pass our name from the face of the earth! Begone! hence, base man!—words can not speak how I despise you! Begone, wretched man, and tremble!"

"Nay, tremble rather you!" he cried, rushing furiously toward her—"for lo! you are alone, and in my power, and that you will not grant par amours, I will have by force!"

"Never! God aid me, never!" and with the words she snatched a long two-edged carving knife from the board, and raised it, with a flashing eye and a lip quivering with wild enthusiasm. "Stand off, base villain! for if my hand be too weak, as I think it is not, to drive this steel into *your* heart, it has the strength at least to reach *my own!* Stand back—or see me at your feet, slain by my own hand, but by your guilty deed!"

The fierce, strong man was overcome, but not melted.—It

was dismay, not pity, that checked him for one moment. His brow grew black as night, and his scowling eye shot forth a ray of hellish spite and fury.

He shook his clenched hand at her furiously—

"I would have saved you," he cried, "but you would not! your blood be on your head!—blame not me that you perish!"

And he rushed from the room, and locked the door behind him as he left it.

CHAPTER XXIII.

THE CHARGES.

The rest of that eventful day, and the long, weary night which followed it, was passed by the gentle and unhappy maiden in a state of mental perturbation and anxiety which it were easier far to imagine than describe.

As soon as her tormentor left her, the enthusiastic courage, which had nerved her for a moment, failed, and was instantly succeeded by that faint and nerveless exhaustion, which is often produced by the reaction of unwonted mental efforts.

She wept long and painfully, though perhaps scarcely conscious wherefore she was weeping.

Hours elapsed before she found even the strength to fall upon her knees, and thank the Giver of all good that he had heard her prayer, and shielded her against the violence of the oppressor.

But when her heartfelt thanksgiving was ended, she was no longer calm and hopeful as before. Every sound now came full of terror to her ears. Every footstep that echoed through the long passages was fraught with apprehensions of new peril.

Not a door clapped, or a window rattled in its frame, but she fancied the approach of her dreaded enemy.

No lights were brought to her, nor did any person indeed approach her chamber-door that night, although full fifty times she started from her chair, with blanched cheeks and clasped hands, in an agony of consternation.

There was no means of securing her door on the inside, nor was there any piece of furniture in the room, which she was able to move, of weight sufficient to prevent its being opened from without, during the hours of darkness.

She did not therefore dare to lie down upon her bed, or to lay aside any part of her dress, or voluntarily to close her weary eyes.

At times, indeed, she would fall into a troubled and restless doze, as she sat erect in her chair; but scarcely had her mind lost the consciousness of her real position before a thousand wild and hideous phantasies would take possession of her thoughts, and with a start she would awake again to a sense of her helplessness and danger.

Terribly this long night passed away; nor, when absolute stillness succeeded to the occasional sounds which had disturbed her solitary watch, were her fears less vivid.

Not the hum of a musquito in the silent night air, not the rustle of a timid mouse behind the arras, but her fancy conjured up the whispered tones, and stealthy footsteps of her persecutor.

But hours of agony, although protracted to the utmost, as well as the brief minutes of ecstasy, must have their end. And to poor Ruth, as the tardy morning crept up the eastern sky, and shed a pale and ghastly light into the gorgeous chamber, hope returned, and a sense of security and reliance in her own firmness and fortitude.

It was not, however, in the proud mansion of the royal governor, as in the humble house of her childhood, where the first clamor of the early cock summoned all from the light slumbers of innocence and health, and the dawn never broke upon sealed eyelids.

Here, though the usages of the yet unsophisticated colony were matutinal and simple, the sun was high in the heavens before any stir announced that the members of the household were afoot, and about their wonted avocations.

And when the sounds of life were audible, after the silence of the dark, no step or voice came near her door, until it was well-nigh noon; and from congratulating herself on her freedom from farther persecution, she had begun to feel some apprehension that she was forgotten intentionally, and left alone perhaps to be starved into compliance with the unholy will of her tormentor.

But even as this fearful fancy suggested itself to her mind, her confidence in the support of Heaven, her gratitude for the Divine protection by which she had been shielded from perils far more terrible to her pure soul than any dread of death, were by no means diminished.

And, whereas she had knelt before to return thanks for that protection which is never withheld from those who seek it humbly; she now mingled with her morning orisons an earnest supplication that strength might be vouchsafed to her to resist the temptations which she imagined to be gathering about he..

Little did she know what those temptations were, or what the ordeal to which she must be soon exposed.

Just as the clocks were striking noon, a greater bustle was audible without the dwelling than any she had heard since her arrival. The measured tramp of infantry, the clatter of accoutrements and arms, and the word of command came clearly › her ears above the hum and clamor of what seemed to be a large and angry multitude.

She ran eagerly to the window in order to see what was passing, but, looking out as it did upon the walled garden only, it commanded no view of the streets, nor gave her any opportunity of judging what might be the cause of the commotion.

Not long, however, was she destined to remain in ignorance. For suddenly the measured tramping ceased, and was followed by the heavy clank of the grounded musket-butts upon the pavement, as the men stood at ease.

A minute afterward, there was a stir through the house: and the loud tread of many feet came up the staircase, and through the corridor, and paused at the door of her apartment.

The key grated in the wards—the door was thrown open, and as the blood rushed back tumultuously to her heart, leaving her face as pale as death, a strange group was presented to her eyes.

The first person who entered the room was a tall, thin, hard-favored man, of sour and puritanic aspect, dressed in a closely-fitting suit of black serge, with a broad, falling collar of white linen, square-toed shoes, a steeple-crowned hat, and a long, straight sword suspended from a girdle of unornamented leather.

He carried in his hand several papers, to one of which was appended a large seal, and wore an air of harsh and presumptuous authority which spoke the puritanic magistrate, as clearly as the pinched, sour aspect and sanctimonious air of the person who accompanied him, clad in a rusty suit of black, with large surpliced bands, denoted the intolerant and fanatical divine.

Behind these personages, a stout, blunt-looking man, with hard features, relieved somewhat by an expression of dogged honesty, paused on the threshold.

He wore a doublet of buff leather, with a bunch of keys

swinging from his belt, and a pair of bright steel manacles hanging across his left arm.

Behind him, again, appeared two privates of the governor's foot-guard, with their red cassocks, and bright-barrelled muskets shouldered.

At first, the poor maiden stood aghast, and wonder-stricken, at the appearance of these strange and unaccountable intruders; but soon perceiving, by the dresses of the two principal personages of the group, that they were of her own creed, and probably of her father's political party, she began to fancy that they were friends, and that their errand might be for her liberation.

"Oh! you have come—you have come to take me hence," she cried, clasping her hands joyously together. "Praise to thy name, O Lord! that thou hast heard thy servant's prayer so early, and set her free from this tyranny."

The magistrate gazed at her for a moment, as if he did not understand her; but, in a moment, with a bitter and sardonical smile distorting his grim lip—

"Verily!" he replied, "we have come to take thee hence, but whether it is cause for rejoicing seems to me somewhat more than doubtful. For it is not to set thee free at all, but to bind thee with chains, that we have come, and thy wrists with fetters of iron."

"It is enough," answered the poor girl—"it is enough that you come to take me hence; the heaviest chains, the deepest dungeon were preferable to the noblest palace halls, where one is subject to the vile solicitations of that foul fiend incarnate."

"She hath confessed it! Lo! she hath confessed it, brother Boanerges!" exclaimed the magistrate, turning toward his clerical associate and adviser.

"All glory be to Him, who saith 'out of thine own mouth have I condemned thee!'" cried the fanatic, who rejoiced in the euphonious and singularly appropriate appellation of Boanerges Bangtext.

"Fetter her fast, Mark Holdfast—fetter her fast, ere the foul fiend, with whom she hath confessed her unholy commerce, interpose to preserve her."

The jailer, for such was the profession of the man in the leathern doublet, advanced, but apparently with little goodwill toward the task, and locked the handcuffs round her slender wrists—before she had recovered her senses sufficiently to ask—

"Of what is it, then, that ye accuse me? What is that ye say I have confessed? Surely I have confessed nothing, but that this base and carnal-minded governor would have forced me to sin and shame."

"Avaunt! Get thee behind me, Satan!" thundered the preacher—"Leave turning the frail wretch, thou hast seduced from that better way to which she was inclined! And do you, witch accused, cease from endeavoring to deceive, and think not that denial can avail thee aught—nay, rather shall it gain thee torments only that shall extort once more the truth."

"Once more, of what am I accused?" cried the unhappy girl.

"Of witchcraft—of unholy commerce with the evil one—of rescuing by glamorous arts the bloody regicide, thy grandfather, from his pursuers—of summoning up fiends with hideous howls and groanings, to daunt the stout heart of the true believers. Of practising strange magic upon the most noble, the vice-regal governor; and last, of working the strong man Henry Cecil to amorous and lustful admiration of thy fleshly charms, and so to rank rebellion against his rightful rulers—"

"Have you done?" she exclaimed, interrupting him indignantly, "or is there more of this foul mummery? I see from whose quiver this shaft has been culled; and I see that the aim is deadly; yet is thine eye, O Lord, sleepless to mark the innocent, and thy hand strong to save the pure of heart. Lead me hence, men of falsehood and of blood! Lead me hence, if it be to die, this instant! Better to perish at the stake this moment, than to endure again the torture of that bad man's presence!"

The priest cast up his eyes, and muttered what might have been a prayer for mercy toward her obdurate and stubborn heart, but what sounded far liker to a curse. The magistrate turned up his hypocritic eyes in silence.

Firmly she passed out of that hateful chamber, the jailer holding her firmly, but not disrespectfully, by the arm; the guard fell in around her; and a few moments only passed before she was in the crowded street, when all the force of the escort was needed to keep back the infuriate and howling mob, who, but for the armed soldiery, would have torn the unhappy, pale girl piecemeal.

Men and boys, maids and matrons, gray-head grenadiers and little tottering children, possessed by some strange frenzy, passed, whooping, yelling, whistling, invoking curses on the head of that innocent young victim, who smiled, as she passed along, serene compassion on their blind and senseless frenzy; and still the tumult and the cry waxed louder and more furious—

"To the fagot and the stake! Death to the witch! Death to the foul fiend's paramour! Hurrah!"

Had there been far to go, the multitude which was increasing every moment, might well have prevailed over the guard; but happily the public jail was close at hand, and the iron leaves of its dark gate was soon interposed between the unhappy Ruth and the brute populace.

Then, when the doors were closed and barred behind her, the courage which had hitherto supported her gave way, and she fell in a death-like swoon into the arms of the blunt jailer, happy to lose the consciousness of her misery, if it were but for one moment.

CHAPTER XXIV.

THE PATRIOTS.

It was perhaps ten o'clock of the morning following that on which Ruth was led from the government-house to the common jail, that her brother Gideon stopped at the door of an old wooden house on the common, and looked about him rather anxiously, as if he were uncertain whether he had found the place of which he was in search.

It happened, however, that no person to whom he could apply for information was passing at the moment; and after some slight hesitation he knocked at the old-fashioned hatch door-way.

A fine and sonorous voice immediately replied desiring him to enter, and as he did so he found a person, whose appearance left him no cause to doubt that he had come aright, sitting alone in a small parlor which communicated with the hall in which he stood.

He who had called on him to enter was an exceedingly old man—one who had exceeded by nearly twenty years the term of threescore and ten allotted to humanity by the inspired writer; his hair, which he wore very long and flowing over his shoulders was literally as white as snow, and as lustrous as silver. His fine calm face was marked with many furrows and deep lines of age; but the eye was bright as some large serene star; and all the comely features were hard and calm, and full no less of grand intellect and moral fortitude than of benevolence and a certain proud humility.

He was dressed handsomely but very plainly in a suit of the finest black broadcloth, faced with velvet of the same color; with black silk hose, and silken roses in his square-toed shoes. A broad collar of exquisitely white linen was folded down over the shoulders of his doublet; and a small cap of black velvet set lightly on his snowy hair completed his attire.

As Gideon entered, he raised his large, lustrous eyes from a ponderous folio bible, which he was reading without glasses, and looked at him for a moment with an inquiring expression; then seeing that the young man was apparently embarrassed, he spoke to him with a kind and encouraging tone—

"Ha!" he said, "this is well, young man; this is very well. You are somewhat before your time, and next to being quite punctual, that is the best thing. I did not look for you earlier than eleven o'clock. So you wish for a mate's birth in the barge Good Hope. Of a truth, you are somewhat young for such a trust, yet—"

"I crave your pardon, sir," replied the young man, who had been hitherto unwilling to interrupt one so many years his senior, and of so reverend an aspect. "I think you are mistaken, since you could not have looked for me, nor have you, I imagine, so much as heard of me at all before."

"Then, certainly, I am mistaken," answered the old man, with a pleasant smile. "I thought you were young Hugh, the son of worthy Master Nelson. But since you are not he, pray tell me who you are and in what I can assist you.

"To begin," said Gideon, respectfully, "in order to avoid further error, permit me to ask if I speak to the ex-governor, the good Simon Bradstreet?"

"My name is Simon Bradstreet; and I was governor before his majesty was misled to abrogate our Massachusetts charter."

"My name is Gideon Whalley, replied the youth, with a deep, reverential bow; "and but that I come to you on a sad errand, and a bearer of sad tidings, I were both proud and happy to stand before a man whom I have learned of my father to revere so highly."

"Alas! all tidings are sad now-a-days. It is long since there has been aught of joy sounded in Boston streets; and I heard that which made me sad but now; how they have trumped up a vain charge of witchcraft against some poor young girl or other, and got the people mad between cruelty and superstition, which still walk hand in hand. I have sent out my man but now to learn the particulars; and thence it is that I am alone. I would fain therefore that your tidings had been good. Sit down, good youth, sit down, and tell me all that you have to tell, though I partly surmise even now to what your tidings point. You are the son of Merciful, the grandson of Edmund Whalley, one of the judges of him they call Charles the Martyr."

"Even so," answered Gideon. "My father has now fled away, conveying the aged exile whither he may be safe until this tyranny be overpast; and ere he went he bade me come and tell you all that hath befallen us, and then do as you shall think good to direct me."

"Ay!" answered the old man thoughtfully. "Ay! I heard how Sir Edmund had taken orders to arrest your grandsire, and, whatsoever I may think of the justice of the deed for which they pursue him, I know that Edward Whalley is a sincere and upright man; I heard that he had escaped his enemies, and I was glad."

"Then you have not heard all, Master Bradstreet," said the boy, "or you would not be glad. You have not heard that they have burned our house to the ground, at sight of which my mother died of a broken heart in one moment," and his voice faltered as he spoke, and he dashed away a tear with the back of his hand from his clear blue eye—"that they have shot our poor servant Tituba, and carried off my sister Ruth a captive."

While the boy was speaking, the old man's face had been gradually lighting up with an expression of concentrated indignation; but as he heard the last words the angry light died away in a minute, and was supplanted by the keenest and most painful anxiety.

"*Your* sister Ruth!—a captive!" he exclaimed, speaking rapidly in a half-smothered voice. "Who—who?—speak, boy! Who carried her off captive, and on what pretext?"

"The governor, Sir Edmund Andross—he who first burned our house, and slew our mother. God's curse upon his—"

"Hush! hush!—swear not at all!" said the old man very solemnly, pointing his hand upward. "Leave vengeance unto Him. It is his: he will repay! Yet this is very, very dreadful! But tell me on what pretext?"

"A hostage for the surrender of my father, within three days' space. But for an officer they call Sir Henry Cecil, he would have haled her hither, while our poor mother lay unburied."

"Gracious Lord!" cried the old man, now excited beyond all bounds. "Poor boy, poor boy, you come to me for aid and consolation, and I have but fresh coals of fire to heap upon your head. It is your sister, Ruth, of whom I spake. It is she whom they have charged with witchcraft! I see, I see it now; he hath done this thing so to avoid delivering her up when your father shall return. Tell me, boy, is your sister fair?"

"Beautiful! she is beautiful!" exclaimed the boy, aghast at this new blow, "and sweet as the flowers of spring, and innocent and gentle as the saints of heaven!"

"Oh! villain, villain, villain!" cried the old man, striking his hands forcibly together, and speaking to himself, unconscious for the moment that the girl's brother heard him. "Again the old tale, insatiate, ruthless lust! By terror, he would compel her to sin and shame;—but this time, this time, help us only thou most Merciful—this time he shall find his villany at fault—"

But Gideon had caught his words, and jumped instantly at their full import. He sprang to his feet, with clinched hand and flashing eye—

"By the great God," he cried, in tones of solemn fierceness, "who made and sees us both, were he ten times the governor, he shall die by my hand!"

And, with the words, he would have rushed from the room, intent on instant vengeance. But the old man caught him by the arm, and said in accents so impressive that they awed his rash anger into silence.

"Again! again! Is this your reverence?—is this your obedience? Hast thou not read His awful mandate, 'Thou shalt do no murder,' presumptuous and wicked boy? Insane, moreover, as presumptuous and wicked; for to do any violence would doom her, you would save, past hope to the gibbet, if not to the scaffold."

"But will the people," cried the boy in agony, "but will the *men* of Boston endure to see this thing?"

"I might reply to you," answered the sage, "that they have endured more than this already; that they have endured to be themselves degraded, almost to be enslaved!"

"My poor, poor sister!" cried the boy, his high courage giving away before this extremity of evil.

"The people, the *men*, as you call them, of Boston are they, are the very men, who will clamor the most loudly for her doom, if we can not arouse them—"

"And can you, great God! Master Bradstreet—can you arouse them?"

"By His aid who forsaketh not the just man at any time, I trust that I can arouse them."

"And save Ruth?" gasped the boy.

"And save Ruth, incorrupt and scathless."

"And will you—will you?"

"The Lord pardon you the question," answered the old man, much affected. "I would give the last drop of blood that is left in this poor frail body before one hair of her head should be corrupted. But now, peace! peace! let us take council together."

And for a few seconds he paused in deep thought; then suddenly—

"When will your father be here?" he inquired.

"This very night he promised to return," answered the boy. "To-morrow he must give himself up in exchange for my sister."

Again the old man meditated long and anxiously.

"Sir Henry Cecil! Sir Henry Cecil!" he began again, "said you not that he interfered in your sister's behalf?"

"But for him," said the boy, "Ruth would have been dragged away from our dead mother's side. He is good, and noble!"

"Yes! yes!" said the old man pensively. "And he has resigned his commission, they tell me. Yet the soldiers love him. His family, too, are God-fearing folks, and friends of liberty and the true cause. Yes! yes! he will help us."

At this moment the outer door opened, and a grave-looking man entered the room.

"I have done your bidding," he said, "good Simon. I have learned all. It is—"

"I also have learned all! This is Ruth Whalley's brother."

"But do you know that she shall be tried to-morrow? and that they are fitting up a gibbet even now? and that the people cry for her young blood?"

"No! no! are they, indeed, so fierce in their malignity? But they shall be frustrated yet, or my name is not Simon Bradstreet. Hark you, good Andrew! Go forth again and send me hither Waterhouse and Foster, as quickly as may be. And then go find Sir Henry Cecil, and pray him come and speak with me forthwith—and then go you, and take as many of your friends as you can find, and spread it through the crowd how Edmund Andross but two days since murdered this poor child's mother, and now trumps up this false charge against her to force her to become his concubine. Spare nothing to excite their pity; deal with the women chiefly; and if you can prevail with them to listen, move the good people to come and ask me to speak to them."

"I will perform your bidding," he said bluntly; and, without another word, departed.

"Fear nothing!" said the old man, taking the boy's hand kindly in his own; "fear nothing; we will save her at all hazards. Only I wish this thing had fallen out a few days later."

As he spoke, the door was again thrown violently open, and a sea-faring man rushed headlong into the room with an expression of wild, eager joy in his bold, sunburnt face.

"I have seen it!" he cried. "I have seen it! Glory to God! with my own eyes I have seen it!"

"Seen what, Charles Nelson?" asked Bradstreet in vehement surprise, but with his whole form dilating, as it seemed, under the influence of some strong expectation. "What have you seen?—speak!"

"The orange flag!—all glory be to God!—the orange flag at the fore! She is becalmed off Buzzard's bay. And when I showed our friends the private signal, they hoisted it at once, but lowered it again in a minute. She will be here, if the wind makes, to-morrow; but beyond any doubt, the next day."

"The Lord hath stretched out his hand; the Lord hath saved his servants! Down on your knees, Charles Nelson. Down on your knees, Gideon Whalley. Let us pray! Let us praise the Lord who has wrought this deliverance for Israel."

And though he knew not, nor could at all divine the meaning of that venerable man's strange words, the boy hesitated not, but fell down upon his knees, and clasped his hands fervently together, so certain was he, from those impassioned tones, that some great thing was indeed accomplished, and praised the Lord in the strength of a confiding faith, ignorant wherefore.

And in truth a great thing had been accomplished; nor was his faith in vain. Is it vain ever?

CHAPTER XXV.

THE COUNCIL.

THE morrow had arrived—the fatal morrow!

The court was assembled which were that day to decide upon the fate of the young, the innocent, the beautiful Ruth Whalley. O mockery! O shame! to speak of deciding that which was determined so soon as the accusation was preferred.

Had the accusers not been the creatures of the brutal and licentious governors; had the witnesses not been to a man suborned to perjury; had the judges not been to a man the sycophantic nominees and pliant tools of Andross; still was the fate of Ruth determined or ere she was brought to trial—for fanaticism and superstitious awe, and credulous terror—than which there is no passion of the human heart so cruel—had maddened and hardened the hearts of the people, and to be accused of witchcraft was in fact to be condemned without trial—to be slaughtered without respite or appeal.

But on that morning there had assembled beside the court another and a nobler council.

In the rear of Simon Bradstreet's garden, and adjoining one of the principal wharfs of the city stood a long, half-deserted warehouse, with a private entrance from a blind and unfrequented alley. Above it, in the third story, ceiled with the rude, bare rafters, wainscotted with rough, unplaned boards, lighted only by a skylight, for the three dormer windows, to the sills of each of which was attached a large telescope, were closely shuttered so as to exclude alike both prying eyes of humanity, and the garish light of day, was a large loft sometimes used by the old patriot as an observatory.

In that apartment was the patriot-council assembled. And yet so singular and so desolate was the whole aspect of that apartment, that, had it not been for the charts which hung here and there against the panelling, and for the globes and large telescopes which stood on elevated stands in various parts of its ample area, it might well have given rise to suspicion.

The sun had not long risen, when the party which I have mentioned, came together in that place, so well fitted for that purpose.

For that party consisted of the patriots, or liberty-men, of Boston, and that purpose was the emancipation of their native province at once from the domestic tyranny of the oppressor Andross, and the bigoted and despotical sway of England's second James.

In the arm-chair, at the head of the board, clad as he was on the previous day, sat Simon Bradstreet, worthy, by virtue of his great intellect as of his long experience, to be the president of such a meeting. Next to him, on the right, sat stout Charles Nelson, the bold, hardy seaman, who had brought the glad tidings to old Bradstreet; and below him, and opposite, at the president's left, two well-known and much-esteemed citizens, Foster and Waterhouse, who had been colonels in the old Boston train-bands.

Besides these, several other aged men, magistrates of the city, under the old charter, were seated at the board, and below them, two or three stout youths, among whom Gideon Whalley was perhaps the most remarkable.

All these men were dressed simply, some in the garb of merchants and lawyers, others in the every-day apparel of artisans, mechanics, and sea-faring men; and it was remarkable, that, at a time when all persons who laid any claim to gentle birth or station wore swords as a part of their ordinary dress, with one exception only, there was not a weapon of any kind in the room.

That one exception concerned a person who occupied the seat facing Simon Bradstreet, and whom I have not as yet described. Nor, in truth, is any description of him necessary, for it is none other than our old friend Sir Henry Cecil.

He was attired with his wonted elegance and care, although no longer in a military habit. His long, curled, and perfumed hair, his velvet coat with diamond buttons, his red-heeled shoes, and gold-hilted small sword, presenting a singular contrast to the cropped hair and plain, sad-colored clothes of the steady burghers.

The council had, it would seem, been for some time in session, for Bradstreet was saying, apparently in conclusion of an important debate —

"We understand one another, therefore, perfectly. We may depend fully on your influence and success with the soldiers, Sir Henry Cecil."

"Under the circumstances you have stated, certainly!" replied the young gentleman. "But you must understand me fully, too. I must be made certain beyond the possibility of doubt, not only that William of Orange has landed in England, but that he is acknowledged the king, and that James has fled the land. I will support the government of England at all hazards, nor will I stir a hand to aid any rising here against the mother-country. I do not reflect upon those who may wish to do so—but England is my country, and England's king is my king. I may wish that William were that king rather than James; and were I at home, might strive to have it so. But being here, and knowing how a premature effort may disconcert the wisest plans, I will be a good subject to James until I shall know that William is my king de facto."

"You are wise, although young, Sir Henry, and you speak very well," answered Bradstreet, calmly; "and in all that you have said, I think you are quite right—but William of Nassau *is* now William of England, that I know; and ere this time to-morrow you shall know it likewise. You would have known it now, but that this rascal Andross has intercepted your despatches—"

"Indeed, indeed—do you *know* that?"

"I know the man who has seen and read them."

"It may be so, indeed," answered Cecil, thoughtfully.

"It is so," replied the old man. "Andross is well assured, even now, of the news which this vessel brings. She will be boarded in the outer bay, and the messenger made a prisoner. But he will be re-captured from the pinnace; will he not, Master Nelson? The troops will be under arms; but we have troops also, ha! Masters Waterhouse and Foster? We will not ask you to stir hand or foot, Sir Henry, until you shall have seen the proclamation of the kings William and Mary. —Then we will claim your services."

"And you shall have them. Let me but see that, and I will answer for it that not a trooper shall draw a trigger on the people."

"And if they do, may God help them!" said Waterhouse sternly.

"And if they do, may God defend the right!" said Sir Henry, solemnly.

"And which will be the right, Sir Henry?" asked Foster, with a smile; not that he doubted or misunderstood the young man, but that he saw a cloud on the brows of some of his confederates, and feared any misconception.

"The cause of the king and the people!" answered the noble soldier. "The cause of England and America!—not of Rome! The cause of King William and Simon Bradstreet! —not of King James and Edmund Andross!"

At these stirring and spirited words, there was an evident disposition to cheer, among some of the younger men present; but it was checked instantly by the graver and more wary leaders.

"All then is understood touching this matter?" asked old Simon.

"All!" replied Henry Cecil; and "All! all! clearly! without doubt!" was re-echoed from every side of the apartment.

"And now," said Bradstreet, "touching this poor girl—"

"Villain and tyrant as he is, I can not think," answered Cecil, "that he will break his faith so basely. He pledged his word to me, that on her father's surrender to the hands of justice, Ruth should go free. I can not think—"

"And for your thinking, or not thinking, shall my sweet sister die?" Gideon Whalley interrupted him rudely. But the young soldier looked at him with an eye both compassionate and full of grave dignity, and paused before he answered—

"I understand your anxiety, good youth. But come what may of it, your sister will not die, or I will not be living. I shall deem it no wrong to interrupt the execution of your sister on any sentence for witchcraft by the strong hand, let who may be the king, or who may be the governor. And that not because she is your sister, or because she is Ruth Whalley; for, as God is my judge, I would have done the same for any one of those poor wretches who were so barbarously murdered at Salem under the plea of law, had I been in the province. Moreover, I have a hundred stout veterans, who have served under me in other lands, and in hotter feuds than this is like to be, who will stand by me to the last, if I give the word, I well believe, in any cause, in any righteous cause I am certain."

"And will you give the word, Sir Henry?" cried Gideon Whalley eagerly.

"So surely as I shall see need for it. But I still hope, and still believe, that without stroke of sword, or drop of bloodshed, this great crime may be averted from the people—this great peril from your sister."

"Amen!" replied the venerable patriot, bowing his head in approval. "Amen, so be it! and in what does your hope rely, for though you may hope and believe religiously in the faith of divine things unseen, you are too wise I think, in the things of this world, and its every-day workings, to hope much or believe anything without warrant. In what, then, doth your hope reside?"

"In the might of the right—in the overruling majesty and weight of the English law—in the honor of English judges. I will myself be in court within an hour, who was a witness on the spot, and can adduce such evidence of this bad man's daring guilt, and deliberate falsehood, that for their souls they dare not convict her!"

"You lean upon a broken reed, Sir Henry," said Bradstreet. "Think you that juries, whose fears have made them madmen—judges who have received the wages of blood, and agreed to condemn the innocent before trial—care one straw either for evidence or law?"

"Moreover, look at this, Sir Henry Cecil," said Waterhouse, throwing a paper on the table. "I saw the original document an hour ago, of which that is the copy. See if you *can* go into court."

It was a council-warrant for the arrest of Sir Henry Cecil, on charges of insubordination and high treason.

The paper fell from the hands of the young soldier, and he gazed round the room in angry wonder.

"His plans are well arranged," he said, at length.

"Whose plans?" asked Merciful Whalley, almost fiercely.

"The governor's!" replied Cecil.

"Here is the governor of Boston," said the Puritan, laying his broad hand on the shoulder of old Simon Bradstreet.—"As I came up the bay, ere it was light this morning, returning from New Haven, I boarded the good ship Two-Friends at anchor. The wind that brought me up was too light to carry her against the tide of ebb. I saw the messenger who bears the glorious tidings. God hath looked down upon his people! This tyranny is overpast! William and Mary are the kings of England! James Stuart hath fled without stroke of sword! Our charter is restored!—and noble Simon Bradstreet is the governor of Boston! Letters, good master Bradstreet! Letters, Sir Henry Cecil!"

And, with the word, he threw down several large packets on the board.

A moment was enough to satisfy Sir Henry. He cast a quick glance toward the venerable patriot.

"It is all true," he said. "The Lord be praised. I am the first to tender you my service and my sword," he continued, taking off his hat and unsheathing his bright blade—"I await your orders."

"They are brief, Sir Henry, and easily obeyed," answered the old man, with a smile. "You must tarry here all this day, in concealment. He must not arrest you or your friend Whalley, here, to-day, on any account, and to-morrow——"

"He may arrest whom he can!" interrupted Waterhouse, bluntly.

"Even so," replied Bradstreet. "And now, to make all certain, go you, my good friend, and have your regiment ready to act at a minute's notice. Let them be on the common well armed at the first clang of the statehouse bells. You, Nelson, know your duty! You, Foster, have all the train-bands in preparation at midnight, but show no force until the signal! Who is to lead the soldiers from Charlestown and Chelsea?"

"Shepherd, the schoolmaster of Lynn!" answered Waterhouse.

"None better," answered Bradstreet. "Farewell, then, all! To your posts—be prudent—peaceful, and silent! So all will certainly go well! Ha! what now, Andrew?" he continued, as the old servant entered the room cautiously, and with a sad expression in his face.

"The court is dissolved—the maid Ruth is condemned! The governor's assent is given! She shall be hanged at noon to-morrow."

"That she shall not," said Bradstreet. "At what time, Merciful Whalley, will the Two-Friends weigh anchor?"

"When the breeze rises, which it will with the evening tide of flood at nine of the clock. She will be here in the morning twilight—but the Rosebud, the pinnace, lies just below the castle."

"Will there be much wind, Whalley?" asked Charles Nelson.

"A topsail breeze I will a-warrant it; and like enough a capful!"

"Then I will answer for the pinnace," said the other.

"And I will answer, by God's grace," said Bradstreet, "that before noon, Sir Edmund Andross shall hang no one!"

"Unless it be himself!" added Waterhouse; and with a grim laugh the council was dissolved.

CHAPTER XXVI.

THE PRISON.

The night had set in dark and gloomy. The sky was overcast with heavy clouds driving in from the seaward rapidly; and a thin small rain fell noiselessly, as is usual at the commencement of a blow from the southeast. The streets of Boston were, however, if not crowded, at the least far more frequented than was common at so late an hour, and in weather so inclement. For it was nearly midnight, and far from abating, the storm appeared to increase every moment. The people in the streets also seemed to become more numerous instead of dispersing for the night; and there was singularly restless and uneasy state of feelings made manifest by every word and movement of the gathering groups.

It was not exactly what would be called excitement, much less was it turbulence or riot; for there was no general noise, nor indeed any loud talking; but there was an air of gloom and discontent very nearly universal; and it would seem that the authorities had taken the alarm, for in addition to the ordinary watch, who were out in their full strength, several small parties of soldiers were abroad, patrolling the streets, though they interfered with no one; and it was rumored that there were double sentries at the guard-house, and that the men were mustered under arms in the castle.

It was about the prison-doors, however, that the greatest number of persons were assembled; and here alone there might be said to be a throng; and that throng somewhat loud and tumultuous, though still peaceable; indeed, what noise there was, seemed to proceed rather from a confusion of eager queries and replies, than from any riotous disposition of the people; and the two sentinels, who walked to and fro before the heavy gates, had found no difficulty in keeping the space clear, which they were stationed there to defend.

Midnight had struck some time, when a tall man, wearing a slouched hat and wrapped in a thick cloak, made his way through the crowd, not without some exertion, although he was preceded by two peace officers, and followed by a subaltern's guard.

As he entered the clear space, however, before the prison gates, which was dimly illuminated by a large lamp, he was recognised by the people for the governor, and room was made for him immediately. There was no cheering from any of the crowd, which was composed for the most part of well-clad, substantial looking burghers and mechanics; but there was no disposition to insult him shown by any one, nor did they manifest their disapprobation by groans or hisses. If they were angry, it was with that calm, resolute, and determined wrath, which is ten thousand times more dangerous, because it is so silent and so thoughtful.

The regular formalities having been executed, the password demanded and given, and an order from the proper magistrate displayed, the governor entered the prison-door alone, his escort standing at ease, with their muskets grounded in front of the gate, between the two sentinels and the people. So long a time elapsed that the crowd, unexcited by any new event, began to drop away one by one ; and then after a while some whispered word ran through the scattered groups which alone remained, and thereupon they also hurried away in the direction of the harbor, and left the front of the prison, deserted by all but the watchmen and soldiery.

Within that cheerless building, in a small stone cell, with a single grated window, a pallet bed, one chair, and a small table, whereon were placed a lamp, an open bible and a stone jug of water, sat Ruth Whalley.

She had been brought thither sometimo before noon, from the court-house, where, in the space of less than three hours, she had been tried, convicted, sentenced to die for witchcraft, and left from that hour until now, alone and unvisited by any one but the jailer.

She was to die at noon on the morrow.

To die ! It is a dark and fearful thing to die, even for those who are aweary of their lives ; who have proved all the disappointments, the vanities, the woes of human life ; who look upward from a world of anguish and of sin, to one of immortal purity and bliss.

What must it be then to one in the first flower of youth and health, and beauty, with all the fresh world bright before her.

Even when honored and beloved, full of years and glory, surrounded by troops of weeping and adhering friends, it is a difficult thing to die ! Even to him, who is powerless, friendless, hopeless, alone on a foreign land, all human pleasures melted and weighed and found wanting, still it is difficult to die—how bold the heart, how firm the faith soever, there is yet something in the mysterious void, whence no voice hath ever come to tell its secrets—something which the soul burns to know, yet coldly shrinks from knowing!

What must it be, then, to die, a death of agony, of shame, of horror—a felon's death on a gibbet? And that for one so young, so tender, and so untried, in the world's school of torture? What to look forward for long hours to such a fate, alone, unsupported by a single friend, unwept, unprayed for, unconsoled?

Can mind of man imagine aught more terrible?

Yet this was the condition in which that beautiful, pale maiden had sate there alone since morning. Hearing the strokes of the fatal bell, each stroke proclaimed that her life was ebbing fast away, fast as the sands in the glass of time.

It is a strange thing, that it is often the weakest and frailest natures which support trials, not moral only, but physical, such as are generally supposed to require physical power to sustain them, better and with more fortitude than sterner and more hardy characters.

So it was with Ruth Whalley.

At first she had been stunned by the suddenness of the false charge, the mass of perjured evidence, the cruel and iniquitous proceedings, the dark, disgraceful sentence—she had been stupefied and unable to comprehend that she was indeed to die—to die a felon's death on the morrow. Slowly and gradually the dreadful truth dawned on her—and for a while she wept, wept bitterly in terror and regret—in terror of her awful doom, regret for the vain promise of her untimely-ended youth.

But it was not long that she yielded to that weakness.—She called to mind the glorious promises of the Redeemer, and she turned the eyes of her mind with a gaze so steady to that exceeding great reward, which the Almighty has himself revealed, as awaiting those who are prosecuted for his sake, that all the terrors of the brief passage from time into eternity, all the weak ties that bound her to this earthly sphere, were unseen and unheeded.

For all the proffered consolations, to all the kind inquiries of the blunt but kind-hearted keeper, who wept for her as if she had been his own child, she had but one answer—

"She needed nothing—she feared nothing—she was exceeding happy."

So passed the day, neither fast to her nor slowly, so steady was her pulse, so confident her gentle spirit.

She had eaten of her prison fare; she had taken her leave of this world; she was in peace with all mankind; she put her whole trust in the mercy of her Redeemer; in a few little hours she was once more to be with her dear mother, never again to sorrow or to sin.

Why should she not sleep soundly?

She had bound up her beautiful fair hair, and was about to seek her lowly pallet for her last sleep save one; but she had yet to undergo one trial.

The door of her cell opened and closed suddenly, giving admittance to a tall man, whose form and face were both muffled in the folds of a dark cloak.

But muffled as he was, Ruth knew him on the instant as by a fearful instinct, and shrank back with dread into the farthest angle of her prison.

"Do you fear me, pretty Ruth?" said her tormentor.

"Should I not fear you?" answered the hapless girl. "You who, for your mere pleasure, have slain or banished all my kindred; and now have slain me also with a lie."

"Hard words, Ruth!" said the governor, for he it was who had come to trouble her last hours. "Do you not fear to use such terms to me?"

"What should I fear—I who shall die to-morrow?"

"Ay! die, and that before another sunset."

"What, I say, should I fear? you can do me no ill more than you have done."

"Perhaps, I can do you good."

"Perhaps," she answered calmly. "But if you can, you will not. Wherefore, I pray you, trouble me no farther. If I have wronged you, you have your revenge—to triumph over a weak girl is pitiful; I pray you leave me."

Even the insolent and brutal Andross was staggered by her gentle and serene fortitude; and it was a moment before he was collected enough to ask her in a voice half-trembling, half-admiring—

"Do you not fear to die?"

"No! Can you say as much, and truly?"

"You must, I think, desire it, that you dare thus taunt one who has the power to smite or to spare."

"There is but ONE who hath that power; and to him I have resigned myself already. If it be his will that I perish, thou, vain man, hast no power to spare. If he stretch out his arm to save I shall not fall for all thy writing."

"Dost thou desire to die, then, that you so scorn me?"

"I scorn no man, no creature of his hand," she answered calmly; and then added, "What I desire signifies nothing—but no living thing desires to die that is in health and reason."

"Ha! you relent, pretty one! I thought your boasting was too loud to be lasting," answered the tyrant, with a coarse and triumphant laugh. "And would you do aught, my sweet saint, to escape hanging; you may yet go free, if you are wise and gentle."

"I would do aught," she answered, "that is lawful. Seeing that I have no right to advance my appointed hour by one minute. But this avails nothing. You have not come this night to spare me."

"By my honor! — by my soul! — I have come for no other purpose! You are too young, too fair, too innocent, to die. I *have* come to spare you."

Her pale cheek was flushed for one moment, her eye was kindled with a ray of hope. She clasped her hands, and spoke, no longer firmly, but in a tremulous and agitated voice —

"You can not — no, you can not be mocking me!" she said. "No man *could* mock a woman at such an hour as this.— What must I do, that you shall spare me?"

"That which I asked of you, the last time we met," he answered triumphantly; and, as he spoke, he drew nearer to her, confident that she was on the point of yielding.— "Grant me that, and you live! refuse me, and you die! Your answer?"

"I would have died *then*, by my own hand, rather than yield, or grant it! Are you answered?"

"Ha! is it so, proud wench?" he cried, furious at finding himself frustrated, when he deemed success certain. "By Him who made me, you shall yield it *now*, and yet die to-morrow. There are no knives here, whether for my heart or your own."

And with the words, he rushed furiously toward her.

Hopeless of aid, and in extremity of terror, the miserable girl uttered a shriek, so loud, so full of agony and horror, that the stout soldiers started at their posts without the gates, and trembled.

And though she looked for no aid, it came, instant, in time to save.

The door flew open, and the stout jailer entered, quiet and grave, though with an angry flush on his blunt brow, and a fierce spark in his deep gray eye. He held in his left hand a heavy partisan; and two large horse-pistols were stuck in his leathern girdle.

"Sir Edmund Andross," he said firmly, "my prisoners are under my charge—and my charge alone, until the time arrive when I must yield them to the sheriff. Until that time come, no man shall wrong them."

"*Shall?*" exclaimed Andross, haughtily. "*Shall* to me? Are you mad, fellow?—know you to whom you speak?"

"Yes! *shall* to you, Sir Edmund, when I am in my place, and you out of yours. Mad! no, I trow, not I. And for knowing—I know well that you are an English governor, and I a Yankee jailer. What of that? I do my duty: you have forgotten yours. But enough of this—lock-up hours are past; and you stay here no longer. I think your *honor*"—and he laid an ironical emphasis on the word—"had better withdraw peacefully. If not, I call the prison-watch, and enforce your departure."

Andross scowled on him furiously; but though his soul was full of fierce and fiery hate, and threatening words were burning on his tongue, he had enough of reason left to perceive that he was powerless and in the wrong; and enough of self-control to restrain his feelings in the hope of avoiding scandal.

He turned therefore slowly on his heel, and moved toward the door. "Advance your light," he said, "and show me the way, sirrah. And, be you sure, that I shall remember this night's work."

"And I am sure that I shall not forget it," answered the sturdy officer, doing as he was ordered quietly, but keeping a quick eye to the other's movements.

Andross strode forward haughtily in dark silence, until he reached the threshold, then he turned round, and shook his finger at the maiden, who had fallen on her knees, with clasped hands and upturned eyes, in gratitude to Heaven for that deliverance from peril worse than death.

"Girl," he said, "make your peace with God! for in his

presence you shall stand, ere the sun sets to-morrow." There was a bitter and sardonic smile on the scoffer's lips as he spoke; and he added with a sneer—"What answer you to that?"

"Amen!" she replied, looking at him calmly, "and may He pardon you, whose name you take in vain!"

If a look could have slain, there would have been no hangman needed to wreak Andross's vengeance on that gentle head upon the morrow.

But it fell harmless as the curse which quivered on his lips unspoken; or recoiled on his own head, urging him on to deeds of fresh madness, and greater desperation. "Whom the gods destine to destruction, they first deprive of reason," said Rome's sage—how sagely, let every felon's fate bear witness.

The door of Ruth's cell closed behind him. No trouble more came nigh to her that night. Innocent, she slept soundly, and in her dreams was happy.

CHAPTER XXVII.

THE "TWO-FRIENDS."

It was yet dark, although morning was nigh at hand; a thick, gray mist hung over the city, and filled the streets and narrower thoroughfares with wreaths of turbid vapor. But over the wharfs, and on the surface of the water the fog was packed so densely that it was not possible to see the largest object at the distance of twenty yards.

Still, in despite of the inclemency of the weather, and the impossibility of descrying anything to seaward, there was a considerable crowd collected on the docks and that apparently in eager and anxious expectation.

But hour after hour passed away, and the dawn grew gradually brighter, and the sky clearer overhead, without the murky fog diminishing in the least below, or anything occurring to justify or account for the eagerness of the people.

Yet as the day grew more apparent, and the sun rose, the number of persons who gathered down to the water's edge increased; and not their numbers only, but their eagerness, although they were perfectly quiet and orderly.

At length, there came a quick fluttering motion in the air, a long cool breath, and the mist waved and shook like the folds of a vast curtain. Then again all was still. A minute passed thus, and then, in an instant, a strong fresh breeze poured in, and the fog was dissipated in the moment.

The fair, broad bay lay visible in its beautiful expanse before the eyes of all, with the great orb of the new-risen sun hanging, mighty globe of lurid fire, upon the eastern verge of the horizon, and shedding a long stream of crimson light over the dancing ripples.

Afar off, on the bosom of the deep, there was however a dark, inky shadow, rushing in rapidly toward the shore—the growing roughness of the waters lashed into life by the stiff and increasing breeze—ere long that inky shadow was broken by spots and flakes of white foam, which became constantly more regular and more continuous, until at length they came rolling in, line after line, of tall, snow-crested billows.

Over the surface of the roughened bay, many a white sail, many a toping hull was discernible, fishing-boats beating seaward, coasters close-hauled, or running in before the wind; but only one large vessel, if the Rose frigate be excepted, which lay motionless, before the castle, at a single anchor, with her yards accurately crossed, and every rope in its place, but not a speck of canvas to be seen, nor any sign of movement or activity upon her guarded decks. Just as the mist cleared off, however, and the sun lifted his gorgeous head above the glowing waters, the dull roar of an unshotted gun broke the silence, and up soared to the gaff-end the snow-white banner of St. George with its resplendent cross of red, up to the mast-head rushed the fluttering pennon, and both streamed out before the joyous blast triumphant and invincible.

The other ship was a tall merchantman, coming in gallantly with every sail set that would draw, into her native harbor—her white canvass bellying in the breeze, and the foam heaped beneath the bows like the froth of a cataract.

She was perhaps a mile distant from the shore when she was first descried; and every moment brought her nearer to the shore, and increased the eagerness and excitement of the people.

"It is she, sure enough," cried out an old sea-dog, who had been contemplating her with a careful and knowing eye. "It is she, by those new cloths in her maintopsail ?"

"The Two-Friends ?" asked a grave citizen. "Are you certain it is she ?"

"Yes, master, it is she sure enough."

And the words the Two-Friends spread rapidly through the concourse, and were greeted by a hum of applause, and then by a regular and partial cheer.

Scarcely, however, had the slight tumult which this news created in some degree passed over, but a fiercer and more stirring excitement succeeded it.

A sharp, rakish-looking pinnace, with the pennant of a man-of-war flying from her mast-head was seen darting like a falcon on her prey, as close to the wind as she could lie, across the course of the merchantman as if to intercept her ; although she was so far distant, and the merchantman was coming in so rapidly, that it seemed more than doubtful, whether she would not weather her pursuer, and come into port before her.

Every moment rendered this possibility more probable ; and ere long the fact was evident to those on board the pinnace, as was proved by a sharp flash a puff of white smoke from the larboard bows, followed by the roar of a heavy gun, though no missile was projected from its muzzle.

Still the tall ship stood on unheeding.

Another flash from the pinnace—another puff of white smoke, and a ball skipped from ridge to ridge of the curling waves scarce twenty feet before the cut-water of the Two-Friends.

Still she regarded not the summons, but stood onward, scarce now a quarter of a mile distant from the crowded wharves of Boston.

In the meantime, between the ship and the docks, a very large, light-laden schooner had for some time been getting under way, in the most lubberly and unseamanlike way that can be imagined ; she was apparently very short handed, for only one man and two or three boys had been seen upon her decks, yet she had no less than five boats towing in the water behind her, one of them a sharp clipper with her tiny masts stepped, and her sails flapping idly in the wind.

Some merriment had been excited among the crowd, while the large ship was at a distance, by her lubberly movements and dull sailing, but now that events were thickening, and something strange was apparently in progress, the attention of the multitude was diverted from her, and few persons observed that although yawing and keeling about strangely, she was steering a course, which, if she held it much longer, must bring her into collision with the Two-Friends.

Meantime, the pinnace had again fired a shotted gun ; and

this time a large rent in the ship's maintopsail showed that the shot had been aimed directly at the object.

Alarmed by the firing, the frigate's crew now came passing up through the hatchways, and her decks were crowded with blue-jackets. The next moment her drums were heard beating to quarters.

Still the Two-Friends held sullenly and obstinate to her course, taking no notice of the firing of the pinnace, except to show two or three English ensigns in various parts of her rigging, and a large orange flag at her maintopmast, as if it were a private signal.

It would, however, seem that this private signal had more than a private meaning; for the instant it appeared a long, loud cheer of joy ran along the crowded wharves, and up the streets, and was re-echoed faint and far from the centre of the city, and from the heights of Charlestown, and from the brow, bloodless then, of Bunker's Hill.

At the same instant, flash after flash, roar after roar, a whole broadside burst from the batteries of the pinnace.

Sails flew in wild disorder, yards fell, a topmast toppled down, and unable any longer to neglect warnings so pregnant, the Two-Friends backed her sails and lay to, to await her captor's pleasure.

Meantime the pinnace lowered her boats, and some ten or fifteen men, well armed with boarding-pike and cutlass, might be seen scaling the tall sides of the merchantman.

Before, however, the crowd on the docks had time to think upon what was passing, the clumsy and ill-managed schooner, as if by accident, ran foul of the ship on the opposite side from the pinnace.

Then, in an instant, grapplings were thrown on board, and at least three hundred men, rushing up from below, burst like a living torrent over the schooner's bulwarks, ran up the rigging, dropped from the yard-arms to the deck of the Two-Friends, and for a moment all on board was confusion and dismay.

A few pistol-shots were fired, and cutlasses flashed in the air, and shouts were heard on board; but all resistance was at an end in five minutes; so thoroughly were the men-of-war's-men overpowered.

Then the crowd was seen to rush back on board the schooner, leaving the ship at the mercy of the pinnace, with her crew hailing eagerly and deprecating hostile measures.

On the deck of the frigate, meanwhile, all was tumult and confusion; sail after sail was let fall, and sheeted home, her cable was cut, and in the shortest time conceivable she was under way, and in pursuit of the schooner, which, having cut away her boats, was beating slowly out to sea.

For a while the abandoned boats tossed about carelessly on the waters, until the pinnace had passed them unheeding, and the frigate, her cable cut, and a sail or two set, was swung off in an opposite direction.

Then the clipper-rigged boat showed for the first time that she had men on board her. For her sails too were trimmed, and right before the wind she came bounding to the shore, unnoticed and unhindered.

And yet she bore the prize for which all were playing.

As she came within eye-shot of the docks, a tall man stood up in her bows waving the orange flag, and again peal upon peal outburst the thundering acclamations, "till every steeple rocked, and the fair hills re-echoed the shouts of an enfranchised people rejoicing in their new-born freedom."

Another moment, and the man stood upon the docks with Nelson by his side. The latter tossed his cap into the air, and shouted —

"William and Mary are your kings — Simon Bradstreet

your governor! Shout, boys of Boston, shout! England and liberty for ever! and down with James Stuart and Sir Edmund Andross!"

There was no need to repeat the order; for such a cry arose of triumph and rejoicing, as told the tyrant and his minions, that their reign in America was ended.

CHAPTER XXVIII.

THE MUSTERING.

Scarcely had that last shout risen on the air, before the long roll of the English drums was heard beating to arms. A gun was fired from the seaward bastion of the castle, and signals were exchanged rapidly with the frigate, which, immediately leaving the pursuit of the schooner, altered her course, and made all sail homeward.

In the meantime Nelson and his companions hurried through the dense streets to the abode of the old patriot governor, bearing the messenger of good tidings on their shoulders. There the old man with Sir Henry Cecil, and Waterhouse, and Foster, were in session, and many others with them, both officers of the provincial train-bands, and magistrates under the old charter.

The proclamation of William and Mary was immediately laid before these worthies, and there was not a moment's doubt now of the truth of the good tidings, which had so long been anticipated.

"You see, Sir Henry," said the old man, "that I pledged myself to nothing but what was strictly true, and which the event has borne out."

"And you shall see, my excellent good friend," replied Sir Henry, "that I pledged myself to nothing that I will not perform. I said that I would answer for the soldiers, and I will."

"But what must we do first, Master Bradstreet?" exclaimed Waterhouse. "This Andross is a man of nerve; and is resolved doubtless to carry the matter on unto the end. The soldiers are Englishmen, and will obey their officers, and do their duty to the last. If we act not at once, it may well be that we shall be all surprised severally, and made prisoners ere a blow is stricken."

While he was speaking, Bradstreet had been employed writing eagerly upon a strip of paper, although he appeared to write every word that his friend uttered. When he ceased speaking he turned round, and handing the paper to his serving man, said, "Make all haste. Give it to no one but himself. He is at his post."

Then turning to Waterhouse, he answered, "Yes. You are quite right, my good friend. What orders have your men? and yours, Foster?"

"To be ready for action at a moment's notice," replied Foster.

"And to muster upon the Common, at the first clank of the statehouse bell," cried Waterhouse.

"How many firelocks?" asked Cecil.

"Five hundred," was the prompt reply; "and eight hundred pikes!"

"That will do," said Sir Henry. "That will do. They will not feel their honor hurt in yielding to such odds."

"Well, gentlemen," said Bradstreet, "you had better make all speed to the common, or your men will be there before you."

Then, as he saw the wild and astonished looks of the officers, he added,

"The time has come, the statehouse bell will sound ere you

are there. As soon as you have mustered your men, Colonel Waterhouse, you will send a hundred men with a captain hither to escort us to the town-hall. Hold the rest of the men firm, assailing no one, but if assailed, yourselves resisting to the utmost. How now, Green?" he added, as a stout powerful man, somewhat above the middle age, entered the room hastily, with his faced flushed, and his dress disordered by the haste with which he had come from the docks. "What is the matter?"

"The frigate has returned to her moorings," he replied, "and has run out her guns, and cleared her decks. I think she will fire upon the town. I fancy she waits only for a messenger from Andross."

"Then let no messenger go off to her. You and your sturdy shipwrights, can take heed of that," said Bradstreet.

"And what if any one land from her?"

"Make him your prisoner! Arrest him in the name of King William, even if it be Captain George himself. There is your warrant, sir," and he gave him a sealed paper as he spoke. "Now," he continued, "here is a task of a little peril — who volunteers for it?"

"I — I and I," exclaimed several voices in a breath, the foremost and most audible of which was that of Merciful Whalley.

"No, no. You will not do at all, good Merciful," answered the governor elect; "for you are angry, and not without a good cause; and angry men make evil councillors. Besides you mistake; there is no active danger in it, and I think that is what you look for."

"Verily you have said it, Simon Bradstreet," answered the Puritan. "Place me in the first rank against the Philistines. It is there I fain would be."

"I warrant it," said Bradstreet. "But what I want now, is one to bear the copy of this proclamation, which your good friend Solsgrace, here, has well nigh finished, to Sir Edmund Andross and summon him to yield his power."

"I will do that, Master Bradstreet," replied Sir Henry Cecil.

"We can not spare you, Sir Henry. You are not to be risked so lightly. For he were sure to apprehend you on the instant, and we want you to deal with the soldierly."

"I will bear it, my good friends," said an old man rising fully from the board. "I need not tell you that I will not be angry. My years will bear me witness for that. And, for the rest, if he takes my life there is no human being in whose veins my blood runs, nor will there be any left to mourn me."

"My good friend, Sturtevant," answered the governor, "most thankfully do I accept your offer, not for the reasons that you give. But simply because in all Boston there is no man so well qualified as you to do this duty. I will beseech you to set forth at once, without loss of time, for ere long—ha! there it goes," he continued, as the keep sound of the bell from the town hall broke out, first in slow, measured, awful tones, increasing still in volume, and thickening on the ear, and quickening into one continuous and startling clangor—'there goes the voice that shall stir every heart in Boston, in America. You, Gideon Whalley, you, Simeon Langdale, go with good Master Sturtevant unto the governor. He is in council now."

No more words were required. The embassy went forth, but went on a fruitless errand. Meanwhile church after church, and steeple after steeple, took up the song of freedom, till leagues and leagues away, far into the heart of the great continent, the joyful tidings were sent forth.

The villages around poured one continuous stream of men, all armed with pike and match-lock, wielded by hands inured to deadly strife with the wild beast or wilder Indian, into the capital of the Bay Province.

The drums beat through the streets—the boys ran to and

fro with clubs and stones, and doors were barred and shop windows closed, and all was tumult and confusion.

Meanwhile the captain of the frigate came ashore in his barge to confer with Andross, and was made prisoner in a moment.

About the same time the messenger returned to Bradstreet, from the governor, refusing to give up the reins of power, and asking for a conference.

"It is of no avail. We will go forth to the town-hall, and read the proclamation," replied the good old man.

And with the words the conference broke up, and they passed out into the street. Just as they reached the common, the English regiment came up with its drums beating, and its colors flying, and its superb and serried lines resplendent in all the pomp and pageantry of warfare—stout hearts as ever wielded weapon, brave hearts as ever dared the shock of battle. But there, directly in their course, lay unexpectedly, the Boston train-bands. Three times their force—brave men, and disciplined, and used, a part of them at least, to Indian warfare.

Sternly they met each other front to front. No word was spoken, no order given, but on both sides the lines halted, and gazed on each other face to face, for a deep, breathless pause of several minutes! Then suddenly, yet steadily, and as if by a simultaneous, and preconcerted movement the muskets rose on both side to the level. Every eye in each line was glancing over the polished tube. Every finger was on the deadly trigger. Another moment and blood had flowed in torrents. But ere that moment came, Cecil sprang forth from the side of Bradstreet, and as he stood with his stately form aloft and his clear voice commanding them to "Hold for your lives"—the peril passed away—the crisis was over!

CHAPTER XXIX.

THE STRUGGLE.

Never, perhaps, though Cecil was an eloquent and able speaker, accustomed for years to address bodies of men and bend them to his will by the persuasive force of words, never, I say, had he spoken with such energy, such fire, such melting pathos as he did at this perilous moment.

His words, not in long, wearying sentences cloying the hearer's understanding with their very sweetness, but in short, terse Saxon phrases, forcing their way wedge-like into the apprehension of the dullest brain, and carrying conviction with them.

Beloved, as no other officer of the regiment, by his comrades, loved and respected by the men, in more than an equal ratio, there was not, perhaps, a man in the world, who would have been listened to by those bold martialists on such a subject.

For his words, had they been unsuccessful, were such as would have gained for him, beyond a doubt, the appellation and the punishment of a rebel, the deed to which he incited them was no less than mutiny.

"Hold," he cried in those deep and impressive tones which penetrate the heart more deeply than a trumpet's clangor. "Hold, men and brothers. You, men of Boston, lower your muskets, ground your arms, I command you! You, fellow-soldiers, hold, I entreat you, hold! If you would spare yourselves endless anguish! if you would save your souls the guilt of causeless bloodshed—ay! Ravensworth, I said *causeless.*

For who are you but Englishmen, but the king's soldiers? And what cause is it that ye would maintain, but the cause of your country and your king?

"Brothers, and fellow-soldiers, you have known me for years, both in peace and in warfare, and well ye know that not to earn a kingdom would I descend to a falsehood. Now, mark me, this, which you think a civil and a public rising, is but a poor domestic quarrel. Were this the time, were this the ground of battle betwixt the cause of England and the freedom of America, God is my judge and witness that as an Englishman my every energy should fight for my king and my country. Not for that grand, that holy, that most divine of all earthly things, a nation's freedom, would I lift hand against my own, my glorious country. Brothers, will you unsheath your sword against her, for a poor minion's cause, in a depressed and fallen tyrant's quarrel? Ye stare on me, with eager eyes, and astonished faces, as though you understood me not — as though you would ask me, 'Who is the minion? who the deposed and fallen tyrant?' Sir Edmund Andross, the *ex*-governor of this Bay Province! James Stuart, the *late* king of England! Ay! start not, it is so! England has risen to a man — church and state, peers and commons, army and navy — ay! fellow-soldiers, that very navy which once he led so well — have turned from the last Stuart in his madness Nay! his own children have forsaken him. He hath fled from the land, without the stroke of sword, basely abandoning his sceptre, even as he did wield it cruelly. England is a free country. England has chosen her a free king — a king not of monks, and cowls, and rosaries — but of stout-stricken fields, of camps, and of armies. Anon I will call on you to lift your voices with him to the God of battles, who has given to you a soldier's king of England in William of Nassau!"

The truth fell sensibly upon their hearts. Rumors of what

was in progress had reached the officers long months before, and they were in some sort prepared, for that which was to follow.

With the army the bigot king had ever been popular—Andross was hated as a tyrant and a martinet.—What cause had they to strike, to bleed for him?

Well satisfied with what he saw, Cecil proceeded, and as he went on, every breast went with him, and the good cause was won.

"These men of Boston," he continued, "are here in arms at my call, mine, and the governor's. Ay! comrades, start not at the word—the governor's. Edmund Andross is such no longer. The good, the noble Bradstreet is now the governor of Boston! and these good men are here, with English arms in their stout hands, and English blood in their brave hearts to strike, if needs be, for the liberty of England! Will you, natives and sons, sworn soldiers of her soil, strike parricidally against them? Will you, men of England, do battle to enslave England, against Americans who are here to strike, one blow for the freedom of their own America, in striking for the freedom of our England?"

"No, no! not we! we will not!" shouted a thousand manly voices. No! never! Cecil for ever! Cecil and England!"

"Speak to us! speak to us, Sir Henry! What would you have us do?"

"Ground your arms, brothers! The muskets which you carry are King James's. Ground your arms! Strike your colors!"

Before the words had well left his lips, the butt of every musket rang upon the pavement, and the proud color which had never bowed before the foeman's fire, was lowered to the earth.

The officers had lost all power over the men had they

desired to exert it. But few there were who did so. There were two or three of their number, personal friends of Andross, who would, if they dared, have done battle in his cause.

But the immense majority of numbers arrayed against them now, with the conviction that a victory even, would avail them nothing, since in the end all England would be arrayed on the other side, held them speechless and motionless.

Only when the men had lain down their arms, and Cecil had ceased speaking, the major of the regiment advanced, his officers all following his example, stepped out from the ranks, and walked directly up to Sir Henry Cecil.

"May we take this—all this, I mean, that you have spoken—as true upon your word of honor?"

"Upon my word and honor, as a man and a soldier," replied Cecil.

"That is sufficient," answered the other. "I tender you my sword, Sir Henry. I am King James's soldier, not King William's!"

"Keep it, sir! keep it, and use it for King William as gallantly as I have seen you use it for King James, or promise, at least, you will never draw it against the King of England! One word more, gentlemen—the governor is there among the people, he will show you, if you are unwilling to take my word, the king's proclamation and his own commission."

"We are well satisfied enough, with your word, Sir Henry Cecil, which no man ever doubted!" exclaimed several of the younger officers; but the mayor and several other of the superiors desiring to be fully satisfied, went up to Simon Bradstreet, and convinced beyond the possibility of doubt by the production of the papers, tendered their swords again, and were again requested to retain them until such time as the oath of allegiance to King William could be duly and legally administered.

Meanwhile, Cecil, fearful of losing time, had again harangued the men with words of fire, and bade those who would be soldiers of King William take up their arms again, and display once more England's royal colors.

And as a single man the regiment resumed its arms, and as the blazoned standard floated again on the free air—three deep, full-mouthed huzzas, the glorious cheer of England, whether gay festive board, or on the field of death, rose on the air—three cheers for King William—William III. of England."

Just at this instant, having heard that which was in progress, Andross came galloping down the street on a superb black horse, in his full array as the royal governor, with a dozen officers, his own particular friends and followers, behind him.

He was prepared, as he came down, to put himself at the head of the soldiery, strike a bold blow for his king, and, if need be, die boldly in the cause which had made him.

But all was lost before he reached the ground, and, as he perceived it, he turned to the nearest of his followers, and, exclaiming "All is lost here! our only hope is in the castle and the frigate!—one bold charge for the castle!" he set spurs to his charger, and made a desperate attempt to cut his way through the crowd.

But as he did so, a tall man dressed in black clothes rushed forward and caught his charger by the bridle.

"Hold, man of Belial!" he exclaimed. "Hold, man of blood! We have a score to settle, and in God's name let it be settled now!"

And ere the words had well passed his lips, the score was settled.

For with the speed of light Sir Edmund Andross snatched

a horse-pistol from his holster, set its muzzle to the man's brow, and drew the trigger with a firm finger.

One flash, one loud report, and Merciful Whalley, for he it was—the only man who fell in that bloodless revolution—Merciful Whalley was but a clod of motionless and senseless clay.

But not unavenged was he in his fall, nor was his score long unsettled with his foeman. For his bold charger reared at the close flash and report, and the dead man clinging to the rein with the tenacity of death itself, stumbled and fell headlong.

Ere Andross could regain his feet, he was seized, disarmed, bound, a captive to the people he despised, and the man he hated. To his proud spirit a doom worse than death!

Meantime the proclamation was read to the people from a balcony, peace was restored, and with the loss of but one life that glorious revolution was accomplished.

Within three hours the frigate was mastered, the fortifications yielded, the castle taken, without a single shot.

Boston was free, and William of Nassau was king of America and England.

CHAPTER XXX.

THE DEATH-BELL.

Hours had passed like minutes during the progress of that fierce and terrible excitement.

None know or can imagine, save those who have been engaged in such scenes, how the mind is whirled on from point to point, forgetful of all, in that passionate and spirit-stirring tumult—of all that is dearest and nearest to its best affections.

So was it now with Henry Cecil.

Had any man told him, the previous night, that ere the next day's noon he should have forgotten Ruth Whalley—forgotten her love, her innocence, her truth, her peril, he had told him he lied.

Yet it was so. In the heat of the revolution, which, if he had not wrought, he had at least hurried to its close in order to preserve that sweet girl from a felon's death—he had forgotten all—all but the zeal of his present purpose.

And the moment was now at hand. The fearful preparations were all made. The minister had prayed with his victim, the last hymn had been chanted, the funeral service of the dead had been performed over the living, who should be living, soon, no longer.

And Ruth was resigned and calm as ever. The last drop of gall, the last pang to her fond and trusting heart, was in the conviction that forced itself upon her soul, that Sir Henry Cecil—that her soul's idol—had abandoned her.

But that black drop she had plucked from her heart, that last anguish she had confessed.

And now she sat alone in her narrow cell; alone, for the last time, with her ears listening, as mortal can listen under such circumstances, only for the sound of that awful bell which should soon announce the last hour of time, the first of eternity—with her eyes fixed and straining, through the small, iron-grated loop-hole, on that far heaven, wherein she hoped ere long to live in bliss for ever.

At that same moment, pride in his heart, and glory in his eye, Sir Henry Cecil stood beside the aged governor upon the ramparts of the castle, gazing over the bright bay and the fair province, which his own skill and manhood had dared so much and done so much to enfranchise.

Suddenly, he turned as pale as death, he staggered, he would have fallen headlong from that steep parapet, but for the ready hand of Bradstreet, which caught him on the brink to the descent.

"Great God!" cried the old man, "what ails you?"

"The bell! the bell!" cried the young man pointing, pale, conscience-stricken, and in agony, worse than the agony of death toward the city, "the death-bell! Ruth—sweet Ruth! —our negligence has slain thee!"

Headlong down the steep stairs of the bastion, the young man rushed, rallying his forces as he went—his stout companions followed him. Horses stood at the gate saddled and housed for war, with pistols in their holsters and half a dozen men of Foster's troop of horse, lounging about, ready for instant action.

To summon them, to leap into the saddle, to spur through the echoing archway of the fort, was but an instant's work; but many a minute passed before they reached the esplanade of the prison-gate, and all the while that fearful bell was clanging in their ears and chiding them, as it seemed, for their delay!

They reached the esplanade, the gates of the jail were open, and through the iron portals, solemn and slow, filed out the dark procession.

But they were yet in time!

A faint shriek burst from the white lips of the lovely girl, as she beheld her lover; for such in her hour of anguish her heart had confessed him, spring from his horse and rush toward her, while his attendants quietly overpowered the resistance of the sheriff and his officers.

But ere his ready dagger had severed the bonds which fastened her fair wrists, she had fainted in the excess of surprise and joy.

When her eyes again opened to the light, she lay in her lover's arms, in the apartment of the blunt keeper of the prison, with none but friendly faces gathered around her.

Reader, my tale is ended — and dead must be your heart and feeble your imagination if it can not supply the rest — if it tell you not that the first ship which sailed for merry England, bore over the laughing waters, their every peril, every trial ended, Sir Henry and his fair young bride;—if it tell you not that ere many months were passed, a stately castle in one of the fairest shires of fair England was proud to claim as its mistress, Ruth Whalley, the Fair Puritan; — Whalley and Puritan no longer!

END OF THE FAIR PURITAN.

POPULAR WORKS

PUBLISHED BY

J. B. LIPPINCOTT & CO.,

PHILADELPHIA.

WILL BE SENT BY MAIL, POST-PAID, ON RECEIPT OF PRICE.

Forgiven at Last. A Novel. By Jeannette R. HADERMANN. 12mo. Fine cloth. $1.75.

"A well-told romance. It is of that order of tales originating with Miss Charlotte Brontë."—*N. Y. Even. Post.*

"The style is animated, and the characters are not deficient in individuality."—*Phila. Age.*

The Old Countess. A Romance. From the German of EDMUND HOFER, by the translator of "Over Yonder," "Magdalena," etc. 12mo. Fine cloth. $1.

"A charming story of life in an old German castle, told in the pleasant German manner that attracts attention and keeps it throughout."—*The Phila. Day.*

"The story is not long, is sufficiently involved to compel wonder and suspense, and ends very happily."—*The North American.*

"An interesting story."—*The Inquirer.*

Bound Down; or, Life and Its Possibilities. A Novel. By ANNA M. FITCH. 12mo. Fine cloth. $1.50.

"It is a remarkable book."—*N. Y. Even. Mail.*

"An interesting domestic story, which will be perused with pleasure from beginning to end."—*Baltimore Even. Bulletin.*

"The author of this book has genius; it is written cleverly, with occasional glimpses into deep truths. . . . Dr. Marston and Mildred are splendid characters."—*Phila. Presbyterian.*

Henry Courtland; or, What A Farmer can Do. A Novel. By A. J. CLINE. 12mo. Fine cloth. $1.75.

"This volume belongs to a class of prose fiction unfortunately as rare as it is valuable. . . . The whole story hangs well together."—*Phila. Press.*

Rougegorge. By Harriet Prescott Spofford. With other Short Stories by ALICE CARY, LUCY H. HOOPER, JANE G. AUSTIN, A. L. WISTER, L. C. DAVIS, FRANK LEE BENEDICT, etc. 8vo. With Frontispiece. Paper cover. 50 cents.

"This is a rare collection."—*Chicago Even. Journal.*

"Admirable series of attractive Tales."—*Charleston Courier.*

"The contents are rich, varied and attractive."—*Pittsburg Gazette.*

The Great Empress. An Historical Portrait. By Professor SCHELE DE VERE, of the University of Virginia. 12mo. Extra cloth. $1.75.

"This portrait of Agrippina is drawn with great distinctness, and the book is almost dramatic in its interest."—*N. Y. Observer.*

Nora Brady's Vow, and Mona the Vestal. By MRS. ANNA H. DORSEY. 12mo. Fine cloth. $1.75.

"These interesting tales describe Ireland and her people in ancient and modern times respectively. 'Mona the Vestal' gives an account of the religious, intellectual, political and social status of the ancient Irish; and 'Nora Brady's Vow' illustrates the devotion and generosity of the Irish women who live in our midst to friends and kindred at home."—*Philada. Ledger.*

Helen Erskine. By Mrs. M. Harrison Robinson. 12mo. Toned paper. Fine cloth. 1.50.

"There is a varied interest well sustained in this story, and no reader will complain of it as wanting in incident. Higher praise we can give it by saying that the tone is pure and elevated."—*The Age.*

The Quaker Partisans. A Story of the Revolution. By the author of "The Scout." With Illustrations. 12mo. Extra cloth. $1.50. Paper cover. 60 cents.

"It is a story of stirring incidents turning upon the actual movements of the war, and is told in an animated style of narrative which is very attractive. Its handsome illustrations will still further recommend it to the young people."—*N. Y. Times.*

One Poor Girl. The Story of Thousands. By WIRT SIKES. 12mo. Toned paper. Extra cloth. $1.50.

"A deep interest attaches to the volume."—*St. Louis Republican.*

"It is a moving story of a beautiful girl's temptation and trial and triumph, in which appears many an appeal which Christian men and women might well ponder."—*Watchman and Reflector.*

Aspasia. A Tale. By C. Holland. 12mo. Tinted paper. Extra cloth. $1.25.

"It is a very interesting sketch of a life of vicissitudes, trials, triumphs and wonderful experience. . . . It is well worth reading, and we commend it to extensive circulation."—*St. Louis Democrat.*

The Professor's Wife; or, It Might Have Been. By ANNIE L. MACGREGOR, author of "John Ward's Governess." 12mo. Fine cloth. $1. 75.

"The story is admirably related, without affectation or pretence, and is very touching in parts. Miss Macgregor has great skill in drawing and individualizing character."—*Phila. Press.*

Only a Girl. A Romance. From the German of Wilhelmine Von Hillern. By MRS. A. L. WISTER, translator of "The Old Mam'selle's Secret," etc. Fourth edition. 12mo. Fine cloth. $2.

"This is a charming work, charmingly written, and no one who reads it can lay it down without feeling impressed with the superior talent of its gifted author. As a work of fiction it will compare favorably in style and interest with the best efforts of the most gifted writers of the day, while in the purity of its tone, and the sound moral lesson it teaches, it is equal, if not superior, to any work of the character that has for years come under our notice."—*Pittsburg Dispatch.*

"Timely, forcible and possessing far more than ordinary merits."—*Phila North American.*

True Love. By Lady di Beauclerk, author of "A Summer and Winter in Norway," etc. 12mo. Fine cloth. $1.25.

"Is a pleasing little story well told."—*N. Y. Independent.*

"This pleasantly told love story presents pictures of English society that will repay the reader."—*Pittsburg Gazette.*

"Many of the scenes of her novel are drawn with truth and vigor. . . . The interest is sustained throughout the story."—*Hearth and Home.*

Carlino. By the author of "Doctor Antonio," "Lorenzo Benoni," etc. 8vo. Illustrated. Paper cover. 35 cents.

"It is beautifully written, and is one of the best delineations of character that has been written lately."—*Phila. Day.*

"It is a capital little story. . . . A simple and wholesome story charmingly told."—*Brooklyn Eagle.*

"Strange and deeply interesting."—*N. Y. Hearth and Home.*

Walter Ogilby. A Novel. By Mrs. J. H. Kinzie, author of "Wau-bun, etc." Two volumes in one vol. 12mo. 619 pages. Toned paper. Extra cloth. $2.

"One of the best American novels we have had the pleasure of reading for some time. The descriptions of scenery are spirited sketches, bringing places before the reader, and there is nothing strained, sensational or improbable in the cleverly-constructed incidents. Even the graduating week at West Point, though a hackneyed subject, is presented with the charm of freshness as well as reality. This is a thoroughly good novel."—*Philada. Press.*

Askaros Kassis, the Copt. A Romance of Modern Egypt. By Edwin de Leon, late U. S. Consul-General for Egypt. 12mo. Toned paper. Extra cloth. $1.75.

"This book, while possessing all the characteristics of a Romance, is yet a vivid reproduction of Eastern life and manners."—*N. Y. Times.*

"He has written us this thrilling tale, based on miscellaneous facts, which he calls 'A Romance of Modern Egypt,' and in which he vividly depicts the life of rulers and people."—*Chicago Advance.*

Beyond the Breakers. A Story of the Present Day. By the Hon. Robert Dale Owen. 8vo. Illustrated. Fine cloth. $2.

All readers of taste, culture and thought will feel attracted and impressed by it. . . . We have, for ourselves, read it with deep interest and with genuine pleasure, and can say for it that which we could say of few novels of to-day—that we hope some time to read it over again."—*N. Y. Independent.*

Compensation; or, Always a Future. A Novel. By Anne M. H. Brewster. Second edition. 12mo. Fine cloth. $1.75.

"It is an interesting work, and particularly so to those who are musically inclined, as much useful information may be gained from it."—*Boston Post.*

"We recommend this book to all who are not longing for agony; for such patrons it is too gentle and too delicate."—*Phila. North American.*

"The writer exhibits a happy talent for description, and evinces a rare taste and genius for music."—*Boston Recorder.*

Beatrice. A Poem. By Hon. Roden Noel.

Square 16mo. Tinted paper. Extra cloth, gilt top, $1.

"It is impossible to read the poem through without being powerfully moved. There are passages in it which for intensity and tenderness, clear and vivid vision, spontaneous and delicate sympathy, may be compared with the best efforts of our best living writers."—*London Spectator.*

"Mr. Noel has a fruitful imagination, and such a thorough command of language as to link the heart and tongue in that union from which only true poesy is born."—*N. O. Times.*

"Mr. Noel has no rival. He sings with fairy-like and subtle power."—*London Athenæum.*

Breaking a Butterfly; or, Blanche Ellerslie's

Ending. A Novel. By the author of "Guy Livingstone," &c. Author's Edition. With Illustrations. 12mo. Extra cloth, $1.50. Paper cover, 50 cts.

"It is a charming story of English life, and marked by the well-known characteristics of the author's style, in which the gorgeous descriptions of manhood are predominant."—*Buffalo Express.*

"It is intensely interesting, full of life and spirit, and throughout is written in the gifted author's most captivating vein."—*Philada. Age.*

"It is a story which every one will find interesting; and it is written with an easy grace indicative of good taste and large experience."—*Albany Journal.*

The Voice in Singing. From the German of

Emma Seiler. New edition. Revised and enlarged. 12mo. Extra cloth. Ornamented. $1.50.

"We would earnestly advise all interested in any way in the vocal organs to read and thoroughly digest this remarkable work."—*Boston Musical Times.*

"It is meeting with the favor of all our authorities, and is a very valuable work. To any one engaged in teaching cultivation of the voice, or making singing a study, it will prove an efficient assistant."—*Loomis' Musical Journal*

"This remarkable book is of special interest to teachers and scholars of vocal music. It is, however, of value to that much larger number of persons who love music for its own sake. Here, almost for the first time in English, and certainly for the first time in an American book, we have a satisfactory explanation of the physiology and æsthetics of the art divine."—*Philada. North American.*

Abraham Page, Esq. Life and Opinions of

Abraham Page, Esq. 12mo. Tinted paper. Fine cloth, $1.50.

"It is really refreshing, in these days of sensational stuff, to fall upon a book like this, written with the easy, well-bred air of a gentleman, and the grace and culture of a scholar."—*Baltimore Leader.*

What I Know about Ben Eccles. A Novel. By

ABRAHAM PAGE, author of "The Life and Opinions of Abraham Page, Esq." 12mo. Cloth, $1.50.

"Quite a pathetic story, which, without being at all of the kind denominated *sensational*, will enchain the attention to the very close."—*Pittsburg Ev. Journal.*

Agnes Wentworth. A Novel. By E. Foxton,

author of "Herman," and "Sir Pavon and St. Pavon." 12mo. Tinted paper. Extra cloth, $1.50.

"This is a very interesting and well-told story. There is a naturalness in the grouping of the characters, and a clearness of definition, which make the story pleasant and fascinating. Phases of life are also presented in terse and vigorous words. . . . It is high-toned and much above the average of most of the novels issuing from the press."—*Pittsburg Gazette.*

"A novel which has the merit of being written in graceful and clear style, while it tells an interesting story."—*The Independent.*

Siena. A Poem. By A. C. Swinburne. [Republished from Lippincott's Magazine.]

With Notes. 16mo. Tinted paper. Paper covers, 25 cts.

"Is polished with great care, and is by far the best composition we can recall from Swinburne's pen, in more than one of its effects."—*Philada. North American.*

"One of the most elaborate as well as the most unexceptionable of his productions."—*N. Y. Evening Post.*

Recollections of Persons and Places in the West.

By H. M. BRACKENRIDGE, a native of the West; Traveler, Author Jurist. New edition, enlarged. 12mo. Toned paper. Fine cloth, $2.

"A very pleasant book it is, describing, in an autobiographical form, what was 'The West' of this country half a century ago."—*Philada. Press.*

"The writer of these 'Recollections' was born in 1786, and his book is accordingly full of interesting facts and anecdotes respecting a period of Western history, which, when the rapid growth of the country is considered, may almost be called Pre-Adamite."—*Boston Evening Transcript.*

Infelicia. A Volume of Poems. By Adah Isaacs

MENKEN. 16mo. Toned paper. Neat cloth, $1. Paper cover, 75 cts. With Portrait of Author, and Letter of Mr. Charles Dickens, from a Steel Engraving. Fine cloth, beveled boards, gilt top, $1.50.

"Some of the poems are forcible, others are graceful and tender, but all are pervaded by a spirit of sadness."—*Washington Evening Star.*

"The volume is interesting, as revealing a something that lay beyond the vulgar eyes that took the liberty of license with the living author's form, and it serves to drape the unhappy life with the mantle of a proper human charity. For herein are visible the vague reachings after and reminiscences of higher things."—*Cincinnati Evening Chronicle.*

Dallas Galbraith. A Novel. By Mrs. R. Hard-

ING DAVIS, author of "Waiting for the Verdict," "Margaret Howth," "Life in the Iron Mills," &c. 8vo. Fine cloth, $2.

"One of the best novels ever written for an American magazine."—*Philada. Morning Post.*

"The story is most happily written in all respects."—*The North American.*

"As a specimen of her wonderful intensity and passionate sympathies, this sustained and wholly noble romance is equal or superior to any previous achievement."—*Philada. Evening Bulletin.*

"We therefore seize the opportunity to say that this is a story of unusual power, opening so as to awaken interest, and maintaining the interest to the end."—*The National Baptist.*

Our Own Birds of the United States. A Familiar Natural History of the Birds of the United States. By WILLIAM L. BAILY. Revised and Edited by Edward D. Cope, Member of the Academy of Natural Sciences. With numerous Illustrations. 16mo. Toned paper. Extra cloth, $1.50.

"The text is all the more acceptable to the general reader because the birds are called by their popular names, and not by the scientific titles of the cyclopædias, and we know them at once as old friends and companions. We commend this unpretending little book to the public as possessing an interest wider in its range but similar in kind to that which belongs to Gilbert White's Natural History of Selborne."—*N. Y. Even. Post.*

"The whole book is attractive, supplying much pleasantly-conveyed information for young readers, and embodying an arrangement and system that will often make it a helpful work of reference for older naturalists."—*Philada. Even. Bulletin.*

"To the youthful, 'Our Own Birds' is likely to prove a bountiful source of pleasure, and cannot fail to make them thoroughly acquainted with the birds of the United States. As a science there is none more agreeable to study than ornithology. We therefore feel no hesitation in commending this book to the public. It is neatly printed and bound, and is profusely illustrated."—*New York Herald.*

A Few Friends, and How They Amused Themselves. A Tale in Nine Chapters, containing descriptions of Twenty Pastimes and Games, and a Fancy-Dress Party. By M. E. DODGE, author of "Hans Brinker," &c. 12mo. Toned paper. Extra cloth, $1.25.

"This convenient little encyclopædia strikes the proper moment most fitly. The evenings have lengthened, and until they again become short parties will be gathered everywhere and social intercourse will be general. But though it is comparatively easy to assemble those who would be amused, the amusement is sometimes replaced by its opposite, and more resembles a religious meeting than the juicy entertainment intended. The 'Few Friends' describes some twenty pastimes, all more or less intellectual, all provident of mirth, requiring no preparation, and capable of enlisting the largest or passing off with the smallest numbers. The description is conveyed by examples that are themselves 'as good as a play.' The book deserves a wide circulation, as it is the missionary of much social pleasure, and demands no more costly apparatus than ready wit and genial disposition." — *Philada. North American.*

Cameos from English History. By the author of "The Heir of Redclyffe," &c. With marginal Index. 12mo. Tinted paper. Cloth, $1.25; extra cloth, $1.75.

"History is presented in a very attractive and interesting form for young folks in this work."—*Pittsburg Gazette.*

"An excellent design happily executed." —*N. Y. Times.*

The Diamond Edition of the Poetical Works of Robert Burns. Edited by REV. R. A. WILLMOTT. New edition. With numerous additions. 18mo. Tinted paper. Fine cloth, $1.

"This small, square, compact volume is printed in clear type, and contains, in three hundred pages, the whole of Burns' poems, with a glossary and index. It is cheap, elegant and convenient, bringing the works of one of the most popular of British poets within the means of every reader."—*Boston Even. Transcript.*

www.ingramcontent.com/pod-product-compliance
Lightning Source LLC
LaVergne TN
LVHW050529100826
845148LV00002B/488